Thorssen reached out closing his eyes to truly experience the feel of the silver sword against his skin.

It felt *alive* to his touch.

"Does Creed know what was found?" Thorssen licked his lips. He knew what he was looking at. He'd grown up with the legend of Beowulf's broken sword—the great blade that had slain the dragon but broken in two because of the sheer force that the warrior had used to deliver the fatal blow.

"Impossible to say."

Thorssen liked that about Tostig. He never guessed, he never speculated, he just assessed a situation quickly, calmly, and responded to the information he had at his fingertips.

"Then we assume that she does." Thorssen picked a shard of debris from the edge of the blade with a carefully manicured fingernail. The corrosion flaked away to reveal the still-shining metal beneath.

It wasn't as though they could just ask Creed if she knew what had been unearthed. It was a case of damned if they did, damned if they didn't.

"There is only one way we can be sure she won't cause trouble," Tostig said. He never threatened, he simply floated the idea, knowing Thorssen spoke the same language: the language of death.

"Take care of her."

Titles in this series:

ROGUE ANGEL™

Alex Archer

GRENDEL'S CURSE

A GOLD EAGLE BOOK FROM

WORLDWIDE®

TORONTO • NEW YORK • LONDON
AMSTERDAM • PARIS • SYDNEY • HAMBURG
STOCKHOLM • ATHENS • TOKYO • MILAN
MADRID • WARSAW • BUDAPEST • AUCKLAND

HUDSON BRANCH

Recycling programs
for this product may
not exist in your area.

First edition May 2014

ISBN-13: 978-0-373-62168-2

GRENDEL'S CURSE

Special thanks and acknowledgment to
Steven Savile for his contribution to this work.

Printed in U.S.A.

THE LEGEND

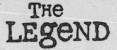

...THE ENGLISH COMMANDER TOOK
JOAN'S SWORD AND RAISED IT HIGH.
The broadsword, plain and unadorned,
gleamed in the firelight. He put the tip against
the ground and his foot at the center of the blade.
The broadsword shattered, fragments falling
into the mud. The crowd surged forward,
peasant and soldier, and snatched the shards
from the trampled mud. The commander tossed
the hilt deep into the crowd.
Smoke almost obscured Joan, but she continued
praying till the end, until finally the flames climbed
her body and she sagged against the restraints.

Joan of Arc died that fateful day in France,
but her legend and sword are reborn....

PROLOGUE

Fiery brands had been driven into the earth to create a path of light from the settlement on the hill to the barrow that would serve as his final resting place.

Tonight there was one more legend to dine with the dead heroes in Valhalla.

Tomorrow there would be one less hero to stand against the creatures of the dark.

Every single one of them, every man with his head bowed low, every woman with her tearstained cheeks, every child wondering how the world could still go on without him, would have killed for the honor of carrying his bier down the path of light.

The clan kings led the procession, followed by his thanes and the men of the Wulfings. He had been one of them and yet he had been more than all of them put together. Skin may wrinkle and bones crumble, but the tales wrapped around the old man were an armor death could never pierce. The stories of his life and the great battles that finally brought peace to the land would live on in the hearts and minds of all of them.

And as the day came and the flames from the path of light turned to ash, the winds would scatter his stories across the world and thus his legend would spread. The path of light was a long and winding walk, but those who walked it now would have traveled to the ends of the earth if he needed them there, such was their love for the man.

The sky glowed red in the east, heralding the sunrise.

Now was the time to say goodbye to their king as he began his final journey—his greatest quest of all—from this world to the next.

His mortal remains would be kept safe, held inside the burial chamber they had constructed deep inside the great barrow that had been built to honor him. He would remain there until the end of time, watching over them, still clad in his armor, his twin swords that had been so much a part of his life at his side. They would whisper, of course, that he would rise again at the time of their greatest need. There was comfort in such thoughts. The mourners had shifted earth to build the great mound; they had carried stone to form to chamber. A few had even stripped the carcass of the great beast he had slain and who in turn had slain him, and used her scales to line the chamber where his body would lie in wait for Ragnarök. Once it was sealed and the earth spilled down over its entrance, no living soul would set foot inside the barrow again.

The clansmen carrying the bier bearing the old war wolf's body paused on the threshold, the sun rising before them. Birdsong filled the morning. There was happiness in it, as though the creatures of the forest and field had come to praise the dead man. The mourners gathered around the bier, one last chance to say their farewells before his body disappeared inside the earth.

A small boy went inside first, his tiny fist clenched around the brand taken from the path of light. He lit the way for those to follow through the low tunnel as it curved and curved again before opening out into the heart of the barrow.

The air was damp and rich with the smell of earth. The light from his torch flickered in the draft, causing the scaled walls to shimmer and shine with iridescent blues and greens. It was hard to believe such beauty could come from such a dangerous beast, but that was the very nature of the dragon. Even in death it was as beautiful as it was terrible. Her flesh had been consumed at his mourning feast, her bones used to fashion tools and weapons for his thanes; her greatest treasure, though, her scales, were his and always would be, shining that last glorious light upon the hero who had slain her.

The boy could not take his eyes from the old war wolf's corpse as they laid him down.

The dead man was dressed in battle-scarred armor. It had been forged, so the legend went, by none other than Wayland Smith. His helmet was placed at his feet, but only when the bearers moved aside were the two blades he had carried in life placed upon his body. There was Hrunting, the thruster, an iron sword with ill-boding patterns wrought into its blade. It had been with him in the mere when he faced the monster and her vile kin. And beside it lay Nægling, the nailer, old and gray but for the jewels studding its hilt. It lay in two pieces now from where it had failed him at the last, broken on the scales of the dragon even as its tip slipped through to end her life.

The last man to enter the barrow carried the dragon's poisonous horn that had delivered the fatal blow. He lay it at the old war wolf's feet while around him the few gathered began to sing the song of mourning.

It was time to seal the barrow.

Beowulf was dead.

1

Karl Thorssen took to the stage like a god. Not just any god, an angry Norse god of old, with flowing blond locks cascading down his back. The silver hammer of Thor was just visible beneath the V-neck of his shirt.

He was met by thunderous rapture.

The assembly didn't just clap, they stamped their feet, they chanted, they yelled his name over and over and over until it rose into a mindless crescendo. There was something else in the chant, too, words she didn't understand, as the room filled with noise. "Quite some welcome," Annja Creed said to the man beside her.

Thorssen stopped center stage and held his arms aloft.

He closed his eyes, threw his head back and embraced the adoration.

It was more like a rock concert than a political rally, she thought, half expecting to see Queens of the Stone Age or Queensrÿche come striding out behind him. The room had that kind of vibe. Alone, each and every one of the people gathered in the theater might have been the nicest person in the world, but together like this the mob took on its own personality. It gave her

the creeps. Annja had seen enough fanatical evange-
lists whip up this kind of fervor in the faithful to know
it wasn't exactly healthy outside of a sports arena, and
even then that was more gladiatorial than devotional.
The comparison was good, actually. There was something almost religious in this, too. Even his stance
mimicked the familiar iconography of Jesus on the
cross, suffering for our sins.

Only, Karl Thorssen wasn't suffering in the slightest.

Here, in front of these people, he really was the
god they were looking for. That was the only way of
describing it.

On either side of the stage Annja marked two thick-
set men, both in matching dark suits, starched white
shirts and pencil-thin black ties. They couldn't have
been more conspicuous. They were just another aspect of Thorssen's carefully manufactured persona.
SAPO—the Swedish Security Service—had officers
in the hall, but they didn't stick out like a sore thumb.
Annja had made six of them in the crowd, watching,
waiting. This pair waiting in the wings were purely for
show. Thorssen wanted people to see them. He wanted
people to know there had been threats on his life, but
no amount of intimidation would stop him from standing up to be counted. That was the kind of man he was.

She'd only been in town for a couple of days and
she already knew that much about him—and it wasn't
all down to her inherent distrust of politicians, either.
The man was headline news. The tabloids loved him.
The broadsheets loved to hate him. The people, she
was quickly coming to realize, worshipped him. Even
from down in the mosh pit she could feel the mag-

netic pull of his aura. The man radiated that magical X factor stars needed to really shine. A bit like Roux, really. That old rascal had a certain something. Right now, that something was probably a big pile of chips on the table in front of him, given that the last she'd heard from him he'd muscled into a high rollers' tournament in Stockholm, part of the most popular poker tour. As for Garin, he'd no doubt found some expensive toys to buy, fast cars to race or faster women to chase. She hadn't heard from him in over a month. That usually meant he was up to no good, but then, wasn't he always?

One of the men nearest Annja was close enough for her to make out the edge of a tattoo of Thor's hammer creeping out from beneath his collar. No doubt the room was filled with similar tattoos and necklaces. The hammer was a common enough branding for fascists in Sweden.

"What does the banner say?" Annja asked the man beside her. Micke Rehnfeldt was an old-school political journalist, the kind of guy not afraid to get his hands dirty if it meant getting to the truth. Thorssen was the current object of his affection. He was producing a television program about Thorssen and his proposed excavation of the Skalunda Barrow down in Årnäs. That was why Annja had made the trip to Gothenburg. How could she not? It wasn't every day the burial mound of a legend was excavated, and that was exactly what Beowulf was. A legend. The Geatish king who had rid the land of demons and dragons in one of the oldest sagas of its type. So while he wasn't a monster, he was still the perfect subject for a segment on *Chasing History's Monsters*.

"*Svensk Tiger Ryter?* It means the 'Swedish Tiger Roars,'" Micke said. "It's a play on the old 'En Svensk Tiger.' You've heard that before, right? It's like the 'Loose Lips Sink Ships' thing the Brits used to say. It's from an old propaganda poster that warned Swedes to be wary of foreigners during the Second World War." Annja didn't see the link so Micke spelled it out for her. "See, tiger is, well, a tiger." He mimed creeping about like a wild animal, and then grinned sheepishly. "Obviously, but in Swedish the verb *tiga,* which is the root of *tiger,* means to keep silent. So 'En Svensk Tiger' could mean either Swedish Tiger or Swede Keeps Silent."

"Ah, clever. A line deeply rooted in the suspicion of foreigners. Class act."

Micke nodded. "No kidding. Thorssen's party is emerging as *the* major force in right-wing politics over here. I don't know how aware you are of the situation in Europe, but he's riding a wave of support that is washing across the continent."

"I've heard bits and pieces, it's hard not to."

"It's only natural. When the economy is in trouble and money is tight, people always blame the foreigners for coming in and taking either jobs or putting pressure on state services. It's the easiest thing to do, blame the outsiders rather than face up to the bad decisions they've made along the way."

"And I'm sure it doesn't hurt that he looks like Adonis's only slightly uglier little brother."

"People will swallow anything a pretty face tells them," Micke agreed.

Sociopolitical stuff wasn't Annja's field of expertise, but they seemed like a reasonable set of assumptions given everything she knew about human behavior.

"Anyway, interesting place for a first date," she joked, grinning wryly.

"Hey, never let it be said I don't know how to show a girl a good time," Micke countered with a grin of his own. It was easy to like him. He had to raise his voice to be heard over the chanting. "Seriously, though," he said, "Thorssen's interested in Beowulf. He's one of the driving forces behind the excavation of the mound. I can think of plenty of reasons why, but rather than just tell you, I thought it'd be better for you to see it firsthand—it's always more impressive that way."

Even with him half shouting Annja could barely hear him above the clamor of the audience. The front few rows had long since stopped applauding, she realized. While most of the room was filled with supporters and fanatics, the front three rows consisted of journalists representing the world's press. She recognized a few faces from Prague, Hyderabad and Paris, but could not put a name to any of them.

"Welcome, my friends," Thorssen began, his words easy, conversational. Annja was relieved to hear he was going to speak in English; her Swedish was limited to saying "thank you" and she'd only learned that a few hours ago. There was more applause. Thorssen gestured for quiet, and within a few seconds the theater was silent.

He had the crowd in the palm of his hand.

"This is the first day. This is a day of new beginnings. This is the day that we claim back our country. This is the day when the Swedish Tiger roars!" On cue the audience roared its approval.

Thorssen smiled.

Annja didn't like the man's smile; it was conde-scending and self-satisfied. It was the kind of smirk she felt compelled to wipe off a face.

"For too long now we've allowed ourselves to be invaded by foreigners…foreigners who have been per-mitted to stay here, to draw from our state and live in comfort without giving anything back. We allowed them to bring with them their own customs, and have tacitly accepted their beliefs. And if we speak up, anything we say is seen as racist, oppressive, against their freedom. I'm all for freedom, and believe me, my friends, I am no racist. I do not differentiate one man from another by the color of his skin or the God he worships. But the plain unassailable fact is these people do not *belong* here. We're a small country. A few years ago we were under ten million, now there are over twelve million people here. We don't have oil like the Norwegians or the British. We cannot support every asylum seeker who comes here. We've been the guilty conscience of the world for too long. Like it or not we have to start thinking about ourselves for once."

Another round of applause rang out.

Thorssen was preaching to the converted and they were lapping up his sermon.

The huge screen behind him changed to show an aerial view of Skalunda Barrow.

"I am sure some of you recognize this place." There was a murmur through the hall. Things were about to get interesting. "And even if you don't, you'll know the name. This is the Skalunda Barrow, believed to be the final resting place of our greatest hero, the old war wolf himself, Beowulf." The screen shifted to show twin swords in place of the burial mound: Hrunting, given to Beowulf by Unferth for the fight with Grendel, and Nægling, the magical blade he claimed from Grendel's cave, having defeated Grendel and Grendel's mother. "He is a true symbol of our heritage. A warrior. A dragon slayer. He killed the enemies who threatened our land…just as the foreigners threaten it now." Annja couldn't quite believe what she'd just heard. Surely it had to be a language thing? A misinterpretation? But the level of sophistication in the rest of Thorssen's language suggested not. "Now is the time for a new Beowulf to arise! Now is the time for someone to drive the dragons from our land!"

Some of Thorssen's acolytes seemed to be on the verge of losing themselves in rapture. They were rocking back and forth on their heels, murmuring, "Yes. Yes. Yes." Only the front few rows seemed to be immune to the craziness. Karl Thorssen was none-to-subtly calling for the people to rise up against immigrants and drive them out of the country.

"Surely this has to be against the law? This is nothing short of inciting racial hated," Annja said, shaking her head. Her companion didn't hear her. He was engrossed by the reaction of the crowd, and pointing his cameraman to where he should direct his focus.

Thorssen had adopted the pose again, clearly enjoying the adoration.

She noticed one of the securing men sprang into action, making his way down the side of the stage into the crowd. He'd obviously seen something he didn't like. Maybe one of the great unwashed wasn't towing the company line? She scanned the crowd looking for signs of dissent, but everyone seemed to be equally enthralled, waiting for the mothership to beam them up to a racially pure nirvana in the stars.

He pushed his way through the faithful, moving his way toward the back doors.

Curiosity might have killed the cat, but it still hadn't managed to kill Annja Creed, though not for want of trying. She gave Micke a nod indicating where she was going, but his attention was already elsewhere. He was wrapped up in his own work, making sure the whole thing was captured on camera for his documentary. There was no denying that it would be good television.

Without another word Annja worked her way through the crowd, until she reached the door, and followed the guard out.

The tattooed man didn't even notice that she was following him.

Once the doors closed behind her Annja should have been isolated from the noise of the auditorium, but she wasn't. It was replicated by a large flat-screen television and sophisticated sound system broadcasting what was going on inside the theater.

Halfway down the red carpet, the bodyguard caught up with the man he'd spotted in the crowd. Annja was too far away to hear the exchange, but it was obvious from their body language that it was hostile in the extreme. His fingers dug into the guy's arm as he twisted him around. He said something—the vehemence behind his words translated even if the words didn't. The man didn't back down. Far from it, he pushed himself up into the guard's face and snarled back, feral, spitting full in the middle of his face and cursing him. Annja saw the scar on his cheek. The guard shoved him away and he went stumbling back two steps, reaching out for a handrail to catch his balance before he fell.

The guard grabbed him again.

"Everything all right here?" Annja asked, walking up behind them.

"Keep out of this," the bodyguard growled. Charming soul. "This has got nothing to do with you."

Annja wasn't big on talking with bullyboys, but wasn't about to leave the man to his not-so-tender mercies. "Look, this doesn't have to be nasty."

The man took her intervention as his cue and pulled free of the guard's grasp, running for the door. The guard didn't stop him. He was looking at the screen over Annja's shoulder as the backdrop behind Thorssen changed. The image of the two blades had been replaced by one of a painted Beowulf standing over what was obviously supposed to be Grendel's mother, the hero holding his sword aloft in victory. It wasn't subtle. But nothing about Karl Thorssen was.

The camera shifted focus, settling on Thorssen. The politician raised his arm, echoing the image on the screen. It was a carefully choreographed move. He was fully in control, playing the crowd until a sudden explosion of noise erupted—through the doors, from the sound system, from the walls around her. The entire framework of the theater trembled, and then the stones themselves seemed to cry out as the building twisted and buckled.

The cheers mutated into screams.

Suddenly people charged through the doors, desperate to get out of the auditorium. Smoke and rubble filled the air. Nowhere was safe. Not in there. Not out here in the vestibule. She looked for the scar-faced man—the bomber? Was that what had happened here?—but he was gone, swept up with the tide of people and carried away with the stampede as they surged toward the street. Smoke. Sprinklers. Sirens. Chaos. Annja pressed herself against the wall to let the flood of people past; she couldn't swim against it. Panic drove people from the theater, but not everyone was so lucky. She could see the screen behind the stage with the image of Beowulf battered and bloody in his chain-mail armor, sword aloft, but beneath it, where Grendel's mother had been, there was only rubble and bodies.

"Micke!" she cried. There was no way he could have heard her but that didn't stop her calling out his name. She scanned the faces desperately, looking for her friend, not wanting to look toward the bodies for fear of seeing him there.

And then she saw him giving instruction to his cameraman. He was pointing at the stage where Karl Thorssen lay. That was the money shot. In all this devastation, the man who would be one of those angry Norse gods of old lay battered and bleeding as two plainclothed SAPO operatives climbed onto the stage, trying to find a path through the rubble to get to the politician. It was an iconic moment. It would be shown on every television set in the world. It would be talked about for weeks. Thorssen rose from the ashes shakily, bruised and bloodied, like the heroic figure on the screen behind him. He breathed in deeply, savoring life amid all of this destruction, and turned to look directly at the camera.

"I am Beowulf," he declared.

2

It was a long night and a longer morning.

She stayed with the rescuers, helping the weak and wounded. Annja pulled at the broken stones, heaving them aside. She heard cries all around her. She couldn't stop. She couldn't allow the horror of the moment to really take root in her mind. Right now people needed her.

Chaos quickly gave way to at least the semblance of order as the paramedics and firemen worked, directing the rescue efforts. To her left three men labored hard, lifting a huge slab of masonry off the legs of a man who wouldn't be walking again for a very long time, if ever. Shock rendered him silent. The rescue workers talked to him constantly, telling him how well he was doing, telling him to hang in there, telling him to be strong, that he was almost out, but not once telling him that everything would be all right. There was a reason for that. The woman beside him was beyond help. He clung to her hand. He must have known.

Annja moved on to where she could be of more use.

A medic crouched over a man who's silver hammer on a chain had torn open his throat, giving him a crude tracheotomy.

She recognized Micke's cameraman. He stood aloof from the destruction, taking it all in with his lens as though the camera gave him the right to separate himself from the dead and the dying, to simply watch and record the tragedy rather than be a part of it. She wondered how he could stand there and do *nothing,* but she didn't wonder for very long. He was coping with it the only way he knew how: documenting it. There was no telling what his camera might pick up that they would miss because they were too wrapped up in the immediacy of the moment, unable and unwilling to just take a step back and *look*.

The worst of it, though, was the smell—that slaughterhouse mix of burned meat and fecal matter that came with death.

So she lost herself in the simple act of trying to help.

Annja was among the last to leave the theater, covered in plaster dust and blood. She must have looked like a ghost emerging from the darkness into the bright sunlight. It could just as easily have been midafternoon as dawn; the sky was blue, without a cloud, the air so fresh in her lungs it stung. They were supposed to be breaking ground in Skalunda in a few hours. There'd be no beauty sleep today.

A stone-jawed policeman came across and started talking to her in rapid-fire Swedish. She didn't understand a word and just shrugged. "I'm sorry. American?"

He switched to flawless English. "Before you go, we need your contact details so we can be in touch to take a statement."

"Of course," Annja said. "I'm staying in a hotel downtown." She pointed toward the hulking shape of her hotel towering over the skyline. It was impossible to miss.

"If you could give your details to the officer." He nodded toward an intimidatingly blonde Amazon of a woman with a pistol strapped on her hip and a peaked cap. She was busy taking details from a line of shell-shocked people. Surreally a radio played in the background, a pop song she didn't know taunting the world to come on and do its worst. She couldn't help but think it had.

Annja joined the line to give her contact info, and then wandered the empty streets toward her hotel, a lost girl in a strange town. She felt her cell phone vibrate in her jeans pocket. When she took it out she saw she had seventeen missed calls, all of them from the same New York number: Doug Morrell, her producer on *Chasing History's Monsters*. Seventeen calls meant he'd obviously seen the news about the explosion at Thorssen's rally and put two and two together. She answered with a not-quite-breezy, "Doug!"

"Annja! I thought you were dead. Answer your damned phone next time, would you? I've been calling and calling. We saw footage of the explosion. Tell me you weren't there."

Doug was a decent guy, if young, blunt and not all that interested in life outside of ratings. She liked him as much as it was possible to like a self-obsessed Ivy League charmer like Doug, which in truth was often just enough to get her to agree to things against her better judgment. He knew it and she knew it. And he liked her just enough in return to at least make the lies and manipulations sound plausible. It wasn't quite a meeting of minds, but in TV terms it was positively synergism.

"Right in the middle of it," she replied, just how lucky she'd been registering as she said it.

"Are you okay? I mean…stupid question…but you know? Two arms, two legs, no bonus bits or bits missing? Every bad word I've ever said, every time I've conned you into doing something you didn't want to do—"

"Don't go saying anything you'll regret, Doug. You know, the kind of stuff that can be used in a court of law." Annja laughed. It was a slightly frazzled laugh. "Because, believe me, I'll certainly hold it against you."

"Okay, good point. You sure you're in one piece?"

"All fingers and all toes in place."

"You sure?"

"I'm sure."

"Okay, I believe you. So, now we've got the mild hysteria out of the way—see what happens when you don't answer your phone?—time for the million-dollar question. Micke had someone in there filming the rally, right?" He paused for a beat, judging her reaction, then added, "Don't get me wrong. It's a tragedy."

"It is."

"But you have to admit it'd make *great* television. An episode on the greatest Norse hero of all, a myth that has continued to fascinate us over the centuries, tied in with the assassination attempt on one of the most charismatic politicians of recent times?" She could hear him marveling at the serendipity that had dropped this in his favorite reporter's lap. "It's pure television gold. I can see it already, can't you?"

Ratings.

It was always about ratings with Doug when it came right down to it.

That wasn't fair, and she knew it. The man who had been terrified when she didn't answer, that had been the real Doug Morrell; the man who wanted the gory details caught on film, that was the TV producer and they were different beasts. It was only now that Doug was sure she was safe that he let that beast out. It was only natural that he did. "Gold," she agreed, halfheartedly.

"Anyway, kiddo, you sound bushed. What is it, one, two in the morning?"

She looked at her watch. It was closer to 5:00 a.m. and she could smell the hit of cinnamon in the air from a nearby bakery. The Swedes loved their cinnamon buns; it was as close as they came to a societal addiction.

"Five."

"You should be in bed. You're breaking ground tomorrow, right? Don't want you looking like you've gone ten rounds with...well, I was going to try and be clever and name some female boxer, but you get the idea. Beauty sleep. That's an order."

"You ever notice you only tell me what to do when there's an ocean between us, Doug?" Annja laughed. "But just this once I'll be good. I'm too tired to argue."

His voice changed. "I'm glad you're okay, Annja. When you weren't picking up..."

"I know," she finished for him. She couldn't deal with mawkishness at 5:00 a.m., not that she was a big fan of it at any other time of day. She walked the rest of the way to the hotel, noting that it was still bright out, and had been for hours. This whole land of the midnight sun thing was a bit unnerving. In the height of the summer it was dark for no more than three hours a night, and if you went far enough north, to the Keb-nekaise massif, you could watch the sun approach the horizon, then just rise again without ever disappearing from sight. As it was, the distinct lack of darkness as far south as Gothenburg was enough to turn a light sleeper into an insomniac and have them climbing up the hotel wall.

An early-morning tram drove by on its way to one of the suburbs. The only passenger had her head resting on the window, still half-asleep. Annja waited for it to rumble off down the street before she crossed the road to the hotel.

The night porter smiled at her as she crossed the marbled foyer and made for the bank of elevators, and her waiting bed. She saw herself in the mirrored elevator doors. It was a wonder he wasn't reaching for the phone to call for the cops.

Two hours of restless sleep later, breakfast skipped, Annja was on-site waiting for Karl Thorssen to grace them with his presence.

There was always something special about that first day on a dig—a sense of anticipation and hope that was almost palpable. Right up until they broke ground, anything was possible.

This was no different.

Beowulf's barrow.

Was the Geatish king interred here?

What, if anything, would they find down there?

Annja grinned despite herself. She wouldn't have traded this part of her life for anything.

Usually the locals were fairly dour and uninterested, but this time it was different. This wasn't just some plot of land where a Roman villa had supposedly stood. This was part of legend. Their legend. Beowulf was more than Gustavus Adolphus, the father of modern warfare; he was their King Arthur. Slayer of dragons.

She couldn't help but think that whatever they found in the barrow had the power to make or break a part of the nation's psyche. What if the bones were deformed or stunted? What if they extracted DNA that proved that he wasn't Swedish at all? She thought of Thorssen driven to apoplexy by the imagined discovery his racially pure hero was nothing of the sort, and smiled. There would be a beautiful irony in that.

Annja shielded her eyes against the sun.

The site was already a hive of activity.

Given the attempt on Karl Thorssen's life last night, it was hardly surprising the press had turned out in force to cover the ritual breaking of the ground. There were local dignitaries, too, businesspeople who provided financial muscle to Thorssen's campaign and, giving their teachers the runaround, a group of schoolchildren who seemed to be everywhere at once, grinning and giggling and pretending to be ancient heroes with invisible swords fighting equally invisible dragons. There were half a dozen television presenters speaking to cameras, each offering a version of the same report. How Thorssen had survived the attempt on his life, how the crowd had gathered for this historic event, how Thorssen was writing his own legend and how the upcoming election promised to be a closely contested thing with a groundswell of support for the right-wing politician in the wake of last night's tragedy.

"Quite a turnout," Johan Cheander said, his camera on his shoulder and scanning the crowd of faces. She couldn't see Micke. Johan was good. He didn't need telling what might make useful footage. Just like the night before, his camera was documenting it all down to the last detail. They'd work out what they needed later.

"You're not wrong," Annja agreed, pointing to the black Mercedes coming across the grass toward them. It wasn't designed for off-road. She'd half expected Karl Thorssen to arrive by helicopter. That seemed like the kind of over-the-top entrance he'd have enjoyed. No doubt he'd discharged himself from the hospital, telling the nurses he couldn't miss this moment for the world. It was the kind of thing that would make good press whether it was true or not.

The sight of the man getting out of the car with one arm in a sling, his rock-star face battered and bruised with any number of minor cuts and abrasions, left him looking like the wounded warrior he wanted to be. The cuts stood out against his pale gray skin. He saw someone he recognized in the crowd and raised a hand in greeting. It took him a second to muster his strength and don the mask of charming affability he'd need to get through the morning, but Annja noticed the occasional wince as he moved, and that he bit on his bottom lip every time the pain threatened to get too much.

Maybe I'm being too hard on him, she thought, watching him press the flesh.

Last night had clearly taken it out of him, but Karl Thorssen wasn't about to be denied the spotlight by something as trivial as an assassination attempt.

That spoke volumes about the man.

Reporters jostled for position as he moved toward the podium that had been set up for the speech, their microphones pushed toward the front. Some were already calling out questions before he reached the lectern. He gave them time to settle down while he gathered himself. He really was good at this kind of thing, playing to the crowd. He wasn't there to address the locals or the schoolchildren. He was talking to everyone on the planet—or as much of it as the news channels would reach. In a viral world that was everywhere there was a screen, a cell phone, a tablet or a laptop. News spread now like it never had before. The reach of microblogging sites was insidious, immense and instantaneous, turning everyone into an on-the-spot reporter. Nothing went unseen. Especially not something like this. Karl Thorssen was a political animal. This was his stage.

He looked up at her and seemed to smile—a smile that was for her and her alone. But of course it wasn't; it was for the cameras.

"Ten bucks says the first words out of his mouth are about politics and have absolutely nothing to do with archaeology."

"I'm not taking that bet," the cameraman said. "Might as well just give you the money."

"Ah, you take all the fun out of life."

"So I've been told."

Annja had heard enough of Thorssen's rhetoric last night. She didn't need to hear any more of it. Instead, she drifted off toward the archaeologists' tents to the side of the dig site. They were more her kind of people. Of course there were plenty of archaeologists out there who didn't think the same of her thanks to the sensationalist nature of many of the segments on *Chasing History's Monsters*.

"Enjoying the circus?" Annja said, moving over to join a small huddle of archaeologists who were intent on something. The nearest looked up. There was a flicker of recognition, but he said nothing. The joys of syndication. No doubt the show was on some obscure cable channel over here.

"Just waiting for the clowns to turn up," his friend said.

"Don't worry, they're here." Annja grinned.

"Thought I heard the natives getting restless."

"Thorssen's just gearing up to do his thing."

"Good," the quiet one said. "The sooner he's done, the sooner we can get on with our job."

"Just consider yourself lucky you're getting to do this at all. We've been trying to get permission to crack open the barrow for years, but have been blocked at every turn. I don't know how Thorssen pulled it off, but the guy's got friends in high places."

"Or some very incriminating photos, more like," the quiet one said, this time with a wicked grin. He stood up and brushed off his hands on his jeans. "You know how it is with the rich and famous—they operate in a different world to the rest of us mere mortals. Lars," he said, holding out his hand to Annja.

"Annja," she said, taking it. She felt the distinctive calluses of someone used to working the dirt.

"Ah, Ms. Creed. I thought I recognized you."

"Occupational hazard."

"Word came down from on high that you'd be doing a feature on the dig."

"On high meaning Thorssen?"

"On high meaning our benefactor, yes. I've been told you've got the run of the place," he said. He didn't sound happy about it, either.

"It's not every day we break open the tomb of a legendary king. It'd be great to get some footage of you guys at work."

"And in return he gets more publicity for his controversial cause. I guess we know who you sold your soul to, Ms. Creed."

Annja took the jibe in the spirit it was intended. She wasn't about to defend her producer's deeply ingrained commercialism, but he was right—assuming the segment was edited together in his favor, they were providing Thorssen with yet another mouthpiece to spread his message. Luckily for everyone, Annja got to do the final edits on her segments. "There's nothing in my contract that says he gets a second of airtime," she said. "I'm not here for the politics—after all, the show's not called *Chasing Modern Politicians,* is it? Our viewers don't care about immigration or racial segregation unless we're talking about soldiers from the Holy Roman Empire. Give me a good old-fashioned monster hunt any day of the week. I leave the politicking to serious journalists."

Lars seemed to like that answer.

She tried to remember his surname. She had it written on a card in her pocket, but could hardly take it out and check.

Lars...

Lars…

Mortensen.

That was it: Lars Mortensen.

"So, what's your deal with Thorssen? He just letting you in on the action out of the kindness of his heart?" she asked.

"Hardly." Lars grunted. "He wants first look at everything we uncover, and any broadcast or press release has to have his name slapped right across it."

"It's all about the glory for him," one of Lars's companions explained, joining them. "The more press he gets, the more he gets to play the benevolent champion of Middle Sweden, the more people will lap up his stupid politics and buy into his send-them-back-home promises. Makes me sick just thinking about it."

He was right; Thorssen's rhetoric was the sort that resonated with certain segments of society whenever there were open borders and high unemployment; the flow of people toward a better life was always one-sided, and with any one-sided narrative it was easy to spin it negatively.

"Well, how about we get one over on him by having you give me a call before anything comes out of the ground, then technically you're not breaking your promise to Thorssen. Saves him getting his hands dirty, too."

"Oh, I'm sure he's quite happy to get his hands dirty," Lars said, though the kind of dirt he meant had nothing to do with the rich soil of the dig site.

Annja glanced across at Karl Thorssen, who was on the podium now, hands braced on either side of the lectern as he leaned forward. His hair fell across his face. He didn't brush it aside for the longest time, then made a show of biting back the pain when he did. It was quite the theatrical performance. He spoke slowly, enunciating each syllable so no one would miss a word.

"Today is a landmark day for this proud nation of ours. Today is a day we embrace the past. Today, as we drive the shovel into the ground to turn the earth, we are forging a connection with the land of our fore-fathers. Think about it. As we open the barrow we are digging through the same ground they strode upon. The same earth. We are tapping into the magic still la-tent within that soil. Heroes walked upon this land, the greatest of which lies buried beneath it. The past and the present are separated by a few feet of dirt. Think about it." His voice carried across the quiet crowd. They were obviously doing what they were told. There was an intensity to his voice that demanded it.

Listening to him, she realized Karl Thorssen was a believer; every word that came out of his mouth, he meant. Yes, it was theater, but weirdly that didn't make it any less *real*.

Believers were always the most dangerous men in her experience. It didn't matter who did the actual dirty work, just so long as it got done. She'd already seen that Thorssen had an army dedicated to his cause.

"Ah, my minute in the sun," Lars said, picking up a pristine shovel that had been leaning against a cou-ple of crates of equipment. "Time to put on a smile for the cameras."

Annja studied his face as Thorssen drove the shovel into the yielding dirt, rested his foot upon it, then pushed down. Not once did he wince or show any sign of physical discomfort. Putting on a brave show for the world? she wondered. Or letting the mask slip to show who you really are?

It was impossible to know one way or the other.

Thorssen turned over the soil to cheers and applause from the small crowd. The cameras had their sound bite and their visual leader for their news segments; his job here was done. He bowed his head, raised a hand in thank you and farewell and allowed himself to be helped back to his car.

A short while later he was driven away, and people were left milling around asking what, if anything, would happen next. It didn't take long for the children to grow restless, several of them deciding that rolling like logs down the hill was a good idea. Their teachers had trouble corralling them, but eventually they were herded onto the waiting coach and whisked away.

The reporters, who only a few moments before had been pressing their microphones forward trying to catch every word Thorssen said, had their backs to the barrow and were doing their final pieces to camera, telling their viewers what they'd just seen and why it was so significant. Fifteen minutes later it was a ghost town. The TV crews had packed away their equipment and driven off in a convoy. Now that Thorssen was gone the barrow was back to being a grassy hill. They'd return if and when evidence was unearthed that Skalunda Barrow truly was the last resting place of Beowulf. Until then, story filed, they'd forget all about it as soon as the next piece of news broke.

"How about I make myself useful?" Annja asked as Lars and his team started to unpack rolls of plastic sheeting from their van. He doled out instructions to others, surprisingly in English rather than his native Swedish, which led her to think that it was for her benefit. He had everything under control, but Annja never was one for being a spectator.

"It's fine, we've got it covered. Unless you fancy a shift with the shovel?"

Annja laughed, assuming it was a joke. Dig sites used mechanical diggers these days to scrape the surface back and mark out the trenches for excavation, not teams of slave labor with shovels. She looked around for the digger, but there was no sign of one anywhere.

"So when is the digger arriving?"

"Digger? You're looking at him."

"Are you serious?"

"Sadly. Yes."

"What? Why?"

"Red tape. We could only get approval to excavate if *everything* was done by hand—minimal impact on the environment, every single sod replaced as close to its current position as is humanly possible."

"Wow. Better grab a shovel, then. We're going to be at this for a while."

"Tell me about it," Lars said. "It'll take us a day to clear out what a backhoe could do in half an hour. But in this as in the rest of life beggars can't be choosers. Lucky for you I've enlisted half of the horticultural department from the university to do the grunt work. Let the big strong farm boys do the backbreaking stuff."

"Nothing wrong with a little extra muscle." She held out her hand. "Pass the shovel."

Lars handed her the shiny new shovel Thorssen had used to break the ground.

"Where do you want me?"

"Over there, we've marked out a trench where, according to geophys results, we believe the entrance to the barrow lies. Have fun."

Annja hefted the shovel onto her shoulder, but before she walked off to lose herself in some good old-fashioned manual labor, she asked, "Do you really believe he's down there?"

"It's been a long time, and there's no way of knowing for sure, but yes. I wouldn't be getting involved in this unless I thought that there was the realistic chance of finding something."

"That's not the same as saying you think we'll turn up Beowulf's bones. We're talking fourteen hundred years for grave robbers, looters, despoilers, defilers, never mind treasure hunters, and heaven knows what else to come along and plunder the barrow."

"That's always a risk," the archaeologist agreed. "We won't know until we're inside. Just as we won't know if this is the tomb of Böðvar Bjarki—the Norse warrior king from the *Saga of Hrólf Kraki,* for instance, whose story mirrors the legend of Beowulf in many significant areas. We know it was from Geatland that Böðvar arrived in Denmark, and moreover, that upon his arrival at the court there, he killed a monstrous beast that had been terrorizing the court at Yule for two years, not unlike Grendel. Of course, there's no evidence as to whether Beowulf was real or not, but his character from the poem does fit seamlessly into the context of his society and Germanic family tree."

"Seamlessly? It doesn't exactly fit the poem, does it?"

"In terms of what we actually know, it's difficult to say anything with certainty. The poem *may* have been composed as an elegy for a seventh century king like Böðvar, corrupting his name over time, but there's little surviving evidence to indicate who it was actually written about, much like King Arthur. It's a legend. And with all poems of the time, it has evolved with the telling and retelling. We have no idea who the original author was. Indeed, there's as much as three hundred years between its composition and the oldest surviving manuscript, which remains unnamed. The poem itself wasn't called *Beowulf* until the nineteenth century. Indeed, from the 1700s it was known as *Cotton Vitellius A.XV*, after Robert Bruce Cotton, the manuscript's owner, and there was no transcription of it until 1818."

She had heard much of this before, but Lars's passion when he started in upon the subject close to his heart made every word fascinating.

"The burial rites described in Thorkelin's Latin transcription bear a strong resemblance to evidence found at the Anglo-Saxon burial site at Sutton Hoo. Likewise Grundtvig's Danish translation and Kemble's subsequent modern English version echo the same funereal rites."

"But wasn't Beowulf's body burned in a funeral pyre on a boat?" Annja recalled having read several retellings of the story as a child long before she'd ever encountered a direct scholarly translation. The image of the burning boat was always one that had stuck with her. If she closed her eyes she could see the flames and feel their heat on her skin. Fire.

"You are correct. The image of the Viking funeral boat sailing out ablaze does provide for a much more dramatic conclusion to the tale. Though I truly believe there has to be a reason why the site of Skalunda has become so intrinsically linked with everything we believe to be true about our hero. Stories don't endure without a grain of truth to them, do they?"

It was a question she couldn't answer, but she wasn't entirely convinced by his reasoning. Yes, it made sense that the poem would have been changed over time. The only extant copy of the original showed at least two authors, and the story itself was riddled with dichotomies of paganism versus Christianity, which supported the notion that each subsequent teller of the epic tale had added their own beliefs to the core story, but was burial really a part of Nordic culture of the time?

"Well," she said wryly, "the answer's only a backbreaking dig away."

3

They had been at it until well into the night, working in shifts and stopping occasionally for food, but now that the sun had finally set and everyone had been sent home, Lars could savor the scene. It was real. It was happening. After all of the paperwork, all of the begging, all of the disappointments, they were finally here, digging down to what could well be the biggest discovery of his lifetime.

He allowed himself a small smile.

Putting the dig together had been a herculean task, and while they were still a long way from finding anything, the sense of satisfaction he felt surveying the site couldn't be denied. They could make do without the backhoes and all of the other machinery. It was all about what was down in the ground now. The team had spent most of the first day clearing the ground, cutting and rolling away a strip of turf a few inches deep to reveal the undisturbed soil beneath, then marking it so the sod could be relaid exactly where it had been. It had taken hours of painstaking work, but the students had put in a full shift, cutting out a trench almost six feet deep, three wide and fifteen long.

It had been a good day, and they'd ended it with a ritual wetting of the site, sharing a beer while they cleared the equipment. It had been one of the students who'd come up with the idea to have that beer out of an old horn, each taking a sip and passing the horn around the circle until it was empty. It was a nice ritual, and very in keeping with the nature of the dig. Then they'd taken a few shots to immortalize their handiwork for posterity, each of them standing beside the deep trench, beer horn in hand. They were all part of this great work, and for him there was no real difference between the workers and the queen. They were all in it together.

Bellis had taken a handful of the team who were bunked up in one of the caravans and headed into town in search of a bar, joking, "Tonight we drink, for tomorrow we dig!" It wasn't exactly a war cry, but then, they weren't going to war so it didn't need to be.

The trailers were still in darkness.

A series of solar-powered garden lights lit up the trench.

Lars sat on the pile of turf that had been carefully set aside in numbered rolls and lit a cigarette. He breathed deeply, savoring the smoke before blowing it out in rings. He'd spent most of the day watching other people work. He was still full of energy and itching to play his part in the excavation. He knew that he wouldn't be able to rest until he had at least got a little dirt under the fingernails. That would make it all seem real. That was just the kind of man he was.

He stubbed out his cigarette and went over to the main tent. The plans were laid out on the central table along with the geophys readings. He'd studied the information diligently and knew it like the back of his hand. The geophys readings were a little more complicated than the ones he was used to looking at; normally they would cover a flat stretch of a field while these ones were trying to plot the three-dimensional shape of the mound itself. He never tired of looking at those images. He'd watched the technicians with their equipment, taking carefully measured steps as the made their readings, one pace after another until they built up a picture of the shape beneath the ground. It was inspiring.

There was every chance that the body—if it had ever been there—would have been placed in a cavity, and sooner or later that would have collapsed in on itself, which meant they would have to deconstruct the entire barrow in the hopes of finding the remains. This wasn't a quick two-week job. They could be here for the best part of a year or more painstakingly going over the ground before they found anything exciting.

Initial ground surveys suggested there was a change in the minerals in the mound, not much farther into it than they already were.

It could be nothing, but the shadow those minerals presented looked too uniform to be a natural phenomena.

Lars Mortensen had spent most of his adult life on digs like this. He knew not to make assumptions when it came to shadows on scans and what they might turn out to be, but he couldn't help himself. He felt that itch just beneath his skin and it had to be scratched. An hour of digging, maybe two, and he'd break through far enough to at least make a reasonable guess as to what the curious shadow-shape was if not know for sure.

He picked up the heavy-duty lantern. Lars angled the beam directly at the scar in the side of the mound as he started to walk toward it. As the light played across the rich soil he thought he saw something *glinting* in the exposed earth. He swung the lantern, causing the light to roll, and again something caught the shifting light for a moment but no more. He played the light across it again, and again until he was sure he'd identified the source.

He assumed it was a shard of quartz that would have been barely visible as the team had worked in the setting sun, but it was worth investigating if for no other reason than satisfying his curiosity.

Lars set the lamp down on the edge of the trench so that its light filled it, and jumped down. It felt good to be right in the heart of it. He unhooked the trowel from his belt and knelt with a mixture of awe and excitement, placing his hands flat on the dirt. He almost imagined he could soak up everything this land had seen over the fourteen hundred years it had sheltered the hero. And for as long as his hands pressed into the earth he felt connected to each and every one of those years.

The glimmering caught his eye again. He knew it would be something and nothing, but he couldn't shake the feeling that the single tiny reflection was calling to him like a beacon in the dark.

He ran a finger over the soil, sending a few tiny crumbs of earth tumbling away.

It wasn't a tiny fragment of quartz or feldspar trapped in the exposed crust, that much was obvious. It was bigger than that.

He set the trowel aside and pulled out a brush. He

knew it was clean. He'd cleaned it meticulously in preparation for the dig. He always did.

He gave the surface the lightest of touches with the tip of the brush, testing how easily it crumbled, if in fact it did.

He brushed aside more particles of earth while pressing his free hand a few inches below the gleam so he could catch every fragment that fell. It took time to reveal that the tiny reflection had come from something much larger than he could have reasonably expected.

With each brushstroke he revealed a little more of the gleaming surface, and the more dirt he brushed away the fiercer the gleam shone, taking on a peculiar blue-green iridescence in the beam of the high-intensity lamp.

He completely lost track of time while he worked.

Eventually he revealed its edge but carried on working around it, trying to find out just how big it was in the hope that it might give him a clue as to its purpose. The color reminded him of an oyster shell, but if that's what it was, then it came from the biggest oyster he'd ever seen, and then some. It took time, but gradually Lars cleared away the dirt enough to make out that it was the size of a dinner plate. He brushed away a little more dirt until it was clear that there was a second one overlapping the first like a gray slate roof tile that had lost most of its luster, but there were still flakes that gleamed with that iridescent blue-green.

He wiped the brush free of dirt before slipping it back into his tool belt, and then reached for his trowel again. He ran its point along one of the exposed edges, working it slowly beneath the lip of the plate. He

pressed gently on its handle with his free hand, testing its resistance before he even tried to work it loose,
but even as he applied the slightest pressure it started
to shift. He felt his heartbeat quicken as he fought
back the rising mix of hope and panic. He had to stop
himself from dropping his trowel to put both of his
hands on the plate, but all of those years of discipline
and training kept him from moving too quickly and
damaging the artifact.

He had secured his trowel in place. As he did, he
felt the plate shift, grinding grit between it and the
overlapping second one. He relaxed his grip slightly
and it started to ease ever so slightly out of the position it had been locked in for centuries.

He felt it give, just a touch, and then suddenly it
came free from its neighbor.

It was heavier than he had expected, despite being
wafer thin.

The edge bit into one of his fingers, slicing it deep
and clean, like a freshly sharpened blade. His blood
smeared across the surface of the strange artifact. He
had no idea what it was—some kind of armor?

He was almost reverential as he lifted the find. He
turned it over in the light to better look at both sides
of it. The underside had none of the brilliance, even
faded, of the topside. Lars reached up and placed it
carefully on grass beside the lamp, intending to clamber out of the trench, and store the strange plate in the
main tent, detailing its discovery and protecting the
site from damp or moisture before turning in, but he
didn't do any of those things. Instead, he knelt back
down in the dirt to examine the raw patch of earth he'd
just exposed, curious to see if the plate was merely

some decorative facing, or if he'd uncovered something more interesting.

He changed the angle of the lantern's beam, shining it down on the newly exposed surface.

There was nothing there.

There was no earth, no stone behind where the tile had been.

Instead, there was a void beyond it.

He played the light inside, straining forward without resting his weight on the edge as he tried to peer down into the hole, but his own shadow made it impossible.

Instead, Lars reached inside, fumbling in the darkness.

His fingers touched nothing but air while the razor-sharp edges of the wafer-thin plates still in situ snatched and sliced at his sleeve, cutting into the fabric as easily as if it was paper, not heavy-duty cotton, as he withdrew his hand.

He reached in again, risking some of his body weight on the plates in front of him, and this time his fingertips brushed against something cold. He couldn't reach it properly, though, whatever it was. He withdrew his arm carefully, painfully aware of just how impossibly sharp the exposed edge was even after all this time.

He tried the lantern, but again it failed to shed any illumination on what was down there, despite the fact that he *knew* there was something to see.

It could be nothing, of course—a piece of rock that had collapsed from the ceiling and fallen away into the air pocket, or part of another layer of lining in the barrow. It was unlikely, yes, but not impossible.

Lars tried to work the second plate out of place to make the hole wider. This time he only succeeded in gashing his hand on its edge.

Gritting his teeth, he tried again, leaning on the wafer-thin plate as he pushed down. It fell and was gone before he could stop it, falling into the air pocket and slicing through his hand as it went.

Lars fished a handkerchief from his pocket and wadded it up around the cut to stem the flow of blood. It was going to need stitches, but it could wait.

He shone the flashlight down through the enlarged aperture, revealing a mound of loose earth and, in the center of it, an uneven shape that lay partially exposed. Soil had fallen through the overlapping cracks in those strange plates to rain down on the treasures below.

He played the light around the confines of the chamber, surprised by how large it actually was— certainly considerably bigger than would have been necessary to house a single body, no matter how legendary the corpse. Colors and shapes reflected back at him as he realized that the whole of it was lined with those peculiar plates. That in itself could prove to be a major discovery.

His blood dripped into the burial chamber.

His handkerchief was soaked with it.

His hand stung as he tried to move it, but that was not going to stop him from being the first man to lay his hands upon the treasures of Skalunda Barrow in fourteen hundred years.

Lars lowered the flashlight inside, clearing away enough dirt to wedge it in place so that it lit up the tomb. The extra space he'd opened up meant he could lean in with his good hand and grasp the tantalizingly close shape in the dirt. His fingers scraped across it at first, before he managed to grip the treasure. Dirt flaked away at his touch, exposing rust-pitted iron.

It was almost as if the treasure sang to him.

Even in that instant, heart hammering, he still had the presence of mind to retrieve his brush and dust aside the accumulated debris of countless lifetimes to reveal the crusted metal rather than just tear it free of its earthly prison. He couldn't reach in far enough to clear it all. He knew he ought to wait for the team to reassemble in the morning, and clear away more of those peculiar plates to get proper access to the barrow, recording everything as they went—everything photographed and logged—but knowing and doing were two very different monsters.

Lars slipped the brush back into his belt.

This is an archaeological dig, not a treasure hunt, he told himself, but that didn't stop that familiar need-to-know hunger from pulling at him. It was why he did what he did. It was why he always knew he was going to make this discovery himself.

He wiped the sweat away from his forehead, trapped in indecision.

After what felt like an eternity he reached in and took hold of the pitted metal.

It was heavy.

Much heavier than he thought it would be.

As he lifted it, the piece of metal broke in two.

He cursed himself, certain that he should have left well alone, followed procedure and photographed it in situ first, but it was too late to stop now.

He gently removed the artifact from its resting place. He needed to use his free hand to support it as it came free of the ground. His blood smeared against the rust. He ignored the pain from more cuts from the razor-sharp plates as they bit deep in his flesh, and reverentially placed it on the ground beside him.

Lars checked the edge of the long piece of metal in the light. Where he thought it had broken in his hands, he saw the edge, too, was encrusted with rust for that to be the case. The edge was corroded, the rust all the way through it.

It made no sense at all.

His blood filled the pits along the length of the metal. The corrosion, he saw, was cracking where it had soaked up the moisture. It appeared to be blistering. He applied the slightest of pressure with the tip of his finger, and a flake of rust broke away. It took him a moment to understand what he was seeing, but when he did, he couldn't quite believe his eyes. Far from being rusted through, the corrosion was more like a protective shell that had formed around the metal. Beneath it he saw a patch of silver metal that couldn't possibly be as pure as it seemed. Lars picked and pulled urgently at the crust until he'd freed enough of the scab to be sure this was no ordinary twisted lump of metal he'd unearthed.

In less than a minute he exposed the impossibly *gleaming* sword. And he was in no doubt that was what he'd found. A sword, or part of one.

He scrambled back to his feet and looked inside the ocular again, seeing the unmistakable outline of the second piece of the sword lying just out of reach. So close and yet so frustratingly far away from his questing fingers. Still, he tried to get it, earning another deep cut for his pains, this one on the ball of his shoulder as he'd leaned in too far.

His only option was to go down through the opening, but he couldn't do that while the razor-sharp edge was exposed so he slipped off his jacket, folded it double and laid it over the strange plate for protection. He had to use his injured hand to support himself as best he could—and it hurt but it was a pain he'd gladly suffer if it meant he could retrieve the rest of the sword. He bit back a scream of agony as blackness threatened to overwhelm him, his head dizzy with pain from the pressure he put on it. There was blood everywhere, smeared handprints all over the dig site and the opening that he'd have to explain in the morning. Still, it would all be worth it, he was sure of that. This sort of find came along once in a lifetime if you were lucky.

Lars Mortensen was lucky.

He dropped down into the tomb itself. It had filled in with sediment and landfall over the centuries. All that remained of the hero's tomb was this air pocket; the rest of it was buried under more earth. He saw an edge of stone and realized it had to be the corner of the bier the warrior king's corpse had lain on. He cursed himself for a fool; his presence here could be doing untold damage to the relics beneath him, but that didn't stop him from crouching to dust away the layer of muck that crusted the second piece of metal before he worked it clear.

He weighed it carefully in his hands.

This sword killed monsters and dragons, he thought, and started to laugh slightly hysterically. Even if he didn't believe the more fantastical elements of Beowulf's story, there was no doubting the fact that the sword in his hands had taken lives.

He shivered and, taking care not to cut himself again, set the second part of the broken sword down beside the first. Then he tried to get a better look at the strange plates that tiled the wall of the tomb. They were unlike anything he'd ever seen before. He had no idea what they were and couldn't wait to get them to the lab for testing. The light seemed to reflect eerily from some of the plates where they weren't crusted and gray, giving the burial chamber a peculiar inner glow. There was no doubting this was the tomb of a hero. The effort that must have gone into fashioning the plates—never mind the genius that had preserved them for an eternity, keeping their edges sharp—was so far ahead of its time it was frightening. This was the work of a civilization that had marauded halfway across Europe, of course. Whatever the Romans achieved, the Vikings matched in their own way.

Lars clambered out of the tomb, savoring the invigorating air as the wind swirled around the mount. He'd never felt more alive in his life. This moment, right here, right now, was why he lived and breathed.

He knelt beside the two parts of the broken sword. It was impossible not to jump to conclusions, but he so desperately wanted to jump: he knew what he'd found. Even with the covering of an age of decay he knew what lay beneath the crust; this was a sword that had been broken centuries before, letting down its wielder when he needed it most. This sword could only be Nægling, the blade that had failed Beowulf even as he'd slain the dragon in its lair.

4

He couldn't sleep.

Lars Mortensen had taken the pieces of the broken sword back to his caravan and cleaned more of the corrosive grime from the blade.

He had a decision to make and he had to make it quickly.

There was no doubt in his mind what he had in his hands, and the ramifications that went with the find.

This was why Karl Thorssen had wanted first look at any finds.

Nægling.

It was iconic.

It was exactly what he needed to tip the balance of the upcoming election in his favor. It was a symbol of everything Sweden had once been—a land of heroes, a land of kings, a land of purebloods and warrior spirits. He could see Thorssen holding it above his head, issuing the challenge to his opponents, rallying his followers.

And that was the last thing he wanted.

How could he possibly let something so culturally

significant, something so historically important, be used for Thorssen's fascist agenda?

He'd been prepared for the discovery of an empty tomb, even the decayed remains of a long-dead warrior, but not this, he realized. Despite everything he'd never really believed Beowulf existed. Who fought monsters and dragons in the real world? No one. But here was the evidence of the man if not the legend, right here on his workbench.

Nægling.

It was one thing to have Thorssen's name attached to a discovery, like some benevolent shadow-figure lurking in the background, a man whose money had made it possible, but it was quite something else to present him with Nægling knowing what he would do with it.

Lars had been on any number of digs over the years, and seen all kinds of finds, but not once had he encountered a find where the years of accumulated grime and decay had fallen away to reveal perfection. Cleaned up, the blade looked as though it had only gone into the ground yesterday.

It was nothing short of miraculous.

But miracles came at a price, didn't they?

He lit another cigarette. Smoking didn't steady his nerves, though. It wasn't some magical cure-all. But it gave him something to do with his hands while he obsessed over the ethics of what he was considering. He'd discovered the sword alone. It wasn't cataloged. No one had witnessed it. There were no photographs. There was nothing to say it had ever been in that hole. He could pretend it had never been found. He could take precautions to make sure it never fell into Karl Thorssen's hands.

He wasn't a doctor; he hadn't taken some form of Hippocratic oath to always present the truth to the world. Sometimes not knowing was better, wasn't it? In this case, given the choice of Thorssen using the blade as a focal point to rally his troops, turning himself into a modern-day Beowulf, surely it had to be, didn't it?

Lars lay in his bunk watching the hands on the clock move impossibly slowly, thinking about all of those immigrant families whose lives would be turned upside down if a man like Thorssen actually rose to power. He thought about the time machine that people often conjectured about when it came to Adolf Hitler, and if they would go back to before his rise in power and kill him if they could. This was his time machine moment. He knew that.

Daylight was already here. It was never far away at this time of year. He still didn't have a solution. All he could do was turn the same things over in his mind.

He needed to get out of there.

The glimmerings of an excuse formed in his mind: he could tell them that he'd tried to open up the tomb himself because he was impatient, and even go so far as to admit a little glory hunting, before he stopped himself. It might cost him his job on the dig, maybe even his tenure at the university if word got out, but it would deflect attention from the truth. He just needed to make the sword disappear, and for that to happen he needed help.

But he had no idea who he could trust.

ANNJA SLEPT LIKE the dead.

Even the insistent beep of her alarm clock didn't rouse her until it had escalated to the point where the guest in the room next door was banging on the wall. She killed the alarm and lurched out of bed. She sat on the edge of the mattress, knuckling sleep out of her eyes. She didn't exactly feel bright-eyed and bushy-tailed. She'd set her phone to silent and turned off the vibrate function before hitting the sack last night, knowing that someone in New York was bound to forget the time difference and wake her up. The first thing she did was check for missed calls.

Five were showing, from two numbers.

Doug Morrell had called four times.

The fifth was from a number she didn't recognize. It had a Swedish prefix, meaning it originated inside the country.

She wandered across to open the curtains while she checked her voice mail.

Looking out on the unfamiliar city she was left with a strange sense of dislocation. It took her a moment to realize which hotel room she was in, in which city; there had been so many over the past few years that it wasn't always easy to tell one from another as they all sort of blurred together.

Annja yawned.

"Hello, Annja? It's Lars. Lars Mortensen. We met at the dig today. You said you wanted to take a look at anything we found…." There was a long pause, like the speaker didn't really want to go on and was fighting himself. She half expected him to hang up. She checked the cruel red glow of the time on the alarm clock while she listened to his mumbling. It was only a little after five, but the room was filled with bright daylight. The city was waking up slowly, too. "I've found something," he said at last. "And I don't know what to do with it. Can you call me when you get this, please? I need to talk to someone and I'm not sure who I can turn to so…you're the lucky winner of tonight's lottery. Oh, right…it's early… Sorry if I woke you." She couldn't help but laugh at the halfhearted apology that ended the call. The message was time coded at 4:32 a.m. It was a ridiculous time to phone anyone.

So what had driven him to call at 4:32 rather than just wait for her to arrive at the site at 8:00 a.m. like the rest of them?

There was only one way to find out.

Annja hit redial and called him back.

"Annja?"

"Hi, Lars, thanks for the wake-up call," she said. "It'll cost you a decent cup of coffee."

"Sorry. I—"

"Couldn't wait to talk to me? I have that effect on men. Well, once in a while, anyway. What's on your mind?"

"We've found something."

"You mentioned. You don't sound thrilled. It's not a clay pot, I take it?"

"No. It's not. But it's best you see it for yourself and make up your own mind, rather than me just tell you what I think it is. Can I meet you somewhere?"

"Now that's what I call an offer you can't refuse. When and where?" There was something about his voice…he sounded agitated. It took her a second to realize he was on the move. She heard a car door slam on the other end of the line.

"There's a café," he said. "Does a decent breakfast." He reeled off directions to a place down by the central station. "As soon as you can make it."

"Give me an hour," she said, despite the fact the address was only a couple of streets away. It wouldn't take long to get showered and dressed; she'd just put her wet hair up and head out. She didn't worry about makeup and making herself presentable; she was very much a take-me-as-you-find-me kind of woman.

"Let's double down, last one there buys breakfast," she said.

"You've got a head start," Lars said, his voice a little more relaxed at least.

"Of course I have, no one said I had to play fair. See you soon," Annja promised, and hung up.

He hadn't spelled it out, but he didn't need to.

He wasn't happy about whatever it was he'd found.

They'd only opened the ground a few hours ago; what could he possibly have unearthed in that time that had him so conflicted?

She thought about calling Johan, but the cameraman wasn't going to thank her for waking him this early so she decided to let him sleep in.

It was only when she was heading out the door that she knew what had been bothering her: why meet at a café? Any find would still be at the site, surely?

What are you up to? Annja wondered, walking out into the early morning to the chorus of traffic sounds, schoolkids and commuters.

His hand was in agony.

Lars slid into the driver's seat of his car.

He had done his best to apply a field dressing and

bind it up once he'd rinsed it in half a bottle of Evian water, but the blood still oozed from the wound and his was getting light-headed from the blood loss and lack of food. He needed to get it seen to but he couldn't waste time with hospitals until he had done something with the broken sword. No one ever died from a cut hand, he told himself, refusing to think about septicemia and all of the bacteria that could have been festering down in that hole. First matter of the day was getting Nægling out of Thorssen's reach; he'd worry about his hand and his shoulder and all of those little cuts after that. He was banking on Annja's connections to get the broken sword out of the country until the election was over and it was no use to the politician. What happened after that was a bridge to be crossed when they came to it.

He couldn't even say why he trusted her, but he did. It certainly wasn't because of the quality of her TV show; that was pure unadulterated drivel for the most part. But while those around her showed no discernible ethics she'd not resorted to their cheap tactics. That was something, wasn't it? It suggested a level of investment in the subject. It wasn't just about making history sexy; it was about getting to the truth. He liked that about her. She wasn't a sensationalist, and right now a level head was exactly what he needed. It almost didn't matter if she looked at the sword and decided it wasn't Nægling. It had been found in the barrow where the legends insisted Beowulf had been buried; people would believe what they needed to believe. It was Nægling if they wanted it to be Nægling.

More than anything, he wished they'd refused Thorssen's money and found some other way to finance the dig. He wished he'd ignored the man's promises to use his connections to secure the hitherto impossible permissions and just continued to bang his head against that metaphorical brick wall.

He looked at himself in the rearview mirror.

Lies. All lies.

He wouldn't have traded the discovery for anything in the world. The only thing he really wished was that it wasn't "dirty," and Thorssen's involvement made it feel dirty. "Beggars can't be choosers," he said to the man in the mirror, but even he didn't believe him. He'd made a choice. He'd always known Karl Thorssen's agenda; he'd just chosen to ignore it to get what he wanted out of the deal with this particular devil. It was only now that he was regretting it, because the sword so obviously served Thorssen's agenda.

Which was why he was considering this plunder, faking an empty tomb rather than deliver the fabled sword into Thorssen's hands. It was better to look like a fool than feed a fascist.

The two shards of the broken sword were on the backseat in a black garbage sack. It wasn't the noblest manner of transportation, but it hid the contents from casual view.

He felt the slick, blood-wet bandage on his hand sticking to the leather of the steering wheel.

He'd already taken more painkillers than he should have, but they weren't dulling the pain.

He pulled up onto a grass verge to check the dressing.

There was nothing he could do with it except unwrap it, teasing the gauze away from the bloody cut before it clotted into the wound, and wrap it again, hoping that would help. He could see the bone and the white of shorn ligaments where the strange plate had sliced clean through the heel of his hand. No wonder it hurt.

He switched on the radio but the news bulletin was still full of talk and speculation about the bombing at Thorssen's rally and the last thing he wanted to do was think about Karl Thorssen so he turned it off again.

The roads were almost deserted, which was unsurprising given the hour and the remoteness of the barrow. He had been driving for another ten minutes before he noticed the car in his rearview mirror. It held back at first, but slowly closed the gap between them.

Lars Mortensen tried to concentrate on the road opening up before him, but he could only think about the car chasing him on the road behind.

5

Lars Mortensen slammed his foot down on the gas.

He really didn't like the fact the car was riding his tail so hard; it was stupid and dangerous. If the joker wanted to pass, he should just pass. Conditions were good, the road wasn't wet, and like most roads in Sweden it was wide because they were designed to be able to function as emergency runways for planes during wartime should the need arise. He knew the road well enough; there weren't any tricky bends up ahead. He gestured in the rearview mirror for the guy to pass, but he didn't: he just tucked in a foot or so behind Lars's fender and gassed his engine intimidatingly even as Lars accelerated.

He watched the needle on the dial climb.

The sound of the engine changed as he shifted gears.

The black car behind maintained the same far-too-close distance.

There were two men in it, both staring straight ahead fixatedly. Staring at him. It wasn't just his imagination; he could feel the heat of their eyes burning into him. It didn't matter how hard he pushed the car, they maintained that same intimidating gap. This wasn't just a couple of guys being jerks, either. Were they part of Thorssen's mob? Was that it? Did he somehow know Lars was trying to spirit away his treasure?

Or was that just paranoia talking?

He took his foot off the accelerator and allowed the car to slow down slightly.

He didn't want to hit the brakes—yet. Doing that would cause his lights to flare and tip his hand. Better they think he's just a slow or erratic driver.

They slowed their pace to match his.

He gripped the wheel tighter. The pain in his hand increased fourfold with the added pressure. The salt from the sweat in the palm of his hand worked its way into the wound, stinging. He gritted his teeth against the swell of agony as his vision swam. He refused to black out, fighting to stay focused as he let the car drift toward the side of the road.

The engine began to strain, whining because it was in the wrong gear, threatening to stall out. He pushed in the clutch and it quit complaining, then slammed on his brakes, forcing the car behind him to pull out and maneuver around him or crash. It slid past at speed, the passenger glaring across at him as it did. The driver cut right across Lars's path, forcing him to slam on the brakes again or plow into the side of them.

Thinking fast, he rammed the gearshift into reverse and tried to get out of there as the passenger door opened. His tires screeched, spitting rubber, and the engine stalled out. Lars twisted the ignition key, jamming down on the gas, only for it to sputter and die again.

The passenger walked toward him. He didn't run.

He was a brick wall of a man in a dark suit, a clone of every villain from every bad movie Lars had seen in the movies, but no less intimidating for it.

He leaned in and tapped on the window, his signet ring rattling on the glass.

Lars couldn't move.

He couldn't even check if the car doors were locked.

He was frozen in place by fear. There wasn't a single muscle in his body that would obey him. It was all he could do to breathe.

It was the pain that finally broke through to end his paralysis. He turned the key over again, shaking like a leaf. The tapping was more forceful the second time it came and he heard a muffled, "You don't want to do that, Mr. Mortensen," as he fumbled with the key again. "Open up."

Reluctantly, Lars opened the window a crack. It wasn't exactly meeting the goon halfway, but he hoped it'd buy him a few seconds to think.

"Leave the key alone, Mr. Mortensen," the goon said, leaning in close to the cracked window. By repeating his name he was laying down a none-too-subtle hint that he knew exactly who Lars was and what he was doing. "I think it might be a good idea if you turned around and went back to the site, don't you?"

"Who are you?" Lars said. It came out more as a plea for knowledge than a demand.

"It doesn't really matter who I am, does it? All that matters is that you don't do anything stupid. Stupidity can be very dangerous for your health, Mr. Mortensen."

The car started suddenly, catching Lars by surprise.

His hands had been working at the key without him thinking about it.

"Don't," the goon said. One word, filled with menace.

That one word said it all.

Lars threw the car back into gear and stamped the gas to the floor, sending his car lurching back.

"You don't want to do that," the goon called out, still calm, still full of menace.

That was when Lars realized the driver hadn't been sitting by idly twiddling his thumbs—even as he tried to peel away from the makeshift roadblock the driver of the black car floored the gas, fishtailing around in a crazy hand-brake turn, and rammed him full-on.

The impact threatened to drive Lars off the road.

The engine grunted and died.

The windshield shattered, showering Lars with fragments of glass.

His hands moved frantically, but he couldn't get the car moving again.

"I asked you not to," the goon said. There was a gun in the guy's hand and it was pointing straight at Lars's face. They were no more than three feet apart. There was no way he could miss. "I'm done asking."

6

The café was nice enough, hand-painted forest scenes on one wall, a rather Rubenesque nude reclining on another. It took Annja a while to recognize the full-figured beauty was actually the woman behind the counter. She smiled as she ordered her latte, admiring anyone who could put themselves out there like that. There were other pictures and hand-painted signage promising forty blends of coffee and a vast array of unhealthy eating options. She refused to give in to temptation, no matter how good the pastries looked. It was too early for anything apart from toast.

There were three other couples in the place, and one lone diner. Lars had not arrived yet.

Some sort of soft jazz hummed in the background, perfectly in keeping with the boho-chic furniture.

Annja checked her watch. Not much time had passed since Lars's call. She took a seat by the window to wait.

And wait.

She didn't know any of the tunes, and couldn't read the newspaper on the counter, so all she could do was people watch as customers came and went, ordering their nonfat skinny lattes and caramel mochaccinos to go.

She could have stayed in bed for another hour, she realized, polishing off the ice-cold dregs in her cup. She wasn't impatient, but it didn't take that long to get from the dig site to town. Forty minutes tops. And he'd already been on the road. Of course she was assuming he'd been at the site when she'd called him. It had been ninety now, if the clock on the wall was anything to go by.

She decided on a refill and a cake, and promised herself she'd give Lars another half hour, and then she was off to the site to see what what was going on.

Annja finally decided she should call him, just to be sure she hadn't gone to the wrong café. The city was full of them, after all. Though surely he would have called her....

She punched in his number.

"What is this, treat 'em mean, keep 'em keen, Lars? I'm here. Where are you? Call me, okay?" she told his voice mail. "I'm on my second cup of coffee and I'm about to gorge myself on cake. This isn't good. There's only so much temptation I can resist. If I put on twenty pounds, you'll pay—just remember that."

She hung up and put the phone on the table in front of her.

"Boyfriend trouble?" the owner asked, offering a sympathetic smile.

"Nothing that a slice of carrot cake won't fix," she said.

"That's lucky, then, considering," the owner said, putting a hefty slice of carrot cake on the table in front of her.

Annja jammed her fork into the middle of the carrot cake and pulled it apart.

"That's the spirit," the woman said, and left her to it.

Annja smiled. If it had been a date she'd have been out of there an hour ago. Work was different. So she waited, concentrating on the carrot cake, which had just the right amount of sweet to take her mind off being stood up.

The pleasure was interrupted when her phone began to vibrate against the tabletop. The screen lit up with Lars's number in the middle of the display.

Annja picked it up and, without missing a beat, said, "You get lost?"

There was a long silence before a slightly accented male voice spoke. "Who is this, please?"

Annja gave her name without thinking. "Who is this?"

"This is the police, Miss Creed. Are you a friend of Mr. Mortensen's?"

"Not really," she said. "I'm doing a segment about the dig that Lars...Mr. Mortensen is working on."

"Dig?"

"Yes, the archaeological dig at Skalunda. You might have seen it on the news last night? Karl Thorssen broke the ground? I was due to meet Lars this morning."

"Where are you at the moment?"

"I'm in a coffee shop in Gothenburg, down by the station. Why?" She struggled to remember what it was called, then spotted the name of the place on top of the printed menu that stood upright in front of her. She had been staring at it for the past half an hour but it had not registered.

"Café Skalunda," she said. Even when she had been making her way there she had not realized that it bore the same name as the barrow. She smiled despite herself. She really was in a world of her own.

And then alarm bells started to ring inside her head. Why did the police want to know where she was? She was about to ask the officer why he was ringing her on Lars's phone when he hung up.

She stared at the phone, trying to understand what had just happened.

Was someone pranking her?

Had something happened to Lars?

She redialed the number. It went straight to voice mail.

That made even less sense, unless the caller was going through his call log to reach out to people, but why would he do that?

As she stared out through the window she saw a car drive past; it was moving much slower than was necessary. Maybe they were lost, or maybe they were looking for something. Or someone. And maybe she was overreacting, but she knew to trust her instincts and her instincts screamed that something was off about the whole thing. She needed to get out of there.

Annja pulled some cash from her pocket, held it up for the woman behind the counter to see, then left it on the table. She took one more bite of carrot cake as she stood up, and mimed that it was good. The woman behind the counter smiled.

She thought about heading back to the hotel room, but it wasn't as if she'd find any answers there. Walking out of the door, she sent a text through to Roux, telling the old man she thought things were about to get interesting. When that was away into the ether, she called Micke's cameraman.

"Johan," she said as a sleep-thick voice grumbled, "Hello?"

So much for being wide awake and ready to rumble.

"Time to get your groove on, sunshine. Action stations. I'll get the car and meet you at the front of the hotel in twenty minutes."

"Twenty minutes?"

"There's an echo."

"It's unholy o'clock—where on earth are we going this early?"

"The dig."

"The dig?"

"Yep. Might be good to get a few shots in the early-morning light."

"Rubbish. You're up to something, aren't you, Annja? Micke's warned me about you."

"Busted," she said.

"It'll cost you breakfast," Johan said.

Breakfast, it seemed, was the global currency of early-morning wake-up calls.

7

Johan stood on the street corner, beneath the hotel's awning.

She pulled up at the curb.

A couple of times on the walk to the underground parking lot Annja had caught herself looking back over her shoulder. She couldn't shake the feeling that she was being watched. She knew it was down to the car that had cruised by the café earlier. Some would have called it paranoia, but for Annja—after everything she'd been through since Roux and Garin came into her life and she first put Joan of Arc's sword into the otherwhere—there'd been no such thing. It was like it had become a finely honed survival instinct. She knew when to act. And when something bad was happening, she wasn't going to sit around and wait to find out what, or just how bad, it was.

She had two options. One, drive out to the dig and start looking for Lars. Someone ought to know where he was. Two, call the police and find out why they'd called her on his phone—if they had.

"So what's the panic?" the cameraman asked as he

climbed into the passenger seat. He'd stowed his gear in the trunk.

She pulled away from the curb. "I want to check up on Mortensen now," she said. "Something's not right."

"Color me intrigued. Love at first sight? A tender moment shared across some decaying old bones?"

"He rang me this morning, early."

"A booty call? I like it. The boy's got style."

"That he might have—but he stood me up for breakfast."

"Ah, a woman scorned, I get it."

"Nothing so clandestine. He said that he had found something, and then he doesn't show up? Seems odd to me."

Winding their way toward Skalunda, Annja saw the glow of red taillights as cars braked and slowed. Odd. She craned her neck and saw a plume of black smoke in the distance followed by a flame that rose high above the roofs of the cars in front of them.

Nothing was going to be moving for a while.

"Keep an eye out," Annja said. "I'm going to take a look at what's going on up there. Slide over. If the traffic starts to move, pick me up as you drive by." She slid out of the car, but before she closed the door she added, "I'll even let you put the radio on if you like."

"Too kind," Johan said, with just the slightest trace of sarcasm in his voice.

She smiled sweetly at him.

Almost every car in the lineup in front of her had the driver's side window wound down, the drivers craning their necks to try and see what the holdup was. A few of them spoke to her as she walked past, not that she understood what they were saying.

It was only as she rounded a bend that had been obscured by thick foliage that she saw the burning car.

Firemen were battling the blaze, struggling to bring it under control before it spread to the vegetation and flamed into a full forest fire. Branches all around the verge had been doused with water but they were still blackened and shriveled from the heat.

A shift in the blaze revealed that the car on fire was a Volvo. There was something familiar about it; but just about eighty percent of cars in this country seemed to be Volvos. Next she noticed a bumper sticker on the back fender proclaiming Archaeologists Do It Down and Dirty. She quickened her pace, reluctant to break into a run, but dreading what she already knew deep down was the truth. An accident would explain so many things, including why the police would call her on his cell phone.

A policeman barked at her, waving her back.

She feigned ignorance, and continued to approach the scene.

He repeated his warning. She reached inside her back pocket for her press pass to offer as some kind of identification, not that she expected it to grant her access to the scene, but it was worth a shot. She held it out like a shield until she was close enough for him to see what it was, hoping he'd think she was a cop.

"Anyone hurt?" she asked, still moving toward the car. She looked around, hoping she'd see Lars wrapped in a blanket, being attended by a paramedic. There was no one.

"The car was already on fire when we got here. Anyone inside didn't get out. We couldn't get near it until the fire crews arrived a few minutes ago."

"But an officer…" She was about to say called me, but then decided against it. There was only one car here, and his partner—another statuesque blonde woman—was working with the firefighters against the blaze. She couldn't see into the smoking car, but it was obvious that if it was already on fire when they'd rolled up, there was no way they could have got Lars's phone out of there. It would have melted in the fireball.

That meant that the call hadn't come from the police, and she'd been right to get the hell out of that café.

A gust of wind took hold of the fire, bringing it roaring back to life. As the flames shifted she caught a glimpse of the windshield. It had shattered, but she saw the shape of a man behind the wheel.

"There's someone in there!" Annja cried, running toward the car.

She knew she was too late to help, but that didn't stop her from trying.

The policeman shouted at her back.

She didn't stop.

Annja felt the heat much sooner than she'd expected. It filled the air and sucked the oxygen from her lungs. Inside five steps it was difficult to breathe.

She could still see the figure behind the wheel, big and bulky, so obviously male and leaning back in the seat as if he'd just fallen asleep, only there was no chance he was sleeping. His skin was charred black and blistered. Some of the blisters had burst and wept down his cheeks only to shrivel under the sheer heat. There was no way of knowing if this was Lars, but she'd seen that bumper sticker on a car at the dig. She was sure of it. It was too much of a coincidence for it to be someone else in there, no matter how many Volvos there might have been on this particular road on this particular morning.

She didn't resist when the policeman grabbed her arm and pulled her away from the overwhelming heat.

"There's nothing you can do. Let the firemen do their job."

She nodded weakly, letting him lead her away from the burning car.

"You know the driver, don't you?" the policeman said.

She shook her head.

She could have admitted her suspicions, but knew that doing so would mean explaining things she didn't really understand and tie her up in knots of endless questions. So she played dumb.

"No. Sorry. I just thought…you know…I could help."

He looked at her, trying to decide if she was telling the truth.

"I think you should return to your vehicle. Leave it to the professionals. It could be some time before we get the road cleared."

"Certainly, officer," she said, "I'm sorry if I…you know…" Annja shrugged and started back toward the car. A few people had gathered on the grass verge, curious. She scanned their faces but didn't recognize any of them. She had no reason to believe the car belonged to Lars Mortensen, save for the fact it had an archaeological joke on the fender, but she couldn't shake the feeling that it was him in there burning and she didn't want to be around when it was confirmed.

"Time to get out of here," she said as she slipped

into the passenger seat, changing the station on the radio as Johan started the engine.

"Hey," he protested.

She shook her head. "I just want some noise. That's not loud enough. The road won't be open for a while. We need to find another route to the dig."

"Already got it covered. Joys of GPS, programmed in the scenic route. Will take about half an hour longer, but we'll get there. What's happened up front?"

"What are you waiting for, then? Let's get out of here."

Johan angled the rental car back and forth, back and forth, until he could swing around in the middle of the road and head back the way they'd come.

"You think that Lars got held up on the other side of that accident?"

"No, I don't. I think he *was* the accident. Now drive."

8

Karl Thorssen's desk was free of clutter.

There were no family photographs, no ornaments or perpetual motion toys, no mementos of any sort; he didn't need any reminders of life outside the office. He couldn't understand those who did. Who wanted to be reminded of something they'd only left behind a few hours ago? You come to work to focus. If you weren't focusing you weren't going to achieve anything close to your full potential. It was as simple as that. Karl Thorssen worked long hours in what to all intents and purposes was a sensory depravation unit of an office, and in those hours he approached a Zen-like balance of body, mind, action and achievement.

He had no time for distractions.

Distractions were for the weak of will.

He had no time for weakness.

The only indulgence he allowed himself was a potted plant on the windowsill. He never watered it. His secretary took care of it. She had bought it for him a couple of years ago—a gift to celebrate his nomination for the party leadership—and despite his best efforts to ignore it, the thing hadn't just survived, it had thrived. There's a lesson in that, he thought, looking at it, in full bloom.

The call came in early.

He had been expecting it.

Ever since he'd first shaken hands on the deal with Mortensen he'd known the man wasn't to be trusted. Inserting two of his own people on the late professor's team had been child's play. It wasn't money that made the world go around. Greasing a few palms with silver would offer them an incentive, but if they loved you—truly loved you—there was no question they'd move heaven and earth to make sure you got what you wanted. And plenty of people loved Karl Thorssen.

And what Karl Thorssen had wanted most of all was eyes on Mortensen day and night.

He had been right to want it, too.

"Don't let it out of your sight." He knew his instructions would be carried out to the letter. No more, no less. Tostig had never let him down before. He would do whatever was asked of him. Thorssen had always been less certain about Tostig's partner, a silent brooding Latvian whose Swedish was poor and his English only slightly better. The man exuded an aura of menace even when he tried to smile. But then as Thorssen had only ever seen him smile when he was hurting people that was understandable. Thorssen had a rule: the Latvian did not come into the office. Tostig could use him if he wanted to, but Thorssen didn't want to know how, where or why. As far as he was concerned it was need to know, and he didn't need to know.

He left the office, nodding to his secretary, and headed for the great glass elevator that took him down the outside of the building to the street below.

He stepped out into the fresh morning—a morning alive with possibilities—and looked for his man. He saw their car parked down the street.

Tostig acknowledged him with the slightest nod of his head, but made no move to get out of the car; it was one of the rules. They never met at the building. They had a place a few streets away, an apartment Thorssen used as a crash pad in the city. And even then they never entered the apartment together. Tostig always made sure that he had allowed Thorssen enough time to get himself to the rendezvous.

Ten minutes covered it.

The two men had no need to exchange any pleasantries. Thorssen liked it that way. There was a table in the middle of the sparsely furnished room. He nodded toward it, indicating that Tostig should relieve himself of his burden.

The big man winced as he laid it down.

Thorssen saw the red raw marks on his wrist. Tostig made no attempt to hide them. Thorssen didn't ask.

What he didn't know wouldn't hurt him. Instead, Thorssen reached inside his jacket for his wallet and pulled out a card. He wrote a number on the back of it and held it out.

"Call this number. Tell him I sent you. I'll take care of any expenses."

Tostig examined the card as if considering the consequences of what taking it meant, then he slipped it into the top pocket of his suit jacket without looking at what Thorssen had written on it.

The package was wrapped in a black plastic garbage bag. There was nothing to indicate that Tostig had examined its contents, though given the fact he had killed to get his hands on it the politician wouldn't have begrudged his man if he had decided to see for himself what the archaeologist had unearthed.

He turned the package over to loosen the sack, feeling the jagged uneven edges through the wrapping as he did.

He took a deep breath before reaching inside the sack.

He knew that whatever it was it had to be important for the archaeologist to risk betraying him rather than hand it over as per their arrangement.

But what was it?

"Nothing's going to come back to us?"

"Nothing," Tostig said. He was a man of few words.

Thorssen nodded, satisfied. "Do we have any idea who he was going to meet?"

"Some woman called Annja."

"Annja Creed?"

Tostig shrugged his shoulders. His massive bulk seemed to move with them. "Should I know the name?"

"If you're a daytime TV fan."

"This is her number." He took a scrap of paper from his pocket. "I disposed of Mortensen's phone."

"How?"

"I burned it right along with the good professor."

He didn't ask for details. There were more immediate concerns, like the discovery on his table. Taking care, he unwrapped the final layer of plastic to reveal Mortensen's find.

He stared at it.

At both parts of it.

Thorssen licked his lips. He knew what he was looking at. He'd grown up with the legend of Beowulf's broken sword; the great blade that had slain the dragon but broken in two because of the sheer force that the warrior had used to deliver the fatal blow.

Could it really be Nægling?

He reached out to touch the fabled blade, closing his eyes to truly experience the feel of the silvered blade against his skin.

It felt alive to his touch.

"Does Creed know what he had found?"

"Impossible to say."

Thorssen liked that about Tostig. He never guessed, he never speculated; he just assessed a situation quickly, calmly, and responded to the information he had at his fingertips, not the possibilities that might or might not ensue. He was like an old analog computer with two settings—do something or do nothing.

"Then we assume that she does." Thorssen picked a shard of debris from the edge of the blade with a carefully manicured fingernail. The corrosion fell away to reveal the still-shining metal beneath. He was no archaeologist, but there was something wrong with that, surely? There was no way that a blade that had lain in the ground for fourteen hundred years could possibly be as honed or polished. It was a physical impossibility. He'd seen swords from three hundred years ago preserved in museums and they were gouged and pitted even if they hadn't been buried in the ground. The iron oxidized and decayed. They just got *old*. But not this sword, seemingly. Beneath its crust of rust and corrosion it was as wonderful as the day it had been made. So surely this had to be some kind of hoax....

"How willing was he to turn the sword over to you?"

"I'd say he'd rather take it to the grave than hand it over."

Thorssen shook his head, trying to understand how it was possible. He picked at another fragment, working his thumbnail beneath it, then held one end of the sword in both hands, studying it. If the sword truly was Nægling, this part must have broken off inside the body of the great beast—*the dragon,* he thought wildly. He tried to wrap his head around the possibility of the mythical creature and grinned—the part of the sword only recovered after the beast's death. If this was the genuine article, not some elaborate fake, it would need to be confirmed before he could reveal it to the world.

It would have been better with Mortensen's stamp of authenticity on the find; the professor had a good reputation among the community and wasn't prone to wild flights of fancy. But with his untimely death Thorssen would need to call in the B team. He'd established contact with various universities across Europe to provide independent analyses of the Skalunda finds; one had been so kind as to promise to validate whatever he needed, for a price. It was always comforting to know just how corruptable human beings were, even those who had dedicated their lives to the betterment of our cultural and historical understanding of these lost civilizations, even the ones with wonderful academic reputations. That was the power of the almighty dollar. There was no money in education. All he had to do was offer a sizable donation, perhaps a named wing at their university, and they were willing to declare him the savior of all things historical.

It wasn't as though they could just ask Creed if she

knew what Mortensen had unearthed. She wasn't an idiot, despite the best attempts of her copresenters to make her look like one by association. If she knew, it would tip their hand, and if she didn't, it would only succeed in raising suspicions. It was a case of damned if he did, damned if he didn't.

"There is only one way we can be sure Creed won't cause trouble," Tostig said. He never threatened; he simply floated the idea, knowing Thorssen spoke the same language: the language of death. To be certain the woman *didn't* say anything was to be certain she *couldn't* say anything.

It needed to be done quickly and with the minimum of fuss. Anything else would lead to more questions and the last thing they needed was some do-gooder cop digging around Mortensen's accident.

"Take care of her," he said.

He started to wrap the two parts of the sword again, carefully folding it within the sheets of plastic. It wasn't exactly the most noble of ceremonies. Nægling deserved better, and in time would have it. But for now he merely wrapped it in the old garbage bag.

He knew that he could leave Creed to Tostig. His man would take care of things as best he saw fit. Thorssen knew better than to try to tell him how to do his job. You didn't stifle an artist, and that was what Tostig was—a death artist.

Tostig nodded his head and left Thorssen alone in the hired apartment with the ancient sword.

Thorssen watched him go. He barely heard Tostig's footsteps on the old floorboards. He never ceased to be amazed at how quietly the assassin moved for such a big man.

9

More than a dozen cars and vans were parked on the grass when Annja and Johan arrived at the barrow.

None of the vehicles were less than five years old. Most were closer to ten. These weren't the cars of the well-off like most of the ones that had occupied the verge the day before. These belonged to students and lower-totem-pole staff from the university. It was still early for the volunteers to be rolling up.

People were milling around aimlessly, looking for someone to give them direction. Without Lars Mortensen to tell them what to do they were lost.

"Hey," Annja said, raising a hand as she came forward to address the main group.

She cast an eye across the cars in the vain hope she'd spot Lars's battered Volvo among them. It wasn't there. It was a smoldering wreck half an hour down the road, his body still sitting in the driver's seat, burned beyond all recognition. She didn't need the coroner's report to confirm it. She knew it was true.

One of the young women gave a tentative wave. She had that young, slightly grungy look that dogged students the world over. Annja thought she'd seen the girl at the ground breaking.

Annja waved back.

She caught Johan's attention, pointing to where she was heading. He looked up from fiddling with his gear, getting it set up for recording, and nodded. She knew he had his rituals; most of these guys did. She just let him do his thing.

"Hi," she said to the girl. "No sign of Lars?"

It was better not to tell them what she suspected; the police would work their way back to the site eventually, and people would remember if she acted weirdly.

"Nope," the girl answered, her shrug lost inside her baggy top. "He'd asked a couple of us to be in early so we could make a start getting stuff sorted for the volunteers."

"You work at the university?"

She nodded. "Sorry," she said, holding out a hand. "Inge Nordqvist. Research graduate. This is part of my project."

"Annja Creed," Annja said, shaking her hand. She had the same rough calluses Lars had had. "Have you banged on his door?"

"His car's not here." Inge waved at the bank of parked cars. "I've tried calling him, but his cell goes straight to voice mail. I guess it's down to me until he gets back."

"I'm sure you'll be fine," Annja reassured her, remembering all too well what it felt like to be thrown in the deep end. It was all about keeping the volunteers busy—give them a bit of direction and let them look after themselves. "Need a hand?"

"Always," Inge said.

Yesterday's work was covered in a large green tarpaulin. They hadn't removed it yet. The air still hung heavy with early-morning mist. As they walked toward the hill, the mist appeared like a carpet of white that clung to the grass. Closer to the tarp, Annja saw that it had been put in place clumsily, rather than being pegged down with precision. The plastic was heavy with dew. It took four volunteers to pull it away, revealing the deep trench, and in it a ragged opening.

"It wasn't like this when we left last night," Inge said, confused. "The horticultural boys had cleared the turf and made a start on the trench, but no more than that."

Annja considered the dark sinkhole and the peculiar slate that seemed to ring it. "So Lars must have worked through the night, or we've got fairies."

Inge bent down and picked up one of the pieces of slate that had come free. She puzzled over it.

"What's that?" Annja moved in closer to take a look. Its edges were too even to be natural. Inge turned it over in her hands. It was dull on both sides, but there was a dark stain along one of the edges.

"Hmm, curious." She rubbed a finger over the stain, then lifted it to her lips.

Annja expected her to say it was blood, but Inge didn't offer any such explanation. Annja had seen enough bloodstains to know what she was looking at. She didn't clarify it, though. There was no need to spook the girl. "And this wasn't there last night?"

Inge shook her head. "The trench, yes, but not the rest of it. But you can see he only went down a couple of inches before he reached this." She held up the plate. "It's hard to believe we were so close to the tomb so quickly. I need to get a lamp so we can take a look inside. Hold on." Inge clambered out of the trench, setting the slate disc aside, and rushed away, clearly excited.

Johan had to do a nifty little step aside to avoid being sent sprawling as the student sprinted toward the cars. Johan looked at Annja and shrugged. His camera rig had a front-facing light, which should be more than adequate to illuminate the shallow hole and record what was down there at the same time.

"What's all the excitement about?" he asked as he hoisted his camera onto his shoulder. He wasn't looking at Annja; he had his eye to the viewfinder. Like most observers he came alive when the lens was between him and his subject.

"You filming this?" she said, brushing her hair out of her eyes.

"Yes."

Her appearance wasn't something she worried about; she'd always been comfortable inside her own skin, and that made her attractive in ways that makeup couldn't. She nodded, switching into professional mode immediately. She wanted to record her initial reaction to what was happening. That couldn't be faked. Whatever she saw when they stuck the camera into the opening she wanted her face on film right there with it, those first thoughts upon seeing what waited down there captured forever. It might be nothing, or it might be the most incredible discovery since Carter broke into Tutankhamun's tomb.

She remembered what Mortensen had said on the phone.

He'd found something.

But before she could wonder at what, she saw the red light on the side of the camera and fell straight into her on-screen persona. "As you can see from the mist clinging to the field, it's a bitingly fresh morning here at the Skalunda Barrow, though no one here's feeling the cold because today we get the first look inside the excavation. Volunteers worked tirelessly yesterday, driven on by the belief that this truly is the last resting place of a legendary warrior king, and they are part of something special. We all feel it. There's something about Skalunda Barrow. And, as you can see over my shoulder, they've got good reason to be excited. It appears that the entrance to the burial chamber was much closer to the surface than anyone could possibly have imagined."

She paused to give herself time to work out exactly what she was going to include in this brief piece to the camera—and more importantly what she was going to leave out. The pause would make the final edit easier. As with most things in life it was easier to just do it rather than leave it out and try and add it later.

"It's been a curious morning," she said in the end. "We arrived a little while ago, only to find that the man in charge of the dig, Professor Lars Mortensen, wasn't on-site, and by the looks of things work had obviously carried on through the night. When the protective tarp was removed to expose the primary trench just a few minutes ago we saw something stunning— an air pocket beneath the hill has been discovered and already broken into."

Johan knew that this was the moment to pan away from her and get a shot of the excavation.

Annja didn't move a muscle even though she was

no longer in shot, careful not to cast a shadow across the trench while he zoomed in.

He recorded for longer than they could possibly need, knowing that when it came to final edits the chances were Annja would change her mind and cut the talking head and go for the establishing shot of the barrow itself, running with her description of the morning as a voice-over. Even though they hadn't worked together before it seemed that Johan could read her mind. He lowered the camera from his shoulder and crouched down over the lip of the trench.

"Okay, let's see if we can get a shot down there before Inge returns."

Johan looked across the fields at the girl heading back toward them. The return journey was considerably less energetic than the run to the car had been.

Annja wasn't worried about the other volunteers trying to stop them; they were too busy worrying about what they were supposed to be doing to pay any attention to what Annja and Johan *shouldn't* be doing.

By the time they'd dropped down into the trench Johan powered up the front-facing light and slung the camera back into position on his shoulder.

He started his shot from a couple of strides away, approaching it from an angle so Annja had the opportunity to peer inside over his shoulder blocking his light.

Excitement and anticipation gave way to disappointment, though, as the camera light filled the air pocket beneath the hill.

She hadn't expected a treasure hoard—that didn't happen outside of action-adventure movies—but some kind of archaeological evidence that this was actually a burial site would have been nice. Gray slate plates tiled around the hollow inner dome wasn't what she would call evidence. Though it was anomalous with everything she knew about burial sites in this part of the world. For a start they were highly uncommon as burial was a comparatively modern concept in the territory. Funereal pyres were much more in keeping with the death rites of the Vikings than any kind of interment, so that there was a burial site at all was surely proof that the dead man had been important. She examined the tiles lining the air pocket. Despite her initial disappointment, perhaps they were the archaeological proof she needed to show the site's significance.

"What's down there? Can you see anything?" Inge Nordqvist asked, coming up behind them. Annja felt the pressure of the young woman's hand on her back and shuffled aside to let her take a look for herself.

"Incredible," she said. "Just look at the construction of this thing. Look at how those pieces of slate overlap and support one another. It's astonishing. I have never seen anything like it. We're talking about a feat of structural engineering far ahead of its time." And again that word, the only one that really seemed to encapsulate everything she wanted to say. "Incredible."

Annja felt an affinity with the girl; Doug might be looking for the spectacular find every time they did a segment, in search of something that would grab the viewers' imaginations and leave them staring wide-eyed with wonder, but that wasn't what drew Annja to the past. It was stuff like this. Simple truths. The barrow itself was an important find. It didn't matter if there were no surviving relics inside it, the structure promised to reveal an entirely new level of understanding about the people who built it. That was important.

But that wasn't what had got Lars so excited.

He said he'd found something—and he'd removed it from the site.

So what was it, and more importantly, *where* was it?

"You got what you need?" she asked Johan.

He nodded.

The other volunteers had all edged a little closer, waiting to get their own glimpse inside. A few had camera phones in their hands, hoping to get a shot of the open barrow as a memento, not that they'd get much beyond dark smears with those low-grade lenses.

As far as Annja was concerned the whole thing raised more questions than it gave answers, which on another day would have made her exceedingly happy. But not today. Not when the man at the root of most of the questions had burned to death in a fireball en route to meet her. Annja didn't believe in coincidences.

"Hey, Inge, you don't happen to have a spare key to Lars's caravan, do you?" Annja asked, trying to make it sound like it wasn't a big deal if she didn't.

The girl shook her head. "Sorry. You looking for something in particular?" Inge's entire demeanor changed slightly, shifting into a more suspicious, defensive mode as her guard went up.

"Nothing important," Annja replied before the girl could get too suspicious. "He'd promised to dig out some stuff on the history of Skalunda for me. I just figured I'd do some reading while I waited for him to get back."

The lie came easy to her lips. She didn't like lying—not like Roux, who could weave a tale so elaborate he'd convince the birds they swam and the fish they belonged up in the sky given half the chance. But sometimes lying was the only option. And it wasn't as though Lars was going to come back and call her out on it, was it?

"Ah, sure," she said. "Of course. He's got all sorts in there. The prof's been obsessed with this place for the best part of twenty years. Have you seen inside his caravan? It's crazy in there. He's a compulsive hoarder. He writes down every thought he ever has, fills dozens of journals, thousands of scraps of paper, the backs of receipts, beer mats, you name it…crammed full of his tight scrawl. It's a disease. Got to be. I have no idea how he can find anything in there, but you can bet there's weeks' worth of reading for you if the prof decided you needed a history lesson."

Annja couldn't help but smile at the girl's obvious affection for her very own nutty professor. The news, when it came, would hit her hard.

Inge shrugged, and then said, "There's a rock near the door. The prof said he'd keep a spare key there in case we needed to go in while he wasn't around. Between you and me—I've been on a couple of digs with him—it's because he locks himself out and can't find his key. I don't think he even bothers locking the door most of the time now. Help yourself."

Inge turned her attention to the volunteers who were still waiting for permission to peer down into the darkness. One by one they lined up to take a look. There were oohs and aahs, but none of the same infectious excitement Inge herself had exhibited.

And, more tellingly, no one mentioned the fact that the dirt floor in the hollow chamber had been disturbed. There were barely discernible signs of agitation in the dust, no doubt down to Lars's brushwork during the extraction of the relic.

She was gambling that Johan's footage would reveal a little more when they went through it back at the hotel.

Right now she wanted to take a look inside Lars Mortensen's caravan before the police arrived. If he was as compulsive a note taker as Inge suggested, maybe, just maybe, he'd left some sort of clue as to what he'd found in the barrow.

10

The key was exactly where Inge had said it would be, but she didn't need it because the door was already open. The girl had also been right about the contents of the caravan; there was little of value—certainly nothing worth stealing apart from a laptop, which lay on the counter, and even that was four years past its prime and outprocessored by Annja's phone no less. There were editions of newspapers dating back weeks piled up side by side with obscure academic journals, stacks of handwritten notes, crushed receipts and who knew what else crammed into the tight space. Dishes were stacked in the small sink, half a dozen mugs ringed with coffee stains of varying permanence.

An open newspaper lay beside the laptop.

Annja scanned the page, looking for anything that might stand out—pictures, headlines—but it was harder in a foreign language even if a few words were almost recognizable. It offered no great insights. She moved the paper, angling it so she could check the date, but as she did she heard something slide across it.

It took her a moment, running her fingers over the paper, to find the fragment but it had fallen into the crease and she couldn't pick it out. She needed better light but neither the sunlight creeping into the caravan or the electric lamp made much difference. She went back to the door.

"Johan, I need you." He looked at her like she was half-mad.

"Are you sure we should be doing this?" he asked.

"Honestly? Yes."

That confused him. She debated not telling him what she'd seen at the accident, but the image of the burning man refused to leave her. She was sure it was Lars. It had to be him. It was more than just a gut feeling. He wasn't coming back to the dig. She could only hope he'd left some bread crumbs for her to follow so she could find out what had happened to him. "I saw a body inside the burning car," she admitted finally. "The car was a Volvo, like his. Had the same bumper sticker on the fender."

"Really?"

"He said he wanted to meet me because he'd found something and a couple of hours later he's dead. I want to know what he found and if he was killed for it, or if it really was just an unfortunate accident. He'd been up all night by the looks of it, so it could have been tiredness."

"Tiredness kills," Johan agreed. "But in my admittedly limited experience what looks like coincidence generally isn't. We really shouldn't be in here if the police turn up. It won't look good."

He was right, of course; getting caught rooting around in a dead man's personal belongings a few hours after his untimely death could look suspicious. But they had only a small window of opportunity before the place was battened down and whatever clues Lars might have left were trampled under the feet of local law enforcement.

"I need your light," she said, pointing to the paper.

"You want me to record?"

She'd been about to say no, but then changed her mind. It wouldn't hurt to have a visual record of everything in this room just in case they never got back inside here. "Do it."

Johan panned the camera lens around the caravan's interior, lingering on the many stacks of papers. He went up the narrow aisle between the kitchen, dining and sleeping area, focusing first left, then right, then returned to shine the front-facing light on the open newspaper.

"What do you think it is?" he asked as Annja pried the fragment up out of the fold with a fingernail.

"Rust?" She picked it up and put it in the palm of her hand, keeping it in the full glare of the camera's light. It wasn't rust. It was more than that. This was *old* corrosion. It had a different quality to it, where the oxidization process had folded in on itself over and over again, building up thick layers like the strata of rock. The corrosive fragment had come off something that had been in the ground for more than just a single season. Carefully, Annja placed it back onto the newspaper and folded the top sheet around it, turning it into a smaller and smaller parcel until she was able to slip it into her pocket without fear of the fragment slipping out.

"You think it's important?" Johan asked, killing the recording. The camera light went out, plunging the caravan into near-darkness in comparison.

"Who knows? We don't have time to go through every notebook or piece of paper searching for clues, and as much as I want to, I'm not sure we'd get away with carrying out his laptop. There's not much else we can do here."

She took one last glance around.

It would be like looking for a needle in a very cluttered haystack, and that was even assuming Mortensen had written down what he'd found, or clues that led to its discovery. It was always possible that if it was such an important find he simply wouldn't have recorded it yet because of sheer excitement. She'd been caught up in that kind of excitement before. And she remembered what the professor had said yesterday when she'd asked about what Thorssen got out of his altruism—first look at anything they dug up. Was that it? Was that why Mortensen had come running to her because he didn't want Karl Thorssen getting his hands on whatever it was he'd found? Or was she just being paranoid?

"Just because they're all out to get you doesn't mean you're not paranoid," she muttered.

"What?"

"Just thinking aloud."

"Want to check the laptop?"

"No, let's just get out of here before the others notice we're in here."

Inge was waiting outside the door for them.

"Any luck?" she asked.

"You were right, we could probably spend a week in there and not find anything if it wasn't pinned to the fridge with our names on it." She turned to Johan and said, "I'll meet you at the car."

He nodded and left them alone.

"Yeah, the prof's a bit…special," Inge said with a smile. "Guess we'll just have to soldier on until he gets here."

"Sounds like a plan," Annja said, offering the girl one of her business cards. "I've got to head back into town. Could you ask him to call me when you see him?"

"Sure."

The purpose of the card wasn't purely masquerade; she wanted to make sure that Inge had her number. When the news about Lars Mortensen's death was made public she wanted the girl to know where she was.

It was purely gut instinct, but she'd learned to trust her gut ever since Roux and Garin exploded into her life. That pair made a habit of turning things upside down, then stepping back to watch others pick up the pieces—Garin especially, and often deliberately. With Roux it was usually a mere side effect of him getting what he wanted from any given situation, the old man mindless of the cost to others. It wasn't selfishness so much as single-mindedness.

Annja wanted to see how the pieces fell here. It was like divination; sometimes the truth was hidden in plain sight and simply by turning the apple cart over and stepping back to watch who scrambled for what you could learn so much more about a situation than if you spent a month asking the wrong questions.

"Well, I'll leave you to get on with things. Have fun," she said, and headed off to join Johan.

"Okay, boss, where now?" he asked as Annja opened the driver's side door and slipped behind the wheel.

"Back to the hotel."

He made an elaborate show of looking at his watch and sighing.

She raised an eyebrow.

"I thought you were standing me breakfast?"

"And I can't buy you breakfast at the hotel?"

"Not on a first date," he said with a grin.

"Good job there's a decent little café around the corner, then."

"Will you be joining me?"

"Sorry, Johan, you're on your own. I want to take a look at the footage you've got so far, see how it's coming together."

"So not only am I paying for my own breakfast, I'm giving you my pride and joy for the privilege? You women…given an inch you take a mile." He smiled, showing he didn't mean it.

11

It had only taken a few minutes to unpack Johan's camera and hook it up to the huge flat-screen TV in her room.

She hung the Do Not Disturb sign on the outside of the door and settled down to watch the footage, skipping through the stuff Johan had shot at the rally before the explosion and the horrific scenes of the aftermath. She didn't want to remember it any more vividly than she already did. Annja had no idea he'd managed to capture so much of it. Not that they'd be able to use it in the segment. It was too hard-core. Every inch of the film was filled with unfiltered suffering. Just knowing that he'd caught the final moments of some of these people's lives made it difficult to watch. It wasn't like seeing it on the news, either. That somehow sanitized it. Made it safe by adding distance to it. This was intimate. Her skin crawled even seeing it flicker by in fast-forward.

She replayed the scenes of the grand opening of the dig, watching Karl Thorssen milk it for what it was worth. The man was a consummate professional, a showman to the core. He knew exactly what he was doing when it came to the camera, wearing his injuries from the botched assassination attempt as a badge of honor and a cloak of defiance. His demeanor gave a very precise message to the viewer: *look at me, I will not be bowed*.

It had been the same when the rescue workers had pulled him from the rubble in the theater.

Theater?

That thought stopped her cold.

Could there be a connection in the theatricality of it all?

Annja began to spool backward and forward through the adjoining scenes, looking at Karl Thorssen in both of them. Something was off, strange, but she wasn't getting it. She ran the film back again, trying to see exactly what it was about him that bothered her.

He addressed the crowd, commanding the room. The explosion, then debris falling as death filled the space. Dust and panic.

Annja watched him being helped out of the building and into the ambulance with blood streaming from his head.

Men shouted and women screamed in the madness as people hurried to get to safety.

She fast-forwarded again, watching Thorssen standing in the shadow of Skalunda Barrow. He was every bit as dynamic as he had been the day before despite the injuries he had suffered—not only unbowed and unbroken but barely touched by the trauma of the explosion, by the loss of his disciples. Bar a few scratches the only trace of weakness was the sling he wore to support one arm.

Annja paused the image as it zoomed in close, his face a little grainy on the screen, eerie in its stillness.

Who are you, really?

And what do you want out of all this attention?

They were big questions. And there were no easy answers to either of them. She'd seen enough of Thorssen on TV to know he was anything but straightforward, but did he really believe that being associated with the rediscovery of a long-lost hero—even one as mythical in nature as Beowulf—would propel him to political success? In the theater she'd thought that he was a passionate man who believed in something and that belief gave him the power to achieve anything he set his mind to. She'd seen that kind of charisma in religious zealots of every stripe, no matter their faith. They were dangerous men capable of whipping others up into an unthinking fervor. It wasn't something that belonged to one particular religion or one part of the world; it manifested itself everywhere there was a need for a leader, everywhere someone with ambition craved power.

There was something else about Karl Thorssen, though, and she knew it.

It was there on the screen in his frozen face.

It was there on the screen in his cuts and bruises.

It was there on the screen as he moved without so much as a wince, caught up in the drama of his performance, despite having struggled so visibly to clamber up onto the platform.

It was there for her to see, if she could just make the mental connection.

But it was illusive, and seemed to mock her inability to grasp it.

What is it?

What am I missing?

Annja's thought process was interrupted by a gentle but insistent knock on the door.

"You do know what Do Not Disturb means, right?" she called, annoyed that the sign on her door was being ignored.

"Police. Open the door, please."

The police? What were they doing here? There was no spyhole in the door, so she couldn't tell who was on the other side.

"Just a minute." She pulled the cables from the television and stowed the camera back into its case, and kicked it beneath the bed. It didn't go all the way under. The knock on the door was more insistent this time.

"Coming," she called quickly, slipping into the bathroom to flush the toilet and run the tap. She answered the door with a damp towel in her hands and a sheepish smile on her face.

"Sorry," she said, letting the towel make her excuses for her. "What can I do for you?"

There were two of them, neither in uniform, both in what appeared to be expensive black suits perhaps a year behind what was fashionable in the cut but no denying the quality. Neither showed any ID.

"I understand that you had a meeting with Lars Mortensen this morning."

Both men were powerfully built. She looked for the telltale bulge of a weapon beneath the tailoring, but both jackets fell naturally.

"No," she said. "I was supposed to meet him for a coffee, but he didn't turn up."

"Can I ask what that meeting was about?"

"I don't see how that's anything for the police to worry about. And anyway, I told you, there was no meeting. He stood me up."

"As that may be, I'd like you to come along to the station to make a statement."

"A statement? Wow, that is harsh. He stood me up—I know I'm special, but missing our coffee date's got to be somewhere below a national emergency in the great scheme of things," Annja joked, trying not to let her concern show. It wasn't easy. She'd already made a couple of mistakes—she *should* have asked for ID, she *should* have questioned the fact the first words out of their mouths were in English, not Swedish.

"We are trying to ascertain Mr. Mortensen's last movements."

"Last? Sorry? What do you mean, last?"

"I'm afraid Mr. Mortensen was involved in a tragic accident this morning."

"Oh…what happened? Poor Lars… I can't believe it. We only talked a few hours ago. I don't know what to say….'" It wouldn't have won her an award, but her performance wasn't terrible.

The second man stepped into the room and closed the door behind him. He didn't say a word. There was something about the guy Annja really didn't like. She'd faced men like him before. Men used to being violent to get what they wanted. She backed up a step. The big man who'd been doing all the talking didn't even turn to look at his colleague. He just shrugged an eloquent shrug and shook his head sadly.

"I had hoped we'd do this with a minimum of trouble. You're lying to us. You know it. I know it. My friend here knows it. It's a pity. A real pity," the first man said. "But if you won't come along for a nice little drive, we'll have to improvise."

The big man stepped passed both of them without making eye contact and strode to the French windows she'd admired so much when she checked into the room. He pushed the doors open and took a deep breath, savoring it, then very slowly and very deliberately he leaned out to take a look at the ground below.

It didn't take a genius to understand the implicit threat.

Annja felt the calm of battle settle over her as her heart rate slowed and a kind of serenity took the place of her earlier anxiety. It was always like this. Her world narrowed to a single point, beyond it there was nothing. She pictured Joan's sword in her mind, and immediately felt the familiar weight of the blade in her hand as her fist closed around it.

She smiled at the men who would try to kill her, enjoying the looks of confusion, surprise and then disbelief cross their faces as she drew the sword from the otherwhere. The sword was like an old lover in her hand, someone who'd not been beneath her touch for so long, someone her body and mind missed.

Craved.

And suddenly they were together.

Joined.

Annja Creed drew the mystical blade in across her chest, its cold, cold metal inches from her lips. It was alive in her hands. Its song sang in her blood. She stared at the men from behind it. The mood in the room had changed. They stared back at her. They were killers, she knew. The pair of them. They would not hesitate to end her life. In turn, she should not have hesitated to end theirs, but Annja had sworn never to kill unless there was no other way. She wasn't a murderer. "Go on," she breathed. "Run back to your masters. You have one chance. Don't waste it. I'm not the kind of girl who offers second chances."

There was a moment of hesitation, then the big man smiled bleakly and reached inside his jacket. "Stupid woman, what good is a sword," he mocked, drawing his weapon.

"One chance," Annja repeated, feeling the thrill of the years coursing through Joan's sword.

She took a step toward the big man, forcing him to take one in turn, moving back toward the door. She felt strong. Good. The vitality of Joan of Arc's fabled sword filled her. She felt invincible.

The man fired once, the shot aimed at her heart.

Body and sword as one, Annja's reflexes were abnormally sharp: the only clue to what had just happened was the ringing of metal. The bullet had been deflected, the blade shimmering in her hands.

"That was your chance," she said calmly. *"Run!"*

She whipped the sword around so fast the displaced air *winnowed* around it as the tip sliced into the big man's suit, parting the threads without so much as nicking the skin beneath.

The man stumbled back, firing wildly. The bullets drove into the wall above and behind Annja, none of the remaining shots coming close to her. His companion, the silent one, reached for the door and threw it open.

Annja lowered the sword, her eyes flicking toward the silent man as he backed out of the room. His partner, empty gun in hand, hurled himself toward Annja.

Instinctively, she stepped backward, catching her heel against the edge of the camera case sticking out from beneath the bed, and, losing her balance, stumbled. The big man threw himself at her, the impact driving the air from her lungs.

She hit the floor hard and then he was on top of her, her sword arm trapped beneath his bulk.

She fought to pull it free, but it was as though time stretched. The big man swung a fist down at her, but it came so slowly she had an eternity to think, to act. Annja used every fiber of her very being, every ounce of strength, to buck against his weight and throw him off—he barely moved an inch, despite her violent thrashing, but it was enough to unbalance him.

As she bucked, his punch went wide, catching Annja with a glancing blow instead of shattering her nose. Even so, it stung. Her warrior's instinct took over. Ears ringing, she drove her knee up, crunching hard between his legs. There was no finesse to it. It was a move meant to disable her attacker and it did just that. He didn't scream, he just curled up and fell away, rolling off her, clutching his groin, gasping as though he couldn't swallow any air no matter how hard he tried.

With the pressure lifted from her chest, Annja was able to breathe again but she didn't waste time enjoying the relief; she didn't have the luxury.

The silent man found his courage and rushed Annja, but stopped dead in his tracks as she rose into a crouch, sword in hand.

"You had your chance," Annja said. "Really, how difficult can it be to do what you're told? I hate it when people don't listen to me."

"You talk too much, woman," the man said, breaking his silence. "It will be the death of you."

"Touché."

She swung, her only intention to ruin his balance. There was limited space to fight in the room, the low ceiling and proximity of the bathroom and bed making it difficult to maneuver with any kind of grace. She lanced out with the blade, pushing him back, and again, until he was half in the doorway, half out, caught between running and fighting, and that indecision was his undoing.

Annja pulled the sword back, two hands wrapped around the hilt, inviting him to attack. He obliged, stepping in close and throwing a fist as Annja rocked on her heels and then countered with a two-handed drive, hilt first. His momentum carried him into the trap she'd set, and even as he tried to pull out of the blow, the pommel of Joan's sword struck him on the side of the head.

He fell awkwardly, his head cracking off the side of the narrow dresser beneath the TV mount. He didn't move.

"Annja? Annja? Are you okay? What the hell is going on?" Johan stood in the doorway. She knelt to check that the quiet attacker was still alive. She felt a weak, fluttering pulse in the vein at his neck. Weak was better than nonexistent.

She looked up at the cameraman. The sword was gone, back to the otherwhere. She had no idea if he'd seen it, or witnessed its return.

"Is he dead?" Johan asked.

"Not yet."

Johan looked over at the big man who was still bent

over. "Remind me not to get on the wrong side of you."
The big man started to move again. Annja turned,
looking back over her shoulder to see him coming up
behind her far quicker than he should have been able
to, all things considered.

He grabbed her around the neck, driving his knee
into the base of her spine as he did. All it would take
to kill her was one sharp twist of the head and her neck
would snap like a dry twig. His grip tightened. She
felt his fingers crushing her windpipe. Soon she was
choking, spots of light sunbursting across her vision.
She couldn't call out. She reached up, hands clawing
at her attacker's hands, trying to pry them away from
her throat, but his grip was vicelike.

Applying pressure under her chin, he forced Annja
to rise. Then he used his extra height to keep her rising until she was barely on her toes, so close to kicking empty air as he pushed her toward the open French
doors.

Annja knew exactly what he intended to do, and
he was so incredibly strong, lifting her like a rag doll
and carrying her closer to the long drop.

Johan appeared to be frozen in fear.

"Johan!" Annja cried, arching her back as she tried
to butt the big man in the center of the face, but he anticipated the backlash and drove his free fist into the
base of her spine brutally.

The blow took the wind and the fight out of her.

Annja felt the tears of pain sting her cheeks.

And embraced the pain.

Pain was good.

Pain meant she was alive.

Pain meant she still had a chance.

Her hand closed around the sword. She felt it solidi-fying in her grasp, but let it slip through her fingers. She didn't need it. Not yet. She jackknifed her body again, ramming her head straight back and up, her skull cracking off the side of his Neanderthal brow. It hurt her more than it hurt him, but she didn't care.

"Get the gun!"

She had no idea if the cameraman could even fire a gun. It didn't matter if Johan even moved—it was all about casting doubt in the big man's mind. Giving him a second enemy to think about meant two points of attack.

Annja could feel the cool breeze on the side of her face.

They were already on the threshold; two more steps and it would be too late to do anything but learn how to fly.

It was a long way down, but by no means far enough for evolution to conjure up wings before she hit the concrete parking lot below.

One step.

Annja felt the iron railing dig into her side as the big man twisted her around. She scrambled, kicking out with her feet uselessly, unable to stop him as he heaved her up toward the drop—and then her legs were on the other side of the railing and there was nothing between her and the parking lot.

She tossed her head frantically left and right, trying not to look *down,* but there was nothing she could use to break her fall, not even slow her descent.

The big man released his hold on her.

Not suddenly—he didn't fling her away from him, he didn't pull back his hand and leave her to the mercies of gravity—he just relaxed his grip so Annja started to slide away from him as though he could no longer hold on to her.

She twisted in a tight half turn as her arms were freed, grabbing for the railing as the grip of his meaty hand slipped. Flailing, Annja snagged ahold of something—his legs? The balcony railing?—and hung there for a heartbeat, but even as she did, it started teetering.

Annja used her body weight to bring him over the top of the railing. She let go, willing her momentum to carry her the precious inches to safety as he tumbled silently past her.

Annja's fingers caught the rough concrete, but with nothing to hold on to started to slip.

And then she felt a hand close around her wrist and saw a pale-faced Johan straining as he leaned over the railing.

"Hold on," he said.

She wasn't about to argue with him; any relief she felt at her sudden salvation was tempered by the sound of the big man hitting the concrete. She didn't look down. She didn't need to. He wasn't going to be getting up again.

"I've got you," Johan reassured her. "Careful, careful, okay…" Annja hooked her foot over the edge, and reached up to grab the guardrail and scramble back to safety.

Annja just stood there, feeling the solidity of the floor beneath her feet. She felt a twinge in her shoulder where she'd strained it hanging on for dear life.

Johan held the gun in his hand. He didn't know what else to do with it, she figured. She hadn't heard a shot, she realized, but security would be coming soon, anyway.

Gunshots and a body in the parking lot below: there were going to be a lot of people swarming over her room in a second.

"I wasn't expecting you to hit him with this," Annja said, taking the weapon from the cameraman. She weighed it in her hand. Was it heavier now that it had taken a life? Weighed down by the big man's soul?

"I killed him…" Johan said. He couldn't stop shaking. She wanted to calm him, but they had other problems. "We should call the police."

He was right, of course. That was exactly what they should do, but she wasn't big on doing what she was supposed to. It wasn't a rebellious streak so much as it was survival instinct.

"No. I need to call some friends first. They'll know what to do," she said, meaning Roux, meaning Garin. "But we need to take care of sleeping beauty."

The dig would be suspended, that was pretty much a foregone conclusion with Lars Mortensen's death and now the attack on her here, and the dead man down there, if the two could be obviously linked. She'd need to check in with Doug Morrell, too. No doubt he'd consider the whole thing ratings gold. She had questions of her own: Who were these guys, who did they work for and why had they come for her?

The *why* she could guess—they thought she knew something, or thought she *had* something. So either they thought Lars had told her something, or hidden his discovery with her. That was all it could be.

Annja stepped back inside the room, intending to drag the unconscious man into the here and now. She wanted to pry a few answers from him before the cops turned up.

It was a good plan save for one tiny thing: he was gone.

12

Annja looked around the empty room.

"We can't just do nothing," Johan objected.

"We can and we will. Close the French windows before someone looks up and works out which window he went out of." As she gave the instructions she set about closing the door, Do Not Disturb sign still in place.

"Someone must have seen you…seen him fall."

"Maybe, but we don't make it easy for them."

"It's not that there are many rooms he could have fallen from," Johan persisted. There was a rising sense of panic in his voice. If she didn't bring him down, and bring him down fast, he was going to go into shock as the adrenaline fell away.

"Okay, you're right, so we'll go to your room. It's on the other side of the corridor, looking out of the front, right? Come on. I want to take another look at the footage." He nodded, but she had no way of knowing if he actually understood a word she was saying. "I've seen one of those guys somewhere. I know I have. At the rally, maybe. He's got a memorable face. You up for going through it with me?"

Annja stepped past him and went to look down from a window to the parking lot below to gauge the amount of activity, shock and panic playing out down there. The double-glazing in the room was good, so she couldn't hear any sounds of a commotion—no shouts, no screams. Nothing at all, she realized, pressing her face to the glass. She peered down, expecting to see a body spread-eagled against the asphalt. There was a pool of blood—a dark stain—but no body.

"He's gone," she stated at the stain on the tarmac, able to make out the vaguely human-shaped imprint smeared by wheel tracks where the corpse had been moved to a waiting car. He'd used one of those luggage trolleys to move the body, and left it abandoned by the parked cars. As if to confirm her suspicions, an engine started up and a car pulled out of a parking space and peeled away.

"He's survived? How?"

"No. He's dead. Our friend's cleaned up the mess." That was the only way to read the scene. The silent man had moved the body. It helped them in that it meant fewer questions to answer—no body meant no crime for the police to investigate, or at least no crime here, linked to her.

"Let's get out of here, shall we?"

"I don't understand what's going on…. What did they want?" And before she could answer that question, he was already asking another. "Annja, what if they come back?"

"Later. Right now let's concentrate on getting the camera set up in your room," she said, hoping that by giving him some sort of direction it'd distract him long enough to calm down, but she wasn't overly hopeful.

She dragged the camera case out from under the bed, glad the silent man hadn't taken it during his escape. Of course, that thought had immediate repercussions: maybe they hadn't taken it because they didn't care if they'd been caught on film or not.

She and Johan went across the corridor to his room. Annja could hear confusion downstairs, people demanding to know what was going on, had they heard gunshots? She locked the door. His room was the mirror image of hers, but where hers barely looked lived-in his looked as though a bomb had gone off in it with clothes and food cartons making a mess of every available surface. He shrugged and began to hook the camera up to his laptop.

The technology had changed so drastically over the past few years that digital video footage had a core hyperrealism to it that surpassed even film in many cases. A couple of cables in place, and Johan began the process of transferring a copy of the recording onto his hard drive. This was his domain. He found tranquility in the process. Annja heard the shift in his breathing while he worked. He executed the command triggers with confidence and told her, "I'm just going to upload the footage to my cloud account, then they can download it back in the office," he explained. "All things considered, it's better to be on the safe side. I was doing a shoot in Ethiopia a few years back, and didn't send any kind of backup. As I went to leave the country, customs seized my camera, all of my backup footage. When I finally got it from them, the entire thing had been hit with a gauss gun. Completely wiped. Once bitten…"

Annja nodded. He'd just helped a man die, recorded

a bombing where several innocent people lost their lives and was still trying to process the knowledge that one of his subjects had burned up in a crash this morning. There was an element of "death comes to us all" about it, but in this case it felt like death was in a hurry to visit, so backing up his footage elsewhere was like ensuring his immortality of a sort.

Peas in a pod, Annja thought, remembering some of her own idiosyncrasies when it came to things like flying: she'd never board a plane with every single piece of work completed, purely because it felt like tempting fate. She liked to leave something dangling, even if it was only a rough cut that needed tidying up before it was screened. The unfinished work was her insurance policy against the plane plummeting out of the sky.

"Right, it's up there, so where do you want to start?"

"At the rally. The last few minutes leading up to the explosion. I've watched it a couple of times. There's something not quite right, but I can't put my finger on it."

"Okay." He started to advance the image in static jumps using the time sequence along the bottom of the screen until he found the right spot.

"Let's see if those two thugs are in there, shall we?"

She and Johan watched in silence as the events unfolded all over again. Annja scanned the faces in the crowd, and then amid the dust and debris, but there was no sign of either of the two men. She'd been sure she'd seen one of them there, even suspected they might have been part of Thorssen's security detail in their neat black suits, but they weren't anywhere in the sea of faces that flocked out of the theater in panic.

"There he is," said Johan, breaking the silence.

"Where?" said Annja. "I don't see him."

He paused the scene and used the touch pad to scroll back until he'd found what he was looking for, then started it again.

Annja watched as Karl Thorssen was brought out of the building by a couple of his security men. He was leaning on them heavily as they pushed others to one side, forcing a path through the injured without a second thought for their safety.

The lens shifted focus as people jostled Johan—he'd clearly struggled to hold the camera steady during the mass exodus—but every now and then it settled on a face clearly. Annja looked hard at each and every one as it came into focus, but she wasn't seeing whatever it was Johan had seen. She couldn't see either of the men in the seething mass of frightened humanity. She stared at the dirt and tear-streaked faces, she stared at the pained and frightened expressions, but none of them looked familiar.

"There," Johan said again, freezing the image this time. He jabbed at the laptop's screen. "That's the guy you knocked out."

Annja stared at the screen. The image was slightly blurred, the movement of so many people barely confined within it, but she knew he was right.

He was in profile.

She hadn't recognized him because she'd been looking in all of the wrong places. She'd been absolutely focused on the people fighting to get out of the theater. He wasn't among them. He *was* outside, though, as people went up to her would-be assassin for help.

He wasn't one of Thorssen's security detail.
He was a paramedic.
Or at least he was dressed as one.

13

Thorssen refused to leave his prize in the office overnight; he needed to take it home with him. It wasn't because he didn't trust the security—his office was one of the most secure locations in southern Sweden. He just couldn't bear to be parted from his treasure.

He had substituted the black garbage sack with a more delicate red silk wrap, and laid both pieces of the broken sword in a fine oak case with sumptuous red silk lining. In the past few hours he had opened the box more than a dozen times to gaze at the sword.

He craved the feel of the metal beneath his fingers. He wanted nothing more than to touch the rust-encrusted surface and pick away at it until it was gone and all that remained was that impossibly *gleaming* metal of Nægling. He hadn't been able to leave the broken sword for more than a few minutes since it had come into his possession. He found himself returning to the safe to make sure it was there, to check that it was *real* and not some fabrication of his febrile mind.

It wasn't.

It was very much real, every corroded crust of it, every gleaming exposed inch of it. Real. Nægling.

Thorssen knew it was *real*. More than real: *genuine*. And that made him restless.

He couldn't just sit in his office pretending it was business as usual.

He couldn't concentrate on anything but the sword, so he packed it away and carried it down to his Tesla Model S parked in the complex across the street. The streets were his. He drove with his foot to the floor, executing each twist and turn out of the city with g-force-defying acceleration until he hit the winding country roads that led up to his home in the hills.

The house was an overblown gingerbread cottage— as though Hansel and Gretel had stolen it from a giant, not a wicked witch—with sprawling grounds, its own lake, ringed by a forest of towering evergreens and an array of modern conveniences that included his own helipad. The protective gates, almost half a mile from the main house, were solid wood, carved with the incredibly elaborate craftsmanship that harkened all the way back to the Viking longhouses with snakes' heads, torcs and, in the very center, the carved image of a warrior, sword in hand, enfolded in a dying dragon's wings.

Music blared on the radio—a mindless pop song telling him to smile if there was anything he wanted. Thorssen caught himself smiling in the rearview mirror, not because he wanted something, but because he had it.

The gates opened as he approached.

Like the rest of the house, they were integrated with a security system that essentially turned it into a defensible fortress.

Thorssen roared up the approach, tires spitting

gravel as he slewed to a halt in the shadow of the house, and clambered out of the car. He carried the wooden case up to his den. The house was far too big for the two people who lived in it, but he'd always promised his mother a large family, and the house was a relic of that promise. Sometimes the dreams of youth were hard to grow out of. He could hear her puttering around in the kitchen as he went upstairs to the den. He closed the door behind him, knowing it wouldn't open again unless he opened it. His mother knew better than to interrupt him when he was in the room. It was his sanctuary.

After his father's death he'd taken her in. He had the room, after all. She didn't intrude, but she was always there, in the background, looking over him. The den was a real "boys' room" with leather couches around a low oak table, a pool table, big-screen television hooked up into satellite relays, posters from old black-and-white movies of Garbo, Bergman and other golden-age sirens. There was a wet bar at the far side of the room, with double-headed axes crossed on the wall behind it.

He set the wooden box down on the table and went to the bar to pour himself a Scotch.

This room was his haven. It offered a barrier between work and home life.

He opened the case and carefully unwrapped the silk covering. He stared down at the pieces of sword, imagining them whole, imagining them in the hero's hand, imagining them slipping between the plates of the dragon's scales to slay the mighty winged serpent. He even imagined the dragon's blood spilling back along the blade as Beowulf raised it aloft.

Is that what the rust is, dragon's blood? Thorssen thought, finally daring to touch the crust again.

He lost all track of time, minutes slipping into hours as time stopped making sense, and was only brought out of his reverie by the groan of floorboards outside the den's door. He realized it was his mother, and could imagine her pacing up and down, wondering if it was safe to knock without incurring his wrath.

"What is it, Mother?" he called out finally, putting her out of her misery.

She coughed slightly, then asked, "Is everything all right, dear? You've been in there an awfully long time." She didn't open the door.

"Yes, Mother. I am fine."

"Dinner has been ready for an hour," she said. "It's spoiling."

"I'll be out shortly."

He could have said that he was busy. He could have told her he really didn't care that dinner was going to waste. He wasn't hungry. He wanted to spend every minute of every day with the greatest treasure imaginable. She would have understood. She would have understood if he'd told her he wanted to watch a documentary or batter around some pool balls to work off his frustration. She would have understood no matter what he told her, without question. That was the nature of their relationship. He thought. He created. He drove them. She understood.

There had been a time when he'd lied to himself and pretended that everything he did, he did for her, to make her proud.

He didn't lie to himself anymore. Everything he did, he did for his own benefit. Just like this.

Thorssen dusted aside the crumbs of rust he'd picked off the two parts of the sword and put them with the other fragments he had collected in small plastic bags. He had no way of knowing if they were worth keeping or not, but wasn't about to discard them just in case.

He ran his fingertips over the sword once more, but this time stopped to take ahold of both pieces of the broken blade and pushed them together, once more imagining what they might have been like in all their majesty.

He covered them once more, left them on the coffee table and went down to join his mother over a meal of Wallenburgers and new potatoes.

He listened as she told him about her day—about the friends she had seen and how busy the shops in the village had been, and how hard the housework was becoming as her old bones began to fail her. More than once he'd offered to employ a housekeeper, but every time he raised the subject she batted the offer away. She didn't want help, she wanted to complain. The conversation died out a few mouthfuls into the meal. They ate the rest of it in near-silence.

He nodded in the right places when she did offer something, but it was obvious he was distracted, so she let him pick at his food and mostly ignore her, but didn't hide her disappointment when he set aside his plate, the meal half-eaten at best.

"Is there something on your mind, dear?" she asked.

"Nothing for you to worry about, Mother."

"But I do worry. I am your mother. It's in the job description."

He smiled at that. "I suppose it is."

"I thought it might have been the terrible news about the car accident."

"And what accident would that be, Mother?" He kept his tone light. Ignorance, when it came to the murder of troublesome little thieves, was bliss. He had deliberately avoided asking how Tostig intended to remedy the problem of the archaeologist, so he wouldn't slip up and give anything away. It was enough that the job was done, and the proof of that was on the table in his den.

"The poor archaeologist from your dig at Skalunda."

"It's not exactly *my* dig, Mother," he interrupted with a self-deprecating smile. "There are dozens of people involved."

"It is yours," she teased. "We both know that. Don't put yourself down. It wouldn't be happening without you. Anyway, I saw on the news today, the man who was running your excavation died in a car accident this morning. I thought someone would have told you?"

"Mortensen died? That's…" he muttered, and shook his head, feigning shock. "We should send flowers. Something."

"That would be the right thing to do, dear. You're such a good boy, always thinking about others. You're lucky I'm here to think about you."

"That I am," he said.

He hated lying to her, and knew in his heart that even if she discovered he was behind the man's accident, even remotely, she would never betray him, never judge him. She trusted him. She believed in the greater good of what he was doing and that there would be casualties along the way. He simply chose not to upset her, and what she didn't know couldn't do that.

She said no more about it as they finished their meal, and kissed him on the forehead as he made his excuses to retreat back to his den to make some calls.

His heart leaped when he saw the sword again.

He closed the door softly behind him and leaned back against it, needing the reassuring solidity of the wood at his back.

"I'm here," he whispered, words he might have offered to an expectant lover reclined on his bed. And that, in a strange way, was how he felt.

There was a comfort in the sword's nearness, a warmth that spread through him.

He crossed the room to the table and reached down to take hold of the hilt where the long rotten bindings had fallen away. He slid his fingers under the blade where the two halves had been separated in battle, and lifted it. The broken halves seemed to stay joined—as though glue had been applied to try to repair the ancient sword—before slowly separating in his hands.

It must have been a trick of the light, an optical illusion, that somehow combined to make him see what he wanted to see. Didn't it?

He placed the two halves down once more and examined the exposed edges, feeling them for some trace of solvent or anything to explain how they had seemed to hold together for that impossible second. There was no obvious change in the surfaces. Nothing apart from the crust of corrosion that had always been there. He started to think about it as dragon's blood again, pushing the pieces together, willing Nægling to be whole again.

But nothing happened.

As his mother liked to say, if wishes were fishes he could have fed an army of loyal supporters for free.

Karl Thorssen turned on the television in the hope of getting some news about the car accident. It wasn't grim fascination; it was purely practical. It would have been equally weird if a friend or coworker died and he didn't know the most rudimentary details. Five minutes into the endless twenty-four-hour news cycle, up came the stark image of a burned-out car, which was replaced by Lars Mortensen's face a few seconds later.

It wasn't as if they were anything more than acquaintances; Thorssen had only met the man on a couple of occasions, and those two times had been more than enough to convince him Mortensen's support couldn't be wholly relied upon. The man was an academic and, with that head full of nonsense, lived in a version of the world with high ideals about the truth, integrity and the relentless pursuit of knowledge for the sake of mankind. It wasn't the real world. And that had made Mortensen the kind of man that needed to be watched. Closely.

It was only a pity that Tostig had to resort to such extreme measures, but the sword couldn't be taken out of the country. It belonged to the people. It was their heritage. It belonged to Sweden.

It belonged to him.

His cell phone rang. He glanced at the display. The name on it was enough to have him mute the television.

"Is it done?"

"No."

"Then why are you calling?"

"There have been complications."

"Do I want to know?"

"You need to know."

"Tell me."

"The Serb is dead."

"Dead?"

"Yes."

"Then why are you calling?"

"To let you know that the Creed woman is more than she seems."

"More than she seems? Very cryptic. In what way is she *different?*"

"For one, she killed the Serb, but it is the how, that's what makes her different."

"I'm growing tired of all this dancing around the subject, Tostig. Spit it out."

"Very well. I don't know how she did it, how it is even possible, but as we moved to finish her, she drew a sword from thin air."

"A sword?" Thorssen didn't laugh. As preposterous as it sounded, Tostig wasn't given to lies or embellishments. If he said that's what happened, then that was what happened no matter how much it defied the laws of physics. He would not have dared mention it if he hadn't been sure of what he had seen. "If she is becoming a problem—and I think she is—she needs to be taken care of. That hasn't changed no matter what peculiar talents she has. I don't care how you do it. I don't care how many people get hurt, Tostig. The only thing I care about is that come dawn Annja Creed has lost more than just the will to live. I will not tolerate failure."

He didn't wait for a response. He ended the call.

Creed was an annoyance, but she didn't possess the sword and, as far as he was aware, had no real understanding of what Mortensen had found, so her death was merely a precaution. But that was the difference between Karl Thorssen and other men of his ilk; he was a cautious man. He planned things out methodically. He controlled the flow of information. He knew what his enemies were thinking before they did. There was little Annja Creed could do to jeopardize his plans. She was like a fly buzzing around his head. He would swat her.

Thorssen closed his eyes and sank back into his leather chair, savoring the feeling of contentment that came with knowing he had factored in every eventuality. He was in control. Even if she somehow discovered Mortensen's secret, even if she worked out what he wanted her to do, even if she managed to piece the puzzle together and make sense of it, she could not touch him, because there was nothing to link Karl Thorssen to the twisted wreckage of the archaeologist's car.

He opened his eyes again.

A yellow ribbon scrolled across the bottom of the silent screen announcing that they were entering the final days before the polls opened and promising exclusive coverage of the candidates' debate.

He hadn't been invited to participate, but Thorssen didn't mind. His exclusion guaranteed him more sympathy than his inclusion ever would have. Sometimes the petty bureaucrats played right into his hands. Besides, he had other things on his mind. Things that would make Lars Mortensen old news.

14

It wasn't so much plan B as plan H, but it was a plan.
Of sorts.

Annja sent a text to Roux, and with one hundred
and forty-four characters to play with she kept it nice
and to the point: Things have gotten weird here. No
matter how good you think your hand is, fold. Come
down and join in the fun. I could do with a friend.
Annja.

Then she'd sent Johan away.

He'd objected, saying she shouldn't be alone, but
she'd assured him she wouldn't be. Instead, she'd told
him she needed him to interview Elinor Johnsson from
the museum of antiquities about Beowulf's swords.
The museum was up in Stockholm, about as far away
as she could send him. Six hours on the train there, six
back, which meant an overnight stay. She took the lib-
erty of booking him into a hotel and, thanks to Micke
Rehnfeldt, managed to snag him tickets to see a jazz
singer she'd heard him mention, who just so happened
to be playing in a small club down by the waterfront.

He saw straight through Annja, but didn't fight her
over it.

"I'll be fine," she assured him. "I've got dinner with Micke to talk about what happens next with his film and our segment, and after that a good friend should be coming into town."

"How good a friend?"

"I trust him with my life," she assured him.

"You'd better…because if that guy comes back that's exactly what you're doing."

It was enough to get him on the train.

The news of Lars's accident had been unfolding all afternoon. The confirmation that it was his car came in first, and within the hour the police had announced that there had been one fatality. Though they had yet to release the victim's name, given it was Mortensen's car, the logical progression to it being Lars's body in the wreckage didn't seem like a big leap, but they needed to get dental records before they could say for sure who the dead man was.

Certain elements in the media were already speculating about what would happen now at the dig, and what it meant for Karl Thorssen, the dig's champion, with an eye on the upcoming election. After all, the timing of the ground breaking, a week before the people went to the polls, seemed to suggest he hoped for some incredible discovery as the votes were cast, surely? And so the talking heads went, opining about the motivations of the right-wing politico, giving vent to their spleens when the word *immigration* came up, and lamenting the use of a legend to feed Thorssen's greedy ambition.

One particularly vile specimen even went so far as to blame Mortensen, pointing out that the volunteers had been drinking the night before, celebrating the ground breaking and wetting the site, the implication being that Lars's judgment was somehow diminished, his reflexes slowed, because he had still been drunk when he got into the car that morning. They edited out the fact that the drinking had been limited to passing around a ceremonial horn, Viking style, and that Mortensen had drunk no more than a mouthful of beer before passing the horn on to the volunteer beside him. But that was tabloid journalism for you.

Micke was already in the restaurant when Annja arrived.

She would have been happy enough to have just met up for a drink in the hotel bar, but when they'd been making the date she'd realized just how hungry she actually was, and when she admitted she'd only had a slice of carrot cake and a couple of coffees since breakfast he'd absolutely insisted they make an evening of it.

"I'm glad you called," he said, rising slightly as she approached the table. "How's Johan working out for you?"

There was already a glass of white wine in front of her empty seat.

"I sent him to Stockholm to get rid of him," Annja joked.

"That well, then."

She smiled. "He's got lousy taste in music, and not much can be said for his personal hygiene when it comes to hotel rooms, but other than that, honestly, I love the guy."

"So to what do I owe the pleasure?"

"Work as always," Annja replied.

He looked down at his watch, like he was about to find an excuse to be anywhere else, then smirked.

"You'll want to hear this, I think."

"Why is it good-looking women always say that and I fall for it every time?" He smiled. It was an easy smile that looked like it belonged there, as if he should not have any other expression.

"Because you're a sucker for a pretty face?"

"That'd be it."

It was only gentle flirtation, but knowing what she wanted to talk about, and with the memory of Lars Mortensen's body in the burning car still painfully fresh, it was difficult to enjoy the moment. She took a deep breath, steeling herself for what she needed to say.

"That sigh sounds serious," Micke said before she could say anything. "Let's order first, then we can devote the attention it obviously deserves. Besides, I know you, if you start talking about something you're passionate about, you'll not stop to eat and I really don't want Doug giving me crap over you starving to death in Sweden. So, tonight we eat like kings, deal?"

She waited until the waitress had taken their order before she shared her reason for wanting to see him.

"Lars Mortensen," Annja said, tackling it head-on. "Do you know if they are going to replace him?"

"I spoke to Thorssen this afternoon—" he began.

"Thorssen?"

"Yep, our little fascist is pulling the purse strings. Straightforward economics—what Karl Thorssen wants Karl Thorssen gets."

"And what does he want?"

"That's the million-kroner question. What does Karl Thorssen want? Do you have any idea how many times there have been applications to excavate Skalunda?"

Annja shook her head.

"I know of at least fifty failed applications. This dig would never have happened without Thorssen. We're not a huge country in economic terms. We have very few megarich—most that reach that kind of wealth leave long before the tax man sinks his teeth into them, but some stay. They don't do it because they love the fifty-seven percent tax bracket. They're given incentives. The government does what it can to convince them to stay."

She considered the implications of what he was saying. "You mean people like Thorssen can hold the country to ransom?"

Micke shrugged. "In practical terms, yes. Some would argue it's a small price to pay if it means Thorssen locates his factories in Sweden rather than, say, Estonia, where he could slash his costs by basically halving his wage bill. He would make a lot more money, but in doing so would make thousands of Swedes unemployed. It's a deal with the devil. He's a big fish here. He says jump, the local authorities ask how high. He's got friends, too. And his friends here are much more willing to pander to him and feed his political aspirations. Like it or not, the guy's saying the kinds of things a lot of people are thinking."

Annja studied her dinner date. He wasn't smiling anymore. He looked troubled.

"And you don't agree with his politics?"

"I don't have a problem with immigrants if that's what you mean. As long as they contribute to society in some meaningful way, I welcome them with open arms. Thorssen's playing on basic fears. He wants his audience frightened. He wants them suspicious. He wants them to embrace all of these base emotions that say different is bad, different doesn't belong, and the extreme right give him a voice. You saw it in the theater. They worship him like he's the Second Coming."

"But the audience was specially chosen, right? Those were his people. Lars Mortensen wasn't one of those, was he? From the little we spoke he didn't seem to have a lot of time for Thorssen's politics, only his money."

"Which, sometimes, ends up being one and the same, I find. But, to answer your question, no, I don't think he did. Our boy Lars was more interested in his books and the politics of fourteen hundred years ago than he was in today's world. I think naive is a polite way of putting it."

"And yet he got into bed with Thorssen."

"We've all woken up the morning after, rolled over and immediately regretted jumping into bed the night before, haven't we?" That smile again. Annja couldn't argue the point. The bad decision process was a rite of passage. "And from what I can tell, Thorssen had a hand in choosing Lars. He can be very persuasive when he wants something, and he wanted Lars."

"You'd have thought he'd have wanted one of his own people in charge, surely?"

"Jobs for the boys? I don't know, he seemed to want someone who wouldn't look as if he was dancing to his tune just in case they turned up something interesting. Which is all academic now as he's decided to shut the dig down. At least for the time being."

"Understandable."

"Maybe. It was hard to tell over the phone. Honestly, he seemed pretty distracted."

"Well, his friend had just burned to death in his car."

"Oh, there was no love lost between them. No. It was almost as if he had started to lose interest in the project. You know what these rich guys are like, it's all chase the next bright shiny thing."

"So you don't think he'll reopen the site when everything calms down?"

"Yes, but I had to threaten him with breech of contract. Even then, it wasn't until I mentioned your name that he began to relent. He's image conscious. He knows that *Chasing History's Monsters* is syndicated in many countries. He's aware of how it would look if he suddenly changed his mind after all the trouble it took to get you guys over here in the first place. So apologies if I used your name in vain, but I think it was the difference between Skalunda being mothballed and closed down indefinitely."

"I'll let you off this once."

"There's a girl who's going to take care of things on-site for the time being and make a record of what's happened so far. Ingrid, Ina, something like that…"

"Inge," Annja corrected him.

"Inge. That's right. I take it you've met her?"

"She was milling around when I went to the dig earlier. She was trying to keep the volunteers occupied while we got some extra shots."

"I'd love to see them," Micke said. It almost sounded like a "can I come up for coffee" line. "How's the segment looking?"

Annja winced. "I've done better. We've probably got enough in the can to piece together a five-minute segment, but it isn't exactly groundbreaking stuff, if you'll pardon the pun. If we can get an interview with Thorssen to talk about why he wanted to support the dig, that kind of thing, and his use of the Beowulf imagery as a hero in his campaign, it'll fill a few more minutes even if it doesn't change the world."

"And you're not worried it'll be a little thin?"

"Not a lot we can do about that if Thorssen shuts the dig down with no relics to talk about. I'll just have to jazz it up with my charming personality. And maybe an excerpt from the poem or with a bit about Grendel's mother coming to avenge her child or something."

If it had been his show, she was sure, Micke would have pulled the plug. It wasn't compelling stuff. There was nothing new to add, no new spin to put on things, even with the footage from inside the barrow. It just wasn't sexy without a find to talk about, because quite honestly there'd be nothing to distinguish it from the dozens of other segments that had trodden the same ground over the years. Her only hope was the Karl Thorssen angle, but would a modern-day would-be Beowulf fascist be something the audience would go for?

She had an idea bubbling, though decided not to share it. What Micke didn't know wouldn't hurt him. Besides, if he knew what she was thinking there was no chance he'd set stuff up for her with Thorssen.

Their food arrived. It looked good and tasted better. Annja hadn't realized just how hungry she was until the first mouthful was digesting in her stomach and by then she was already shoveling the food down in a very unladylike manner. She caught Micke grinning at her. Her plate was already half-empty.

Before she could apologize, her cell phone began to vibrate in her pocket. It rattled against the table leg, making Micke raise an eyebrow. She offered an apologetic face and tried to ignore it, but even after going to voice mail, the caller tried again.

"Sorry." She half expected the display to show Johan's name. He ought to be getting off the train any minute, she calculated, but it wasn't him. She didn't recognize the number. Voice mail kicked in again before she could answer.

"Problem?" Micke asked.

"Don't know," Annja said, giving the caller a moment to leave a message before she dialed into her voice mail. The automated text came through, confirming she had a new message.

"Go on, you know you want to," Micke said.

She phoned in and was greeted by a hesitant voice on the other end.

"Oh, er… Hey…" the woman's voice began. "This is Inge…from the Skalunda dig. We talked earlier today. I'm sure you don't remember what with everything that's happened…." There was a pause, the girl clearly unsure what she wanted to say. "I meant to call as soon as I heard the news. I can't believe Lars is dead. I just…but things have been crazy here with the police and everything…." There was another long pause as she broke off trying to figure out her next words. "Anyway, I just wanted you to know that Lars's mother has been in touch. She's coming to the site tomorrow morning. She said she wanted to talk to you. I have no idea why. I gave her your number…I hope I didn't do the wrong thing. I thought I should tell you. I'm sorry I didn't know what else to do. I couldn't say no…not with her son dying like that."

The call ended without any goodbyes or requests to call back.

"Speak of the devil," Annja said.

"Which devil would that be?" Micke asked.

"Inge, just checking to make sure that I'd heard about Lars and to let me know his mom wants to have a chat."

"I don't envy you that conversation. How did she sound?"

"A little vague. Understandably. She worked with Lars every day. He was her professor at university. I'm thinking there was some hero worship going on."

"Must have hit her hard, then."

Annja nodded. But how hard? she wondered. She was beginning to feel suspicious of everyone involved with Skalunda Barrow. It seemed like they were all tied together in some twisted relationship of money and power, and it all came back to Karl Thorssen.

No one had said that the accident had been anything other than an accident, but to believe that seemed trite and foolish. Maybe it was the insistence the news reports had on laying the blame squarely at Lars Mortensen's feet, talking about alcohol and suggesting he must have been impaired. Add that to the call she'd had from Lars's phone, which must have come in when the car was already burning, and the visit she had from the two guys who'd shown up at her hotel room, and it was hard to deny that something was very rotten in the state of Gothenburg.

What she couldn't prove was that any of this was connected to the dig, although her mind kept being drawn back to that shaky handheld shot of the paramedic helping Thorssen into the ambulance. There was no denying it was the same man who'd tried to kill her in her hotel room.

There was her proof, wasn't it?

15

Tostig took his work seriously. It was the only hope a man like him had to see old age. He didn't trust anyone with the details of a job. He was obsessive and needed to control every single detail no matter how small. That way if something went bad, he only had himself to blame. If he was going to die, it was going to be his fault, not because someone had failed him.

He didn't need instructions. Though he could follow them, of course, if the client demanded it. Thorssen was a preferred client—letting him get on with things without interfering. It usually meant the job went like clockwork.

Not this time. This was his screwup.

Tostig really didn't like it when things went wrong. And there was no denying things had gone wrong.

He wouldn't underestimate Annja Creed again. Once was careless, twice was downright stupid, and Tostig has his downfalls, but he wasn't stupid. This time she was going to die. She would pay for the Serb's death. But before that there was another more pressing matter to take care of.

The Serb was starting to smell.

He'd found the Serb's body on the blacktop under Creed's window. The fact that the Serb had even the slightest pulse was a miracle, but he couldn't have recovered. Bones pierced his skin, his breath wheezed through collapsing lungs, his eyes were empty. There was nothing of the man in there, and no chance for him. Even with a hospital, he wouldn't have made it. Tostig wasn't a sentimental soul. The Serb knew what he'd signed up for when he'd become his apprentice.

It was purely self-preservation. There was an increased risk of discovery if he'd left the Serb to be found, alive or dead. If the police had the body it would have given credence to the woman's story. No body and she was just a hysterical tourist.

He had covered the man's nose and mouth and waited for him to die. It had only taken a couple of minutes and he was gone.

The ground was still too hard to dig a hole deep enough to bury the man, but there were other ways to conceal a body…better ways.

All it had taken was a single call to put everything in place.

He drove toward the lake.

Vänern, the largest lake in Sweden, covered more than two thousand square miles.

Tostig was familiar with the cold water and the potential it offered as a place of disposal.

As a child he'd imagined the lake was as big as the sea. It wasn't, but it was big enough to hide his secrets.

It wouldn't be the first time Vänern had taken a corpse he'd offered, and it wouldn't be the last. The call had been to arrange a small boat to be left for him on a narrow strip of shingle that pointed like a finger into the lake, along with the heavy chains and padlock. Anders Jakobs hadn't asked any questions: he knew better than that. His silence was one of the few things in this life that was guaranteed. One of the first bodies the assassin had dropped into the lake had been Jakobs's wife. She had cheated on him with his best friend. The friend had joined her two days later so they could be together forever and ever long may they rot.

Tostig had laid a false trail that took the lovers to Norway, convincing enough to make it appear as though they were both alive and well long after the eels had started to feast on them. In return, Anders continued to live a quiet and happy life in Mellerud, a small town directly across the lake from where the boat was moored, and when called upon did what he was asked, no hesitation. He was Tostig's man, body and soul. You couldn't buy that kind of loyalty.

The assassin drove slowly along the narrow track, lights out. There was no need to take unnecessary risks, even though the dirt strip ran straight and true all the way down through the trees to the water. No one would have noticed his car at this time of night, but standing out, even if it was only headlights and a revving engine, was not in his nature.

The boat was exactly where promised—an orange dinghy with a decent outboard motor.

He turned the headlights on before killing the car's engine, lighting the area around the dinghy so he could work.

Stuffed inside the belly of the boat was a large sheet of black polythene, the padlock and chain, and underneath the bench seat a bag containing a single item: a brand-new fish-gutting knife.

Working silently, he rolled the Serb into the plastic shroud, securing it with a padlock and chains.

He hoisted the Serb up onto his shoulder, taking the strain in his thighs. He moved unsteadily from the lake bank to dump the corpse into the boat. The Serb's skull made a sickening crack as it hit the bench seat, but the dead man didn't complain. Tostig's sweaty shirt stuck to every inch of his back.

He returned to the car and switched off the lights. While he would have liked them to guide him back, there was just too much risk involved in leaving them on for the hour plus he would be out on the water disposing of the Serb. He would just have to orientate himself from the lights of Mellerud on the other bank and plot a course from them.

Finally, he pushed the dinghy into the water, his fleet splashing in the waves, and clambered in over the corpse to take the oars. The boat lurched alarmingly as he struggled to maintain its balance. He waited, letting the hull drift free of the bank before he fired up the outboard motor and steered for deeper water.

He used the glow from the distant village to guide him out, and gradually, as it changed into a mere pinpoint of light, he cut the engine.

He waited for silence to fill his mind.

The boat drifted in the ebb and flow of the water, the waves lapping against the sides of the dinghy. Tostig patted a hand on his cargo; it was the closest thing he would offer to a fond farewell. He hadn't liked the Serb. They weren't friends. Like and friendship never factored into things. Still, it wouldn't be easy to replace the dead man.

The boat threatened to capsize as he levered the

corpse closer to the side. Moving quickly, he dropped one end of the weighted chain into the water, feeding it through his hands until it achieved momentum. Tostig steadied himself, bracing for the backsplash and, in that moment, before he slid the plastic-wrapped body over the side, used the gutting knife to cut a deep gash through the wrapping and the Serb's guts.

The body slipped beneath the water, leaving a bloom in its wake. The dark stain was barely visible in the moonlight and would disperse in a few minutes. The open wound he'd gouged into the Serb's guts served two purposes: it would attract eels and fish to feed, breaking the body down faster than might otherwise have been the case, and it would prevent the build-up of gases, which in a worst-case scenario could bring the Serb bobbing back to the surface—it was something he'd been told many years before by his own teacher.

He sat for a minute and watched the disturbance in the lake ripple slowly away, the blood dispersing into the blackness, lost to the rhythm of the water.

There was no sign of the Serb.

Tostig fired up the engine again and turned the boat around to head back toward the shore.

16

Karl Thorssen had lost track of time.

He'd spent the night in a leather chair, hunched over the low oak table, picking at the layer of corrosion that marred the sword parts. Just picking, picking, picking, first at one edge, then at the other, until his fingers were bloody. He marveled now at the gleaming metal, unable to believe it could have survived in what was essentially its pure form.

He carefully positioned the two pieces, broken edge to broken edge, and sank back into his chair.

Sleep stole over him. The blood on his fingers dried. The nagging in his brain ceased. The room was in darkness, scant light provided by the dull glow of the moon through the blinds. He dreamed fitfully of victory, of battle, the heady rush of charging headlong toward death, welcoming its embrace even as glory fired his blood, making his sleep fitful. Eventually, he cried out, clutching his side, feeling his lifeblood pulsing out of him only to wake in a fever sweat.

He wiped the sleep from his eyes.

The early-morning sun had replaced the moon.

He didn't move for a long while, gathering his thoughts together.

He needed coffee. He needed a shower. He needed food. But not necessarily in that order, and not before he'd examined his handiwork again.

He turned on the reading lamp beside the chair. Now that the blade had been cleaned it looked as if it could have been forged yesterday but for the fact that the metal still bore some of the scars of battle. There was a nick that had been patched and repaired, reworked and retempered. The workmanship was excellent, especially for its day.

Thorssen ran his fingers along the metal, closing his eyes as he felt its length, trying to feel out the break without success. He opened them again and even in the concentrated light it took a moment to find the faint line that revealed where the two halves had been pushed close together before he fell asleep. The two broken edges were still a perfect fit despite everything the metal had been put through.

He wondered how easy it would be to reforge the two halves and make the thing whole again. Replacing the grip and bindings for the hilt shouldn't prove too difficult, but the blade itself, much harder, surely? It was a complex job requiring specialist skills. Skills that had almost died out in the modern era. Would it be possible to find someone capable of the task? It wasn't his field. The archaeologist would probably have known someone who could have fixed it, but there was no use crying over spilled milk. He would find someone. Money had a way of finding men with unusual talents. Men like Tostig and the Serb. Men like him.

Thorssen imagined stepping out onto the hustings, raising the aged weapon in triumph to the rapturous cheers of his supporters. Just how good would that feel? How powerful would he feel standing there, Nægling in his hand? What an amazing gift it would be to the people—to his people—to be able to put the ancient sword on display to the world.

That would show the world just how important he was, how *powerful* he was.

He imagined himself strong enough to slay dragons.

He picked up Nægling's hilt once more, pretending it was whole.

He cut through the air, twisted his wrist, dropped his hip and cut through the air again, savoring the feel of the sword in his hand.

His connection to it was primal.

Powerful.

It took him a moment to realize that the two parts were still held fast together, and that it wasn't just an illusion.

He laughed, turning the sword in his hand this way and that, and could not stop laughing.

He tested the blade, cutting the air again. The joint held firm; somehow the two halves had reforged themselves while he slept.

They belonged together and never wanted to be parted.

He knew that now, felt the truth of it in his hand.

Thorssen scrutinized the edge of the blade. It was straight as a die, with no imperfections. There was no sign of the joint. It was a weapon for a warrior.

It was a sword fit for a king.

17

Annja woke the next morning with the sour taste of wine in her mouth.

Her head was pounding, but not because of alcohol; she'd only had two glasses of wine. She hadn't been good company after that and had made her excuses to head back to the room. Micke took it like a gent; in other circumstances she might have offered him that cup of coffee, but all she wanted to do was crash.

She rolled over.

Her mind was running slow.

The light from the window came in from the wrong side of the room. No. She'd not slept in her own bed. She'd used Johan's room. Johan had insisted on leaving his key with her, and after the briefest of goodnights with Micke, she'd stood in between the two doors playing a game of eenie-meanie before deciding that should her would-be killer try again, he'd come looking in her room, obviously. The last thing she'd done before getting into bed was to push Johan's giant camera case up against the door. The noise of it moving should have been enough to wake her if her attacker found her.

The alarm clock on the nightstand showed that it was a little after seven-thirty. Annja got up, showered quickly and dressed in the clothes she'd been wearing the night before. She gathered up the rest of her things and went back to her own room.

Her door was ajar.

Annja eased the door open slowly while standing to one side.

She could hear movement inside.

She tensed, readying the sword in the otherwhere, in case she had to fight for her life, only to scare the heck out of a startled maid.

"Oh, miss…the manager is coming."

And then Annja realized that all of her possessions were tipped out of her case, and the contents of the wardrobe had been emptied and dumped on the floor and bed. The room was in complete chaos.

Annja didn't say anything.

"I hope you don't mind. I was walking past. I saw that your door was open and it was like this. I called out, but there was no answer so I came in. I think you've been robbed."

"It's fine, don't worry. I appreciate it." She shook her head, looking at the mess. Her bag was still hooked over the back of the chair. She checked it. Her credit cards were still in her wallet. Meaning, this was no opportunist's crime. The thief had been thorough, but for all that thoroughness he'd almost certainly left empty-handed. She suspected she had what he was looking for: Johan's camera.

"It doesn't even seem as if anything has been taken," she said, but before she could thank the girl and send her away, the manager appeared.

"Oh, no," he said. "I am so sorry. I just…this has never happened here before. I can't believe this. I'll call the police straightaway. Please, Marcy, would you be so kind as to show Ms. Creed to suite seven?"

"There really is no need," Annja said.

"You can't possibly stay here now. Please. Let me at least give you an upgrade. Anything you've lost, we'll bear the cost. Just give me a list."

"It's okay. I have an idea of who's behind this."

It was clearly music to their ears.

If Annja knew who was responsible and didn't want to involve the police that was her decision, one that meant no bad publicity for the hotel. The manager's face lit up at the idea of being able to sweep the whole thing under the carpet.

"If you're sure?"

"I'm sure."

"The suite?"

"To be honest, I kinda like my room, and I'm not good with heights," she joked.

"If you are sure," the manager repeated.

"I really am."

In the silence that followed their leaving, Annja took another moment to look around the room, reassuring herself that nothing had been taken. It wasn't about theft; it was a warning. They could reach her at any time.

Well, good for you, Annja thought. Bring it on.

Annja Creed wasn't some passive victim. They could come for her, they could try and scare her, they could try and silence her, but what they needed to know, to really understand, was that she could just as easily come for them.

And, closing the door on the chaos, that was exactly what she intended to do.

18

A woman was waiting for her in the hotel's reception area.

Annja had no idea of how Mrs. Mortensen had found out where she was staying. It was a little unnerving. And why did she want to see her? It wasn't as though she knew her son particularly well. They had talked for perhaps twenty minutes, but she was probably one of the last people to speak to him, she realized, if not *the* last.

The woman's eyes were red and raw with grief.

It was obvious she wasn't sleeping.

"Miss Creed?" the woman said, coming across the marbled foyer to meet her. "Una Mortensen. Can I have a few minutes? I promise not to take up too much of your time. I just hoped to talk to you about Lars."

"No, of course, let's grab a seat," Annja said, indicating the lounge opposite the reception desk. There was a continental breakfast desk set up, filled with a variety of cornflakes, yogurts and crisp breads along with glass beakers of coffee strong enough and black enough to stand the sugar spoon up in. Annja poured two and joined Una Mortensen.

"My son said that he was going to see you?" Una said.

"That's right, Mrs. Mortensen," Annja started, but the woman interrupted her.

"Una, please," she said. "I've to listen to the police call me that all day, like it was some sort of token of respect when there was none. They think that he was drinking, that what happened to him was his own fault."

"Because of the ground breaking?"

"It's traditional, isn't it? It's not a real party. I'm not saying Lars didn't drink, because he enjoyed a bottle of beer as much as the next man, but he's not a drunk, and he'd never drink and drive, especially after his father died. He was hit by a drunk driver when Lars was fifteen. He wouldn't do it. Everything in moderation, that was my Lasse."

"He sounded fine to me when he called," Annja told her.

The woman's face lit up at this simple statement.

"He did call you, then? That morning? He said he was going to. He said he needed to see you."

"He said that he had something he wanted to show me."

"Well, then, he clearly trusted you. He didn't trust everyone. He said there were people at the dig he was sure were working for Thorssen. He was worried that someone would try to take it from him."

"Take what?"

"He didn't tell you what he found?" The woman sank back into her chair.

Annja shook her head. "He didn't want to tell me

over the phone. He said that he would rather show me what he was so excited about."

"But they haven't found it, have they?" Una asked.

"I don't know. If he had it with him the chances are it was destroyed in the fire."

Una Mortensen looked defeated. It was as though the whole world had suddenly caved in around her and buried her last hope along with it. Annja couldn't believe that she hadn't at least considered the possibility that the artifact had been destroyed, but if she didn't believe that his death was an accident why should she believe his treasure had perished in the blaze along with him?

"Do you know what he had found?" Annja asked. If the archaeologist had confided in anyone it would have been his mother, especially if the find was so important. He would have needed to tell *someone*.

Una shook her head, quashing that notion just as quickly as Annja had quashed hers. "He told me it was the most important thing he'd ever found. He said it would make him famous."

So he had found something, and without any significant signs of excavation after breaking through the shell into the tomb under the hill. Not the remains of the hero; he would never have attempted to remove those bones for fear of damaging them irreparably. No, it had to be something easily portable, something light, just waiting for him to reach inside. Something that would have barely left a trace behind after he'd taken it.

"He didn't give you any clue?"

Una shook her head and sat in silence.

And then her face lit up as a thought crossed her mind.

"He was always so careful. He wouldn't have just taken something. He wasn't a thief. There are procedures, aren't there? Things to establish a chain of continuity for a find. He would have taken a photograph of it before he risked the extraction, wouldn't he? He's done that ever since he started. He's got a picture of every fragment of every piece of pottery he's taken out of the ground, so wouldn't he have done that with something really important?"

"There's got to be a chance—it's hard to break a habit like that, even when you're excited about something," Annja agreed. Archaeologists were creatures of habit; their procedures were so ingrained they'd never break them, given what was at stake.

"He had some kind of fancy phone that took really good pictures," Una Mortensen said, suddenly filled with excitement."

The phone that his murderer called her on, she realized. They were still two steps behind, chasing shadows.

"Gone," she said, not wanting to say the rest of the sentence.

"The phone might be, but that doesn't mean the picture is. He always copied them to his computer so he could show me when he came home. It was worse than looking at his holiday photographs." She smiled softly at the memory, just a little bit more lost than she had been a second before.

His laptop.

Annja remembered that it had been sitting on the table in his caravan, half-buried by newspaper articles and journals and just about everything else he'd been able to amass to clutter such a small space. So if he had taken a photograph, if he had transferred it to his laptop before he left to meet her, that's where it was. If the laptop was still there. Those were a lot of ifs.

Her mind raced through all of the possibilities.

Was that what the burglary this morning had been about? Someone looking for that photograph? If Mortensen was a creature of habit, someone who'd been watching him for a while would know his methodology, and know that there had to be a photograph of the find out there. It made a grim kind of sense.

"It was in his caravan yesterday," Annja said.

"His caravan?"

"He's got a caravan on-site."

"That sounds like Lasse. Once he gets his teeth into something he won't leave it alone. Not even for a minute. I remember him going to Pompeii and the only time he left the camp they had set up was when he was heading to the airport to come home."

"Which doesn't make sense, does it? I mean, why did he want to meet me in town, not out at the site? It would have been easier to get me to come out to the dig. I could have seen the find in situ."

"He was frightened," Una confessed. "I told you. He was frightened someone was going to take it from him."

Annja thought about the implications of what Una was saying. The only someone had to be Karl Thorssen, didn't it? Lars had told her he'd done a deal with the devil and as a result Thorssen had the right to see everything as it came out of the ground. So he'd tried to get the find out of there before word of his discovery got back to Thorssen. It was all starting to make sense.

"I have to go to the police station this morning. They want to explain everything to me face-to-face. I want to see his body but they won't let me. I guess that's what they want to go over, that he was too badly burned in the fire. They want me to identify his medallion."

"I saw the fire," Annja admitted, and waited for the news to sink in.

"You saw him?"

"The police…the firemen…they were all doing everything they could to put the fire out."

"But no one tried to get him out of his car," Una said flatly. It wasn't an accusation.

"It was too late by then. I didn't even spot that it was his car, but believe me, no one could have gotten close enough to help him. It was already too late by the time they got there."

"And that's supposed to make me feel better?" Una Mortensen was unable to meet Annja's eyes. The woman seemed to age fifty years in as many seconds as her resolve broke and the tears started to fall. Her body heaved and shuddered as the sobs raked through her. Annja let her grieve. It was a private thing.

"Are you here on your own?" Annja asked when the woman's sobs finally subsided. She couldn't abandon her. Not if she needed someone. She was barely able to make any coherent sound. Una nodded.

"Would you like me to come with you?"

"Would you?" The words hitched in her throat.

"There's nothing that can't wait. We could go out

to the site afterward, if you like. So you can see what Lars was doing, where he was staying."

"We could check to see if he took a photograph," she suggested hopefully.

"We could indeed."

"You don't think this was an accident, do you?" Una asked the question Annja had so fervently hoped she wouldn't.

She couldn't bring herself to lie.

"No," she said. "I don't."

19

The Creed woman was sitting in the hotel lounge drinking coffee with an old lady Tostig did not recognize. According to Thorssen, Creed was some kind of television personality, which increased the risk of her being known. In the world of cell phones and instant media it was a problem. He had to be aware, careful not to be caught in any celebrity snapshot souvenirs.

It would have been better to deal with her yesterday but there was no undoing the past.

Getting into her room again after he had disposed of the Serb had been child's play. She hadn't been in there. Her bed hadn't been slept in. That had pushed him close to the edge.

He knew he was on the verge of doing something stupid when he snarled, stormed out of her room and raised his foot to kick down the door of the room opposite. As the rage threatened to consume him, he saw himself kicking down every door on this floor and the next and the next until he found her. He couldn't do that.

She would be on her guard. That was going to make things more difficult.

His first problem was getting her alone—or at least luring her away from somewhere quite as public as this.

Tostig was patient. He could bide his time. Watch. Study her. Get to know her when she thought no one was watching. That was when you learned the truth about a target. The car was uncomfortably warm as the heat of the day started rising, but air-conditioning drained the battery while the engine wasn't running. It was a compromise, invisibility for discomfort. He had only managed a few hours' sleep the night before. He only needed a few hours. Like many in his line of work, he'd learned to adapt, to snatch rest whenever it was offered because there was no way of knowing how long it could be until he could next sleep. He didn't take artificial stimulants. A man survived on his wits, on his skill and, if necessary, his fear. He did not survive on amphetamines.

Besides, the thought of his brain being interfered with, of his thoughts racing any faster than they already did, was an entirely different kind of fear for the assassin. Chemicals altered the balance of the mind. There was no telling what demons they would liberate.

He needed distance.

Objectivity.

Making something personal increased the chance of making a mistake.

That meant keeping low profile for now.

His cell phone signaled he had a call. He checked the display. All it said was The Client.

"What?"

"Where is she? Right now?" Thorssen asked, his voice bright and excited.

"In the hotel lounge having coffee with an older woman."

"Mortensen's grieving mother."

That made sense. Creed was a meddler. She couldn't leave well enough alone. "Do they know each other?"

"It seems they do now. That leaves us with another loose end you will need to tie up before this is over, but there is a more pressing problem now."

"A problem?"

"Yes. And you know how I hate problems."

"What do you need me to do?"

"There's a man who knows too much. Now he thinks that his silence is worth something. Surprisingly, I agree with him, but not in the way he'd hope. Silence him. Permanently."

Tostig listened while Thorssen gave him the name and address of the problem. He didn't need to write the details down; he knew exactly where the address was. Tostig had met the man once. If he was talking about things best kept secret that put Tostig in the firing line. He didn't like the idea of that. The assassin took another glance at Annja Creed and Mortensen's mother. Creed was comforting the old woman now.

That was another weakness. Empathy. He could work with that.

Tostig started the car, pulled out into traffic and drove.

The warehouse stood just outside of town.

It was surrounded by farmland.

A herd of cows looked inquisitively toward him as Tostig stepped out of his car.

Every country had its secrets. Sweden was no different. There were enough explosives stored in this building to blow Gothenburg off the map.

The signage declared Grendel Pyrotechnics on one side of the warehouse.

The only other vehicle in the vicinity was a white van bearing the same name and corporate logo.

Tostig had seen the van before; it had been parked near the theater on the morning of Thorssen's call to arms.

He'd noticed that Thorssen became agitated at the sight of it, demanding that the driver move it farther away once he had unloaded his equipment. If Tostig hadn't known what was being planned it might have seemed uncharacteristic and unnecessary, but given what was going to happen, the assassin could all too well see the risks the van's presence constituted.

The reinforced metal door stood open, inviting the assassin to come inside the warehouse.

Tostig strolled past it, taking a tour of the building to get the lay of the land.

All of the windows were of frosted glass and covered with bars to keep intruders out.

They'll work just as well to keep people in, he thought grimly.

The fire exit was at the rear of the building. Tostig didn't want the man slipping out the back and missing out on all the fun. He used a crowbar to wedge the door shut. There was no other way in or out. Having secured the building he returned to the trunk of his car and retrieved the gallon can of gasoline he kept there for just such situations.

The man at the workbench inside didn't see him at first.

Tostig took the opportunity to cast his eyes around the space.

There were boxes of completed fireworks and bins of the raw materials for their construction all around the workshop. Nils Fenström had built himself a nice little business working on special effects for film and television companies in Sweden, and even farther afield after Swedish crime shows became the toast of the world. Fenström was good. Better than good. When it came to blowing things up spectacularly, he was the man. It didn't matter if it was small-scale fireworks for the holidays, or rigging it to look as though parliament was ablaze for the latest action-adventure blockbuster.

"Can I help you?" the man asked, clearly unphased by the fact that he had a visitor.

"Mr. Thorssen has an answer for you."

"Ah, right. So he's agreed to pay up?" The man smiled. It was an avaricious leer. "Come on, then, what is it, a check? A bag of silver? No. A briefcase of used banknotes, right, like out of the movies?"

"There's no money. Not now. Not ever," Tostig replied.

"So you're supposed to frighten me off?"

"No."

"What, then? You want me quiet? That comes at a price. Simple as that. Tell Thorssen it's just business."

"I'm not here to intimidate you," Tostig said, unscrewing the cap from the plastic fuel can.

The man looked instinctively toward the fire exit. The movement revealed the scar tissue that puckered up the skin as far as his disfigured ear. He wanted to bolt, but was rooted to the spot, staring at the gasoline can in Tostig's hand. The assassin could see him solving the equation—gasoline, fireworks, an enclosed prefabricated warehouse and human skin. It all meant so much pain before death.

Instead of running, Fenström fumbled in the pocket of his overalls for something. It wasn't a gun. Not in a place like this. Not when he felt safe. People were never prepared for death to walk into the four friendly walls where they spent the majority of their lives. That was just the way of things. Death was always a stranger. Fenström produced a cell phone, but in his panic, he dropped it to the floor.

The screen shattered on impact.

Tostig could have kicked it away from him but there was no need. Instead, he said, "Go ahead, pick it up, make a call. They won't reach you in time."

He splashed the gas to the left of Fenström, in an arc, and to the right. The man didn't move. He stared down at the stains on the concrete, the stench of gasoline permeating the air. "You can't…"

"But I just did," Tostig said, emptying the can over the pyrotechnics expert's overalls, getting it in his face and hair, before he tossed the canister into one of the bins marked Explosive Material.

"Look…I get it. No money. I won't say anything. My lips are sealed. Mr. Thorssen can trust me. It was a joke, okay? A joke. Not a very good one. I didn't mean anything by it. You called my bluff. He knows me. I'd never take his money. You can let him know that I've got the message. Received and understood. I can call him now." And thinking it would save his life, Nils Fenström dropped to his knees and scrambled about on the floor trying to pick up the shattered phone. Fear made his hands shake so badly he couldn't hold on to the bits of phone.

Tostig took a step back toward the open door.

"I'll pass him the message. Maybe he'll forgive you."

"Yes. Yes. I know he will. He's a good man, he'll get the joke."

"I'm sure he'll laugh when I tell him the punch line," Tostig said. He reached inside his pocket for a book of matches, tore one off the strip and struck it. He used the match to set light to the rest of the box, and as the matches caught fire there was a burst of flame. "Catch." He tossed the box toward Fenström, who scrambled backward, trying to get away.

It didn't matter. The box landed in a puddle of gasoline at Fenström's feet, caught on fire and spread to engulf the man. Fenström tried to beat the flames out with his bare hands, screaming, twisting, then dropping to his knees as the flames raged higher.

Tostig watched the panic transform into certainty in the man's eyes as his body began shutting down to hide from the pain.

Tostig turned his back and walked away, shutting the heavy door behind him. He went toward his car with the echo of death still ringing in his ears.

He slammed the car door, putting it into reverse as the first ear-shattering explosion ripped through the warehouse.

Watching the flames rise, he hit redial on his phone.

It rang once.

"It's done," Tostig declared.

Before Thorssen could ask how, the scream of buckling metal and the roar of gunpowder gave him the answer to every question he never wanted to ask.

Tostig could see the cows stampede to the chaos of exploding fireworks.

He hung up on his employer, and put the radio on. The DJ had a sense of humor: Talking Heads' "Burning Down the House" was followed by The Animals' "We Gotta Get Out of This Place." The assassin found himself singing along as he drove away, fire in the sky behind him.

20

Given how things were playing out, Annja was glad that she'd put Johan on the train rather than handing him the car keys. She was hoping there'd be an element of safety in numbers. Even though she knew she was the object of the goons' affection, she couldn't be sure he was safe. She didn't like that uncertainty. She hadn't heard back from Roux, either, which worried her. Still, she couldn't help her overactive imagination.

She stared at every face as people went by her, just in case she recognized one of them from Johan's footage. It was exhausting. She knew that if she kept it up she'd drive herself crazy, but she couldn't help herself.

Una Mortensen held her hand as they walked to the police station.

The visit proved less stressful than she had anticipated.

Annja caught a glimpse of the young officer who'd been at the scene and had tried to keep her away from the burning car. He showed no sign of noticing her. A wry half smile crossed her lips; the joys of not really being famous.

A female officer was sent down to collect them from reception.

She was as compassionate as it was possible to be in such circumstances, reassuring Una, modulating her tone, keeping it emotionless, offering no extra commentary as she led them to a quiet room and sat with them. The sight of the silver medallion, almost melted from the blistering heat of the burning car, and the chain that had fused into a lump of coil offered a grim reminder of what had happened to her son's body.

"Can I hold it?" Una asked. She didn't reach for it. She sat with her hands folded in her lap, and leaned forward, unable to take her eyes from the ruined chain.

"Are you sure?" the policewoman said, but even as she did, she reached for the evidence bag and broke the seal, emptying the chain and medallion into Una's cupped hands.

"I gave it to him when he went away on his first dig." She said the words like some half-remembered prayer. The medallion, Annja realized, was of Saint Christopher, obviously meant to keep her son safe when he was out of her sight. The fused chain was a very vivid reminder that it had failed him. Una Mortensen held it tight in her fist. Annja knew the old woman never wanted to let it go. There were certain things she had in her own life that made her feel like that, relics from her time growing up with the nuns in the orphanage.

The tears came again.

"Can she keep this?" Annja asked, reasonably sure that the officer would agree with the request. It wasn't about preserving a chain of evidence. Lars Mortensen's murderer would never be made to stand up in court.

"I'd like to go to my hotel," Una said.

"Of course," the policewoman said. Annja didn't know who she was answering.

"It's not far from here," Una said. "I think I'd like to be on my own."

Annja didn't want to leave her, but knew how important solitude was to the grieving process. The necklace had made it real for her. It didn't matter that she'd known for twenty-four hours. This visit stole the last fragment of hope she'd been able to cling on to. Because right up until that moment, holding the twisted silver in her hand, she'd been able to convince herself it might—just might—be someone else's body in the wreckage. Someone else's son.

The old woman stood, shook her hand and left them. She didn't relinquish her hold on the necklace, and the policewoman didn't try and stop her from taking it, so that was her answer.

"I'll call you when I'd like to go out to the site," Una said.

"I'll pick you up at the hotel, just let me know," Annja reassured her. As eager as she was to check out the laptop, she'd just have to occupy herself until the woman was ready. A promise was a promise.

Annja was watching Una's receding back when she heard the distant rumble of thunder—only it wasn't thunder. Thunder didn't sound like that. She knew that sound. An explosion. A massive explosion. The sound dampened as it reached them through the concrete of the station house, but still unmistakable.

She ran to the nearest window. In the distance, above the rooftops, Annja saw the beginnings of a cloud of black smoke pluming up toward the sun.

It took less than two minutes from the crack of thunder resolving until she heard the first siren of emergency vehicles headed in that direction.

Annja's first instinct was to help, but it wasn't her place to. The firemen and paramedics knew what they were doing. She would have just added to the confusion by chasing the explosion.

She had a story to focus on.

She had a man intent on making sure she didn't tell it.

Annja needed to think. There was still plenty she hadn't managed to puzzle through. She also needed a decent breakfast—or lunch as it was quickly becoming—so she left the station house and crossed the street to a small deli, picking up an olive and feta focaccia and yogurt drink to take back to her room. She wanted to run through Johan's footage one more time. She didn't think she'd missed anything. But every time she watched it served to cement the faces in her subconscious, and who was to know how important that would prove in the long run? And the big man's presence masquerading as a paramedic proved it wasn't all about the main people in the shot. It was the people in the background she wanted to look at. The ones who didn't take up a lot of space on the screen. The ones who didn't want to be seen.

The maid had done up her room nicely. There was a basket overflowing with fruit on the desk, and a note from the manager hoping she'd enjoy the rest of her stay. The room felt clean and new again in that way only hotel rooms can. If walls could talk, these ones would have more than just illicit liaisons, or happy vacation chatter. They'd have death and violence to whisper about, too.

Annja knew the big man would be back to try and finish what he'd started. Next time she was going to be ready for him, assuming she didn't find him first.

She turned the television set on as she entered the room. After she changed channels away from the hotel menu the first words out of the speaker were about the explosion. She couldn't understand a word they were saying, but she didn't need to understand. A photograph of a man flashed up on the screen, a thin, rat-faced man with a patch of scar tissue on one side of his face. She didn't know if he was the suspect or victim so she started up the laptop Johan had left with her, and cued up the footage he'd downloaded.

She watched the frames pass again from the start of the rally.

Before she had concentrated on the explosion and its aftermath, but this time she looked more closely at the minutia of what Johan had recorded, especially the shots of people milling around outside as they had arrived.

Johan had filmed hours' worth of material for what might have been thirty seconds in the actual segment, far beyond what he'd need. It went beyond planning and into an obsessive compulsive need not to miss anything that might be remotely important. It was what made him a good go-to guy for Micke, no doubt. He knew he could trust the man not to screw up and miss the good stuff.

As she slowly went through it all again, she spotted a couple of faces she was sure she'd seen at the ground breaking. Of course, that should come as no real surprise. These were Thorssen's disciples after all, it was only natural some would follow him around like little lost dogs. But then she came across another face that stood out for all the wrong reasons.

At first Johan had caught no more than a fleeting glimpse of the guy, just enough for him to look vaguely familiar. However, there was a second shot where he turned his head to reveal the scar tissue on the side of his face. There was no mistaking it was the same man who had been up on the television screen a moment before.

Well, now, isn't that interesting, Annja thought, putting the pieces together. She waited for the news to put up some footage of Thorssen's rally, which they would have done if they were linking the man to it as the bomber behind both. When it didn't come she was convinced she was looking at another victim. And even as she thought it, she realized she'd seen the guy, too, arguing with Thorssen's security man before he was thrown out.

Curiouser and curiouser. She shifted her attention back to the frozen frame on the laptop screen and the scarred man.

She looked at the digital clock over by the bed, annoyed that Roux still hadn't been in touch.

There was one person she could think of to call.

"Annja!" Micke Rehnfeldt sounded pleased to hear from her at least. That was something, considering she'd skipped out early last night. Maybe he hadn't harbored hopes about how the evening would end, after all. "I'd begun to suspect you'd slope off without saying goodbye!"

"I'm sorry about yesterday. Chalk it up to a bad day.

Maybe if you're unlucky we'll get the chance to do it again before I have to head back home."

"Sounds like a plan."

It wasn't hard to hear the smile in his voice, so maybe he was still thinking of them having that coffee, after all. Flirtation was fun and harmless most of the time, but there was a fine line, and as much fun as it was to be flattered, there was something a little uncomfortable about using her sexuality to get what she wanted. She wondered if Micke felt the same way; after all, she doubted many women would have kicked him out of bed in the morning. Did he feel a pang of guilt when it came to using his two-day stubble and deep, serious eyes to get what he wanted out of a conversation? Somehow she doubted it.

"Have you seen the news?" Annja asked.

"It's running pretty much nonstop," he answered. "What piece in particular?"

"The fire."

"You mean the fireworks factory that just went up in smoke?"

"Fireworks factory?" That explained the ferocity of the explosion.

"Well, not just fireworks. There's a guy that does explosions and special effects for Swedish films, all the pyrotechnics stuff. Nils Fenström. He's good. Really good, actually. Very much the go-to guy for anything explosive. We've worked together a bunch of times, last time was a battlefield reenactment. The factory was his place. He's pretty much a one-man band." He broke off for a moment, then finished, "His car was outside. The firemen haven't been able to enter the place yet. If he was in there…" This time he trailed off and didn't say anything for an uncomfortably long time.

"I'm sorry," she offered, knowing it wasn't enough.

"What's your interest?"

"I don't know. Not yet."

"But there's something?"

"There is."

"Right. And you're not going to tell me what?"

"Not until it makes more sense," Annja said.

"Okay, but you'll call me about dinner?"

"You know I will," she promised, her mind already racing with questions. What was a pyrotechnics expert doing at Thorssen's rally? Wasn't it a coincidence that there should be an explosion while he was there, and despite the devastation the one person who should have been the target basically walked away unhurt? If he'd been trying to kill Thorssen he'd made a botch job of it, hadn't he? An explosives expert who managed to basically leave his intended victim safe in what ought to have been the center of the blast zone—unless that was exactly where his expertize had come in… Could he do that?

Of course he could, Annja thought.

And from that, her churning thoughts extrapolated more questions. More what-ifs?

What if the explosion at his factory was no accident at all?

What if it was the tying up of a loose end?

Could Karl Thorssen be that ruthless or was she making him into some sort of maniac that he wasn't?

A man who surrounded himself with dangerous substances all day treated them with respect; he didn't make mistakes. He didn't accidentally burn down his warehouse and himself with it. It was just too convenient.

And it came back to fire.

She hated that elemental force of nature.

It was voracious. Unquenchable. Destructive.

The more she thought about it, the more it felt as though Thorssen was the epicenter of this storm, and anyone who might have helped her grasp the truth of what was happening in this city was being taken care of permanently. First Mortensen, now Fenström, both in some way connected to Thorssen, both dead within days of each other, and then there was her own brush with Thorssen's people, the big man and the silent one who'd gone out of the window. Being associated with Karl Thorssen was proving to be a bad thing for one's life expectancy. The problem was the only man who could answer all of her questions was Karl Thorssen.

Annja needed that interview, but how was she going to get it?

21

The sword had an identity of its own.

It yearned to be set free. If Thorssen held Nægling up to the sunlight he could just make out a flicker of flame that ran along the sword's edge.

This was more than just a relic from a great past; this was a weapon of real power.

It was more than he could ever have dreamed of.

"Did you have to bring that thing to the breakfast table?" his mother asked as he placed the sword, safely wrapped once more, on the table between them. She had no idea what it was. He intended to keep it that way for now. Meal times were sacrosanct. Putting the sword on the table between them broke that pact, but that didn't matter today.

"Really? In the grand scheme of things is it important that I leave it in my den? I can take it back up there if the world will grind screeching to a halt. I wouldn't want to be responsible for a global disaster. Stop the clocks!" He didn't even try to mask the venom in his voice as he said it. His mother was beginning to irritate him. Just because he owed his life to her there was no reason why he should have to put up with her presence. He wouldn't accept the harping and grousing from a member of staff, so why should he accept it in his own home?

"I just thought—"

"I *know* what you thought, Mother. You always think the same thing and use subtle put-downs and prods to manipulate me into doing what you want your good son to do. You're just like everyone else in this damned world—you want something from me. Well, I've had enough of you, Mother." He felt the dam threatening to burst inside him as the tirade built up, his lips twisting into a sneer until he saw the tears glisten in her eyes and pulled back from the brink.

He wasn't sure what was happening to him.

It was a fight to regain control.

He was always in control.

That was how he lived his life.

She didn't deserve this. All she had ever done was want the very best for her boy.

"I'm sorry," he said, placing a hand on hers, but she pulled away.

That hurt.

He looked at the sword, but no matter how much he wanted to, he couldn't bring himself to carry it up to the den. He wasn't even sure that would make amends. "I'm sorry, Mother. You know the pressure I'm under with the election and everything. And the news…I don't know if you saw, but Nils, a friend of mine… he was in that explosion at the fireworks factory. I'm sorry, it's just all…" He let the sentence hang, knowing she wouldn't punish him in the face of such loss. It went against every instinct she had for him.

He was right; there was an immediate shift in attitude as she reached out to take his hand. "Oh, love. I didn't know…. How horrible—first the archaeologist, now your friend. However must you feel?"

The truth was he didn't know how he felt. Feelings seemed so…inconsequential. Nothing mattered apart from Nægling.

The thoughts raced through his head, pushing all other considerations to one side.

It was so hard to hold on to himself when he so much as thought about the ancient blade.

All he could think of now was how he would unveil it to the world.

His pain at upsetting his mother was gone, quashed by Nægling.

And then a stray idea crossed his mind: *If only it had been me…if only I'd found it. If only the two halves were still separate…I could return them, put them back in the ground where they belong.*

But it was too late for that. If wishes were fishes, as his mother liked to say.

The sword had somehow been reforged with its own magical fire—that same heat he saw rippling along its flawless blade—and even the memory of that fire was enough to send a surge of power through him. It filled him with more courage, more strength, than he could have imagined in his wildest dreams. He was like the blade, made whole by it.

He kissed his mother, and rose from the table.

"I'll take it away," he said, his skin crawling even as he made the promise he knew he'd never be able to keep. "Put the kettle on—I'll tell you all about what's going to happen today."

His mother nodded, grateful for the concession.

He retreated to his den, making two calls. The first was to a man who'd come highly recommended from one of his university cronies. "And you have the necessary skills?" he asked. "The handle and binding have suffered considerable deterioration. It will need an entirely new hilt."

"I can do it," the man assured him. "For the right price."

And that was what it was all about, wasn't it?

Nægling would look its best before revealed to the world. "I'm willing to pay more than you could possibly imagine, under three nonnegotiable conditions. One, the work is carried out today. Two, that it is done under my direct supervision. The sword is never to leave my sight. And three, that you are to speak of it to no one. Breaching any one of these terms will have consequences you would not want to incur. Believe me."

His second call was to the office, canceling all of his appointments for the day.

Everything else he determined was inconsequential and could be dealt with by his staff.

He turned on the TV.

The assassin had called with a simple message. It had taken no more than two words to confirm that he had taken care of another problem—two words that said everything and yet nothing. *It's done*. There were no better words in the world as far as Karl Thorssen was concerned.

The news channel was still carrying footage of the fire, replaying the spectacular explosions as the fireworks went up. There was no sign of Tostig's car in any of the footage, and any security camera would have gone up with the factory unit itself so there was nothing to come back on him. With that in mind, he enjoyed the show. High-pressure hoses jetted arcs of water over the blazing building without ever seeming to touch the flames. Three hours on, the fire showed no sign of abating. It would burn and burn, fueled by the combustibles inside.

Watching on the big screen, he wished he could have been there in person to enjoy the assassin's handiwork. The man was a maestro when it came to the act of killing. He wished he could feel the heat of the flames against his face as they grew out of control. He wished he could breathe in the acrid tang of gunpowder and blistered paint. He wished he could fan the flames, spilling them out across the open countryside.

Thorssen hadn't even realized that he'd picked up the sword again. He gripped it with both hands as though about to strike a massive blow.

Flames licked the ancient metal, dancing along its edge. They crackled, looking to leap to anything that might feed its fire.

He felt it burning inside him, too.

Blazing.

Was the sword causing it?

Was the burning inside him igniting the sword?

He was certain that they belonged together. Somehow, one fed the other.

He walked down to the waiting Tesla. The sword was slung across his shoulder like some warrior of old striding out to the battlefield. He rested his prize against the passenger seat as he drove toward the sword smith's. The ancient blade slid a couple of times as the car negotiated the many tight turns between his house and the city. He drove aggressively, accelerating into the corners and out of them, pushing the Tesla to the very limits of its endurance. On a normal day the journey would take the best part of an hour, today less then forty-five minutes.

GPS steered him with its mechanical voice to the smithy.

He only knew the man's first name: Ulric. That was all he needed to know. He was more interested in his skill than being his friend. The smithy wasn't at all what he'd expected—a cramped shed behind a run-down cottage on the opposite side of the city. Ulric's expression went from mildly curious to rapt as he examined the sword.

"Very nice, man, very nice indeed," he said as he held the metal in his hand, turning the sword over and over again as he studied it.

"How long will it take you?"

"As long as it takes. Never rush a craftsman," Ulric said. "First, I need to make a wooden grip to fit here." He drew Thorssen in, pointing out the strip of metal between the guard and the pommel. "And because all of this is fused together I will need to make it in two parts, close it around the metal, then bind it in place. It all takes time if you want it done properly."

"I want it done perfectly," Thorssen said.

"As do I. A piece like this deserves nothing less. You can leave her with me if you have somewhere to be."

"As I said on the phone, three conditions. Break any of them, and there will be consequences. I will stay and watch. The sword will not leave my sight for

a single moment. I will pay you half a million kroner for your skill and discretion. Do we have a deal?"

While it wasn't dollars, half a million kroner was a
huge amount of money for a single afternoon's work.
How could he possibly say no?

"Deal," Ulric said.

"The right answer. Had you said no I would have
been disappointed and I don't deal well with disappointment, Ulric, believe me. Actually, you don't want
to know how I deal with disappointment." Thorssen
laughed.

22

There was still no sign of Johan when Una Mortensen called to say that she was prepared to visit the barrow now. It wasn't her day for people getting back to her. She still hadn't heard from Roux, either, and the more his silence stretched on, the more worried she became. At first it had just been mild annoyance, but since she'd sent out her SOS, she'd at least expected the Frenchman to touch base. If he so much as smirked when he finally showed his face she'd read him the riot act. In fact, for him, it would be better if he turned up with a couple of broken legs and a big sign that said Sorry. Then maybe she'd forgive him.

Meanwhile, Annja didn't want to keep Una waiting. It must have been hard enough to muster the courage to go out to her son's final site. Annja hoped the whole thing would be cathartic for her, but sometimes even the best medicine hurt to take.

Annja tried calling Johan but his phone went straight to voice mail. The train tracks went through some pretty remote countryside between the capital and the second city, though, so there wasn't anything necessarily sinister about his silence.

Rather than try to find her way through the confusion of streets to Una's small hotel, Annja arranged to pick her up close to the police station, which she knew she could find again.

"This really is very kind of you," Una said for the umpteenth time as she slipped into the passenger seat. "You didn't have to."

"But I wanted to. Besides, if you're right and he photographed the find, I want to see it."

"Do you think it might be important…even if it was destroyed in the fire?"

Annja nodded. "Important enough to kill him for? Maybe." And what she didn't say was she didn't think the relic was in the car when it burned. If Thorssen really was behind Lars Mortensen's murder, then almost certainly his killer had recovered the artifact and delivered it to Mortensen.

"So he could still become famous, then, even if it cost him everything?"

Annja glanced across at the woman, but Una was staring out at the road ahead.

Annja realized exactly where they were, and what the twist in the road up ahead meant in real terms: they were driving along the same stretch of road where Lars had died. Annja was angry with herself. She should have followed the alternative route to the site. She gripped the wheel tighter as they reached the spot. The verge was scorched black back to the dirt. The branches overhanging the road were shriveled and stripped of all vegetation. There was no mistaking the wounds of fire. Annja shivered, the memory of the car bright in her mind.

Una stared straight ahead, deliberately avoiding so much as a glance toward the blackened ground.

"We'll drive back a different way," Annja promised by way of an apology. Una said nothing. She didn't need to.

They drove the rest of the distance in an uncomfortable silence.

The dig was just as quiet.

There was a single car parked on the grass not far from the dark caravans and various tents. Annja called out as she clambered out of the car, but couldn't see anyone. "Hello?" she called again, and was greeted by a distant shout. A moment later the girl, Inge, emerged from the main tent dusting her hands off on her trousers. She smiled when she saw it was Annja.

"Oh, hey," she said as they approached, with a wide, genuine smile despite the fact she obviously hadn't expected any visitors. Annja noticed one of the curious slate tiles on the workbench through the tent flaps.

"Inge, this is Una, Lars's mother. Una, Inge was your son's assistant." The two women didn't seem to know if they were supposed to shake hands, hug or merely stand there. In the end Inge lurched forward a little clumsily and hugged the old woman. "Where is everyone?" Annja asked.

"It's just me for the moment, I'm afraid. No one's decided what's happening yet, so while they talk about what they want to do with the site I'm just keeping things secure, doing a bit of tidying up, you know, for Lars."

Annja appreciated that the girl felt the loyalty to her old professor to stick around and do the day-to-day minutia necessary to keep the site viable. "I've brought Una here to show her what Lars was doing, give her a peek at his last work and collect his stuff. We won't get in your way."

The girl paused, obviously unhappy with the thought of them removing anything from the caravan. "What kind of stuff?"

"His clothes, a few bits and pieces. Nothing to worry about. It'll save people sending it on afterward when they clean the caravan out," Annja replied, avoiding any mention of the laptop. No point in giving the girl an excuse to say no. If it came up later, they could say that they took it with the rest of his personal belongings, no need to make a big deal out of it.

"Should be fine," Inge said. "The door's locked now. I'll let you in."

"It's no problem," said Annja, already starting to walk back toward the caravan. "The key's in the same place, right?"

"Er, yes," Inge said, starting to follow them.

"I'll make sure I lock up, then we'll come and find you and you can give Una the full guided tour."

"Okay, sure, come and find me," Inge echoed, and shuffled back a couple of steps, not wanting to leave them alone.

Annja waved to her after she'd rescued the key from under the brick, to show her she didn't need to worry, and opened the door.

Someone had been inside the caravan since Annja had last been there.

It was instinct. There was nothing to suggest it, or at least nothing obvious, but Annja knew as soon as she put the key in the lock someone had been inside. The place gave off a vibe. She realized that it was the rock itself; it had been moved. There was a dead patch of grass a few inches away from where she'd picked up the key this time. She walked back down the couple of steps and kneeled beside the indentation.

"What is it?" Una asked.

"Someone's moved the stone," she said, keeping her voice low.

There were any number of rational reasons why someone would need to go inside the caravan. Maybe it had been Inge herself, looking for notes or instructions amid his clutter. Maybe she'd needed a telephone number or something else about the dig. All of Lars's paperwork was still inside, after all. She had every right to be in there, even if it was only for something as stupid as using his kettle....

Regardless, as Annja pushed down on the handle and opened the door, she couldn't shift the sense of trepidation she felt.

There were more signs on the other side of the door; someone had definitely been inside. The living space was a bigger disaster than it had been when she'd last been here. She wouldn't have seen it if she hadn't been looking for it; the differences were almost imperceptible—papers had been disturbed, the chair had been moved, a small cupboard door left open. It could all have been innocent. The laptop was where Lars had left it. Surely if someone had been in here looking for something they'd have taken it?

Or maybe they'd just fired it up and deleted the incriminating file, Annja thought. It would have been easier, faster and less likely to raise any suspicions, whereas a stolen laptop would lead to even more questions.

She made room for Una to join her inside, then opened the laptop.

"Just like when he was a student," she said as she looked around. "He was always messy. He used to have to crawl over his clothes in his bedroom." She laughed softly at the memory. "Sometimes he could barely get the door open, and would have to jump from the doorway to the bed, but he wouldn't let me move anything because he knew where everything was—or so he said. I always had my doubts. He used to have a sign on his desk about how a cluttered desk was the sign of a genius at work." She poked at the piles, at the journals folded open on old articles, at the newspaper cuttings and stacks of CDs out of their cases. It was hard to believe that there could be any order within the chaos.

Annja smiled and pressed the power button to start the laptop. The smile didn't last long. The log-in screen asked for a password.

She stared at the screen, annoyed with herself for not considering the possibility that he might have protected the files. "Any ideas," she asked. "Favorite books, first pets, anything that Lars might have used as a password?"

"Hmm, I know that he used to use his first girl-friend's name, Kristina," she said, spelling it out as Annja hit the keys.

The speakers grunted and the entire screen shook as access was denied.

There was no indication if they had three guesses or infinite ones before the system locked down, but Annja wasn't about to risk losing the photograph— assuming Lars had even uploaded it.

"No point in trying to guess," Annja said. "Let's just take the rig with us. I have a friend who should be able to get us in. Let's grab everything you want before Inge decides to stick her head in here and ask more questions."

Una picked through his things, throwing his clothes into a sports bag. There were dozens of books but she only selected a couple of them—old well-loved books that had probably been with him for a long time, Annja thought. Amid the clutter Annja spotted a laptop bag. She packed the computer away.

"Annja?" Una's voice was shaky, barely controlled. Annja turned to see her holding a towel with a dark stain streaked across it. It was blood. A fair bit of it. But not to cause concern, was it? Not enough for him to black out on the road and cause the crash.

"Looks like he cut himself pretty badly," Annja said, examining the stain more closely.

"He didn't mention it when we spoke."

"Maybe he didn't think it was worth mentioning."

"Do you think it could have been why he crashed? Maybe we're wrong. Maybe it was just an accident."

"I don't know…I don't think so. It's possible, but it doesn't fit with everything else," Annja admitted.

"Everything else?"

"We don't really have time for explanations here, but I'm hoping the definitive answer to what's going on is on here." She held up the laptop bag.

Una nodded. She took the towel back and stuffed it into a bin, then hurriedly finished what she was doing. Long before Annja had locked up and replaced the key beneath the stone, Una was already sitting in the car, clutching the stuffed sports bag on her lap.

Annja clambered into the car and slammed the door. Before she'd even jammed the key in the ignition, Una asked, "Do you really think you'll be able to do something with the computer?"

"Not me," Annja said, pulling away. She could see Inge in her mirror, standing there, looking confused. "But Garin, my friend, well, there's nothing he can't get done. If he can't do it himself, he's got people falling over themselves to do it for him."

"Must be nice."

"I'm not so sure. But it's useful."

"So, you said you'd explain?"

"Yes. Okay. Bear with me, I haven't said any of this stuff out loud before, so… After I was supposed to see Lars, two men broke into my hotel room. At first I thought they were looking for something. But they weren't. They'd come for me. One of them came back the next morning, before we met, and searched my room. I think he'd come to finish the job, but I wasn't there."

"Oh, my God."

Annja concentrated on the road ahead. "There's more. Johan, my photographer, took footage of a political rally a few nights ago—"

"Karl Thorssen's? Where the bomb went off?"

"One of the men who came to my room was there, dressed as a paramedic. He's dead now. There was another man there who died this morning in that fireworks factory explosion." When she said it like that the links between the three dead men seemed painfully obvious: Karl Thorssen.

"You think Karl Thorssen's behind it all, don't you?"

"I do," Annja said, as though making a solemn vow. "But I don't have the proof."

"I never liked the man…" Una said. "I warned Lasse. I told him to stay well away. Men like him can't be trusted. But he wouldn't listen to me. He wanted to be the one to excavate Skalunda Barrow. It was all he'd ever wanted. He wanted to find Beowulf. And it killed him."

They drove back by the more circuitous route, avoiding the strip where Lars Mortensen had died.

"I hope your friend can get into the laptop and that you find what you need. If there's proof there, use it to bring Thorssen down. Then, maybe with one less fascist pig in the world, my son's death might mean something. Please. Promise me you won't stop trying to find the truth."

All she could do was to promise that she would do her best.

That was all anyone could ever do.

Even with the heavy bag of clothes and personal possessions that Una had packed at the caravan, she still insisted on being dropped off at the same place outside the police station, rather than being driven to her hotel.

Annja spotted the old woman now among the crowd on the sidewalk, bowed down beneath the extra weight of the sports bag. Annja thought of their last conversation, and wondered if she would even find the truth Una Mortensen was looking for.

23

The cut wasn't healing.

Thorssen had sliced his palm on the sword. The gash wasn't deep, but for some reason the blood refused to clot. It continued to seep through the Band-Aid he'd slapped over it, and then through the bandage he'd wrapped around it when that failed.

His mother had fussed over him, concerned that left untreated it would become infected, and urged him to go to the hospital to have the wound cleansed and stitched. And though she only meant well, he lost his temper with her. Again.

It was becoming harder and harder to control the fire inside him.

He didn't know what was happening to him.

His thoughts weren't his own.

Too many times now he found himself closing his eyes, hearing the sounds of battle, smelling the sharp scent of blood. His pulse would race and his breath hitch, and he'd been unable to bite back the surge of power and the need to commit violence that went with it.

He wasn't himself.

His mother fought back the tears, grabbing her coat and leaving the house.

He let her go.

He didn't care where she went.

He didn't care if she came back.

The house echoed emptily around him as he walked through it.

It no longer felt like home. It felt cold. Alien. Like it belonged to some other life.

Thorssen retreated to the bathroom on the second floor, and peeled back the dressing that was now wet with blood. He teased it away from his palm, wincing as the gauze tugged at his palm, and tossed the bandage into the garbage. Gritting his teeth against the pain, he ran his hand beneath the hot tap, washing away the blood.

There was no sign that the cut was going to close.

Fresh blood bubbled up from the wound as he pressed the loose flaps of skin together.

His mother was right; it needed stitching.

But she was wrong if she thought he'd ever reduce himself to joining the great unwashed to be treated. No. Money bought certain privileges, including house calls. He made a call to a private clinic just outside the city and arranged for a nurse to come to the house. They promised that someone would be with him within half an hour.

It was incredible that the blade's edge could be as keen as it was after all that time in the ground; even the fact that the corrosion had somehow protected it didn't make sense when he thought about it. It was the nature of things to decay. But Nægling defied nature.

He had watched Ulric work on the weapon; he

hadn't honed the edge in the slightest. In point of fact, he'd remarked how he didn't need to, and how it was in remarkable condition for such a rare and obviously old piece.

The flesh around the wound had turned white, he noticed, and when he probed at it, felt soft with the swelling beneath it pushing the cut wider.

Thorssen admired Ulric's skill. Nægling was whole again. The two halves of the wooden hand had come together easily, their symmetry perfect in every detail. The completion of the binding had been painstakingly slow, the smith refusing to be rushed, working with the same calm precision until the last turn of the thin strip of leather was tightened and secured. Even then he wasn't finished. The man had fussed and fiddled, making tiny adjustments that, to Thorssen's untrained eye, appeared to be unnecessary, and made no obvious difference to his work, but finally he handed Nægling over, beautiful and complete for the first time in centuries.

Karl Thorssen held the relic in both hands, feeling its weight, testing its balance.

It was *his* sword.

He relished the surge of heat he felt flare up the hilt.

The smith kept his distance as Karl Thorssen cut the air with the blade again and again, feeling a power surge through him, filling him with a hunger that had to be sated. The blade had already tasted his own blood, the exposed metal slicing deeply into his palm when he'd tested it. Now it cried out for fresh blood. Now it cried out for the smith's blood.

Thorssen's grip clenched even tighter around the hilt, forcing the cut in his palm wider still, allowing the blood to flow. The cut stung as the dressing caught in the leather, but the pain only served to make everything more real.

The pain was immaterial. All that mattered was the sword in his hand and the rage it fostered.

He swung again, causing the smith to stagger back a step, barely avoiding the blade as it cleaved through the air where his throat had been a split second before.

"That was a little close, my friend," Ulric said, laughing nervously.

Thorssen closed the distance between them and swung the mighty blade. The tip of Nægling cut through flesh and hit bone, barely slowing the weapon's arc.

"What the hell...?" The man stumbled back again, desperately trying to step outside the reach of Thorssen's swing, but the politician wasn't about to let him escape so easily. The smith was another loose end that couldn't be left hanging.

Now that Nægling had tasted blood again for the first time in more than fourteen hundred years it demanded more, and more, and more, to slake its thirst, and Thorssen was only too happy to feed it.

He and the blade were one.

It was in him. Of him.

It flowed through his veins.

It nourished him.

It drained him, feeding off him like some steely vampire in his hands.

He hacked and slashed at the fallen man long after Ulric stopped screaming. Thorssen gave in to the blind frenzy, cutting, cutting, cutting. His wild swings chased Ulric into the afterlife.

The smith's remains were unrecognizable by the time Thorssen's fury subsided.

His sword arm hung limp at his side.

He breathed heavily.

Sweat matted his hair to his scalp.

It was all he could do to maintain his grip on the sword.

His clothes were soaked with the dead man's blood. He could feel its warmth against his skin.

There was still something inside him, an energy buried deep down, primal, primitive, wild. He roared to release it, raising Nægling above his head.

Something was happening to him, something that was making him more than he was before. More than he had ever been.

And he embraced the change.

24

Sometimes it took an element of luck to make everything go right.

Tostig was only too aware of that. He would never turn his nose up at it, either. Luck could be the difference between nearly and done. Luck could be as simple as the wind direction turning, carrying your scent away from the dogs, to someone turning up in the right place at the right time.

This time luck came in the guise of a call: Annja Creed had been out at the Skalunda Barrow with Mortensen's mother. They would be returning to the hotel soon, giving him a place to wait and watch.

He'd noted the positioning of the CCTV cameras inside the hotel and on the various floors, covering their angles and their blind spots. He knew where he could wait without being seen by hotel staff. Closing his eyes, he could picture the critical path that would take him across the lobby without ever showing his face to the cameras, to the stairwells beyond the bank of elevators, and Creed's room upstairs, but he had no intention of taking a risk.

His good luck continued fifteen minutes later in the

form of Annja's cameraman, Johan Cheander, striding toward the hotel.

It was a question of neatness. Tostig had already decided that killing one of them dictated killing both of them, preferably together, and making it look like an accident. The body count was rising. That was a concern. And two more deaths in a matter of days would have the local police running around like headless chickens. It was an unfortunate necessity, though, and five dead or fifteen dead, it didn't really matter so long as nothing could be traced back to him.

The issue, though, was connectivity. These people had direct contact via one another's lives. They weren't random strangers. Their lives dissected at various key points in time, points that could be identified and prove telling because each and every one of them had links to one man: Karl Thorssen. There was no denying the finger of blame would be laid at Thorssen's door sooner or later, and even if Thorssen didn't care, Tostig did, because if Thorssen talked there was only one man he could talk about: Tostig.

Which meant the relationship had moved into sudden death.

It was time for the assassin to watch his back. Trust his instincts. Protect himself and plan an exit strategy.

He slipped out of the car as the man approached, camera bag hanging over his shoulder, and opened the rear door, all the while careful to keep his face shielded from the lobby camera that just reached the sidewalk through the huge plate-glass windows.

"Inside," he said, motioning for Johan to get into the car. There was no subtlety to it; he revealed the gun in the waistband of his trousers, and pushed the cameraman toward the open door. Cheander tried to pull away, but then froze as recognition hit him. "Don't do anything stupid," Tostig said softly, hand on the gun. The cameraman seemed trapped, wanting to swing the bag at him, to run. He put a hand on the man's back. The touch was enough to deter him from making a break for it.

The man slid inside onto the backseat.

"Wise decision," Tostig said, closing the door behind him.

No one was looking.

"Facedown, hands behind your back," he said, leaning into the car without getting in. "Don't fight me and I won't have to hurt you."

It was difficult for the man to maneuver, but fear made him supple. Tostig forced him down deeper into the footwell behind the front seats and yanked his hands back, slapping a pair of handcuffs on his wrists.

It didn't pay to take chances: he ran a hand over the man's clothes. The quick frisk turned up a cell phone.

He took it from him.

Tostig had a small metal case in his pocket. The case held a syringe preloaded with something that would take Johan down fast. It was a fallback. He would rather not pollute the man's system with anything that might turn up in an autopsy.

The assassin had also replaced the fuel in the gas can and put it in the trunk. He liked to keep things simple. Every day household objects readily available from any hardware store were his murder weapons of choice. They tended not to rouse suspicion in the same way as rare drug cocktails would these days.

They were flashy and obnoxious and would only ever lead to hot trails and big trouble. Why take the risk?

Tostig slammed the door closed behind him and smoothed out the wrinkles from his jacket. He took a look at the phone.

There were a number of missed calls from Creed. It would have been gratifying to phone her now and simply say, "I've got your man. What little is left of his life can be measured in breaths." And hang up, but that wasn't Tostig. It was too showy.

He owed the cameraman for the Serb.

And Tostig was the kind of man who honored his debts, on his own terms, in his own time.

"What's this about?" the man demanded as the car pulled away from the curb. Tostig had no intention of telling him. He wasn't about to engage in conversation with the man. There would be no bonding. No begging. No reprieve. And, for once, the chance to kill two birds with one well-cast stone.

He had just the place in mind.

Having the cameraman's cell phone made things a lot easier.

He adjusted the rearview mirror, keeping the cameraman in view as he tried to struggle into a sitting position. It was almost impossible, given the way Tostig had jammed him down behind the seats, especially without the use of his hands. He hadn't gagged the man, but for now he was silent. Perhaps he wasn't stupid, after all.

Tostig took the same road he'd taken the previous night, then picked up the trail that circled the lake. This was another part of the country he was intimately familiar with. He recognized the holiday homes that dotted the countryside like a braille pattern. His grandfather had lived in one of them. That was his strongest tie to the region, but by no means his only one. It didn't harbor the pull of sentimentality. He'd hated the old man.

He drove on until at last he saw what he was looking for—a unique spire pointing like a finger through the trees.

The white church stood alone, seemingly in the middle of nowhere.

It was still in a good state of repair.

This was a Lutheran church, a house of God for the fishermen who lived around the lake—part place of worship, part sanctuary.

The old church hadn't changed in the slightest since Tostig had last been there more then twenty years before. As he'd expected, its doors were open. There was a heavy iron key hanging on a hook just inside the door so that it could be locked at night. There was an iron spike on the outside wall beside the door where the key would hang through the night in case anyone came seeking shelter. No one was ever turned away. No one would steal from the old church because there was precious little of value to steal.

Tostig assumed there would be no one inside, but he could afford a few more hours' patience to be sure, even if it meant moving his passenger to the trunk. The stain left behind by the Serb would no doubt give the cameraman food for thought.

He drove the car up along the track, following the curve away from the road and stopped the car on a patch of ground beyond the church. The spot was out of view from anyone who should happen to glance toward the white spire as they drove along the road.

"I am going to give you instructions to live. Listen to them carefully. Obey them and you might survive. Move and you're a dead man," Tostig said. "Make a noise and you're a dead man. Do *anything* I don't give you explicit permission to do, and you're a dead man. Do you understand me?"

"Yes."

That was all that Tostig wanted to hear.

Despite what had happened back at the hotel, the cameraman was no hero. The proof of that was plain in just how meekly he was accepting his fate. Perhaps if he knew exactly what Tostig had planned for him he might have been a little less accepting.

He got out and closed the car door softly behind him. Not that he expected anyone to be around. The church was as remote a place as could be found within an hour's drive of the city. But slamming doors startled birds, and a flock of birds erupting into flight drew attention from miles around.

He went inside.

The old church was empty.

The layout of the building was simple enough, as were the furnishings. Most of the interior was given over to the congregation with wooden pews lined up to face a sturdy pulpit beneath a stained-glass window.

Tostig had sat in those pews as a child.

Being forced to suffer through those insufferable sermons had given him a healthy loathing for all things spiritual. The only salvation he was after came in the form of excellence, the only release in death. The two together were the only religion he needed.

The lone door led to a small vestry with a locked cupboard where the pastor stored the components for sharing the Eucharist.

He sat on the first row of pews, and looked at the cameraman's phone, pondering exactly what he was going to say. As in all things, preparation was important.

He wouldn't fluff his lines.

25

"Annja?"

"I need a favor."

"Don't you always?"

Garin wasn't her first choice as a go-to guy, but there was a refreshing honesty about their relationship, and it was a while since he'd tried to kill either her or Roux, so perhaps there'd been a thaw in the immortality relationship stakes. Despite that, and despite the fact he could be a pain at times, she liked him and, perhaps surprisingly, given their history, trusted him.

He was certainly her best hope for getting at the files inside Lars Mortensen's laptop. As she'd told Una, if he couldn't do it, he almost certainly had people who could. That was Garin Braden. He surrounded himself with people who could. It didn't matter what it was, only that they had areas of expertise he could exploit down the line, preferably for monetary gain.

"Where are you?"

"I could ask the same." He sounded like he was at a loud party. "I'm in Sweden," she replied.

"Ah, yes, the Beowulf thing, correct?"

"That's it, 'the Beowulf thing.' What's all the noise?"

"That, my dear, is the collective sigh of thousands of people losing an awful lot of money and enjoying it. I'm at the races. Longchamps. If you weren't up to your knees in mud, I would have asked you over to join me."

"I'm sure you've got half a dozen beautiful women hanging on your every word."

"I do, but they are not you, Annja Creed. You should know that by now. I'd give them all up for an afternoon with you." He oozed false charm like oil. Annja couldn't help but smile. Some women obviously fell for it; after all, he'd had a lot of years to perfect his seduction skills. Couple them with his muscular sportsman's physique and long dark hair and that dangerous charisma of Garin's and it was no surprise women flocked to him. And no surprise he reveled in their beauty and flesh at every hedonistic opportunity.

"So this favor? What do you need?"

"I've got a laptop that I have to access, but it's password protected."

"Shouldn't be too much of a challenge, but next time try picking a password you can remember."

"It's not my laptop."

"Oh, well, things just got a little bit more interesting, didn't they? You know, Annja, you really shouldn't go prying into other people's things."

"He's dead," she said, refusing to let Garin get under her skin. "His mother wants me to see if I can get into it for her."

"Hmm, so it's all completely altruistic, then? I'm sure that I know someone more than capable of cracking it. I mean, I've got my own private army, after all," he joked. "I'll send someone over right away. Where are you staying?"

She read out the address from a sheet of hotel letterhead on the desk.

"Leave it with me."

He hung up with the briefest of goodbyes. Annja was still cradling the handset to her ear.

She didn't know what she'd expected—some techno miracle that would allow him to hack into the laptop from France, opening it up for Annja at the touch of a button, perhaps? How foolish.

Annja passed the time waiting for him to return her call by reading the notes she'd made about the Beowulf segment.

Micke had been right; it looked very thin, and would continue to look very thin unless the dig was reopened. And even then they'd need to find *something*. Otherwise, it was just another show about chasing shadows. Doug wouldn't like that. He wanted glamor. He wanted success. He wanted discoveries that would draw in advertising dollars. He didn't want Annja filling the silence.

Two words written in red ink stood out: *Interview Thorssen?*

Not that he'd ever agree.

And even if he did, he'd want way too much control over what went into the final cut. People like Thorssen were often more trouble than they were worth.

But then, in a week his star could be falling if the election didn't go his way.

What then?

Maybe he'd be grateful of a few minutes of airtime to spread his hate?

Perhaps she could sell it to him with the promise of letting him put forth the background, linking Beowulf as a hero to his own ideology.

Maybe he'd buy it.

Maybe he wouldn't.

There was no way of knowing without asking.

Tomorrow.

After an hour of adding thoughts to the notes, she tried Johan's number again. It went straight to voice mail, which was more disconcerting this time, as he should have been back in Gothenburg hours ago. Maybe he'd retreated straight to his room after the long journey and turned off the ringer so it didn't disturb him. She didn't know him well enough as to whether that was typical behavior for him, or if it was out of the ordinary. Surely he'd see the missed calls on his display and think to check in, though.

Annja was on the verge of going to try his door, even if she risked waking him, when her phone vibrated with an incoming text.

It was from Johan.

Can't talk now. Meet me at the Church of Saint Peter's of the Lake in an hour. This is important. I've got what we need to nail Thorssen.

She tried calling him, but it went straight to voice mail. Evidence? What had he found in Stockholm? The smoking gun? She didn't bother leaving yet another message.

The rack of tourist information leaflets had a small map of the area with sites of interest clearly marked.

It was hardly surprising that Skalunda dominated

the brochures with various guided tours. The standing stones around the barrow appeared in all of the leaflets. Annja scanned through the literature for churches, figuring it had to be a significant one for Johan to not bother with any landmarks in the vicinity. The most obvious one turned out to be the cathedral in central Gothenburg. There was no mention of any Church of Saint Peter's of the Lake in anything she could find.

She picked up the hotel phone and dialed through to reception. "Good evening, Miss Creed." She recognized the woman's voice on the other end. "How can I be of help?"

"Actually, I'm trying to find a church—Saint Peter's of the Lake. Have you got any idea where it is?"

"Certainly," the receptionist said. "It's an old fisherman's chapel about an hour north of here, out near the lake. There's nothing of any real interest out there, though. The cathedral here has a lot more history on offer."

"It's really Saint Peter's I need to find," she explained. "I need some footage for the program I'm making."

"Ah, well, it's easy enough to find once you get onto the lake road, but I'll print off a map for you. You can pick it from reception whenever you need it."

Annja thanked her and hung up. Why would Johan go out there? It didn't make sense, unless someone had tipped him off. She started to speculate about what he could possibly have unearthed up in Stockholm, and wished he'd just used the phone before he went dark to fill her in.

But, oh, no, boys will be boys. They have to be all mysterious and have their fun.

Garin still hadn't called back, but she was going to have to leave now to make it out to the old church on time, so cracking the riddle of the laptop's password would just have to wait until she'd heard what Johan had to say for himself.

26

As promised, the map was waiting for her as she entered the reception area.

Annja left it as late as she could before heading out, hoping that Garin would ping her with a plan for how to tackle the laptop. Best case, reasonably, was to think it would be the morning before anything happened with it. Which gave her the evening to entertain herself—and the main feature seemed to be a trip out to a little lakeside church in the middle of nowhere. She almost called Micke to ask if Johan was usually this cagey about stuff when they worked together, but didn't. Micke trusted him, Johan had delivered for her every step of the way, so why doubt him if he said he'd found Thorssen's secret?

She was already out of the door and in the rental car before she thought to ask the receptionist if she'd seen him, but that wasn't the only thing that was bothering her. Call it gut instinct, call it whatever you wanted, Annja had a nagging feeling that something wasn't quite right here even if she couldn't put her finger on it. But at least she wasn't walking into the lion's den unarmed. She never did these days, not since Roux had first come into her life on that mountaintop in Lozère. Joan's sword was never more than a thought away.

As promised, the map was easy to follow once she understood how to get out of the one-way system and onto the main road to the lake. After that it was a simple matter of keeping a lookout for the white spire of the Lutheran church. The traffic was steady, but the worst of the rush hour had long since moved on home. She couldn't help but marvel at the juxtaposition of modern and old Germanic architecture the city had to offer, with the ugliest glass carbuncles squeezed in right beside some wondrous piece of Hanseatic relic.

There was a glorious array of colors on offer, too, with the facades plastered oranges, reds, yellows and umbers, while the windows were surrounded by white plaster and wrought iron, transforming the old buildings into rows of strangely Gothic faces watching her leave town.

A couple of times car horns blared behind her as she slowed a little too much to get a sense of which lane she needed to be in to follow the traffic out of the city; some drivers were the same the world over. Annja ignored them, letting them work themselves up into a lather before roaring out around her to pass at the first opportunity.

Annja looked for the mile marker that would indicate where she needed to turn toward the water, not really sure what she was looking for. The map said mile marker, not signpost, so it probably wouldn't be a big metal arrow pointing the way.

As it was, the mile marker was actually a faded rune stone with an elaborate Ouroboros and the name of the village she was looking for, so she swung a left onto a much narrower winding road. Within fifty yards she realized there was no street lighting along this stretch of road. The hedgerows grew high on either side, but occasionally broke to offer glimpses of the countryside beyond. She'd been following the narrow road more than fifteen minutes without passing another car when she finally spotted the white building set back behind thick trees. Even knowing it was there she almost missed the track that would take her there.

Annja pulled off the road, scanning the area before she drove any closer. There wasn't another manmade structure for hundreds of yards, and the few that were even that close were down by the lake clustered along the waterfront rather than set back on the hill where the church stood sentinel. Through the trees on the lake side of the road Annja could see the glimmer of the failing sun trapped in the ripples, but that was the closest she came to seeing any signs of life.

Again, the same questions surfaced in her mind: Why would Johan want to meet out in the middle of nowhere like this? What part could Saint Peter's of the Lake play in Karl Thorssen's story?

She put the car into gear and drove down the narrow track toward the church until it opened out into an open patch of ground in front of the building. There was a wooden bell tower outside the church, which she'd seen at a few churches in Europe before. Beyond the bell tower she could just make out the plain white crosses marking generations of the dead.

It was a simple structure, built for the local fishing community. It had a parish of perhaps two hundred people. More than anything it offered a tranquil resting place for those who had lived beside the water.

The door of the church stood open.

There was no other indication that anyone was inside.

Annja continued driving slowly off the track onto a patch of ground that served as a makeshift parking lot and pulled up the hand brake. The engine idled as she stared at the open door for a moment. Finally, she turned the key and the car fell silent.

The temptation was to sound the horn to see if Johan emerged, but it felt somehow wrong to shatter the silence. If he wasn't here, or if something was wrong, not sounding the horn wouldn't change things. She waited instead, assuming that the sound of her arrival would have carried inside the old church.

He didn't emerge.

That was the second warning sign, the first being the remote location.

The sound of birdsong surprised Annja when she stepped out of the car. Even only fifteen minutes from the freeway, she felt utterly isolated. Despite the scattered holiday houses along the road in, it felt as though civilization proper had been left behind.

Maybe Johan had picked the spot for some atmosphere footage. It was a good location with the backdrop of shimmering water and the white crosses on the hillside. Even the bell tower had a nice feel to it that could fit with the segment.

But none of that had to do with Karl Thorssen.

Was this little church linked to the murders somehow?

Was that it?

There was only one way to find out.

Annja took a deep breath and made the short walk to the church door.

She stood inside the tiny porch with its row of coat hooks and a metal umbrella stand showing signs of rust at the bottom where water had been left to eat into its base. There were no coats hanging on the hooks. The umbrella stand was bone dry. No one had used it for a while. A red fire extinguisher stood beside it, ready to extinguish the flames if one too many candles were lit.

Annja crossed the threshold.

Light diffused by grime came into the body of the church through tall arched windows. No amount of cleaning could have scrubbed the crust from the stained glass. It left the interior in a weird half gloom.

There was no sign of Johan.

There was no sign of anyone at all.

And no sign that anyone had been in the old church in a very long time.

It smelled odd—old, stale, but of something else, too.

"Johan?" She called his name, though the word came out as barely more than a whisper.

There was no response, but she thought she heard a rustle of movement. The building was small, offering no place to hide. She checked each pew as she went up the aisle. Nothing. No sign of the cameraman. She was almost at the front of the church before she spotted the door in the far corner behind the pulpit.

"Hello?" she called again, this time a little louder. Her voice echoed eerily in the confines of the church. Again the only response was a rustle of movement that seemed to originate from behind the door.

Annja knocked once, then placed a hand on the iron handle. It turned. She pushed the door open. She started to call for Johan again, but the words died on her lips.

The cameraman was tied in a chair with electrical tape over his mouth and plastic ties that secured his wrists and ankles. The chair had been tipped over. He had a white cloth stuffed inside his mouth that poked out from beneath the electrical tape. That white rag was the source of the strange odor, she realized. Gasoline. She saw the terror in his eyes. Fear, panic, relief, all warring with one another for supremacy.

Every instinct she'd had was right; Johan had been used to lure her here. Before she could question by who, or why, her head filled with pain and the world went dark.

27

It had proved to be disappointingly straightforward in the end.

Tostig had bound up the cameraman, giving him his most loquacious speech, the one in which he tells the victim he only knows two kinds of people, the ones who scream and the ones who don't, but in the end they're all just the same because they give up their secrets eventually, and then they die. The cameraman had whimpered as he stuffed the gasoline-soaked rag into his mouth, understanding what it meant for him in terms of survival. After his performance he'd retreated outside the old church, using the time to move his car to park it outside of one of the empty holiday cottages up the road, and then returned to hide within the huge wooden timbers of the bell tower on the hill where he could watch without fear of being seen.

There were two points on ingress and egress in the old church—the main door that locked with that single huge iron key and a tiny window at the rear of the building. It was what he liked to call a heartbreaker—it offered hope, promising a way out, but was too small for an adult to crawl through. Just as he liked it. There was nothing more satisfying than snatching every last ounce of hope away before the final blow.

He heard the car long before he saw it, and watched Annja Creed follow the road, stopping short herself to survey the scene. She was cautious. And with good reason. But no matter how much care she took, Tostig held the upper hand. He'd baited the trap perfectly, knowing her natural curiosity would get the woman out here. He'd seen her in action before. He knew all about her tricks. His first move would be to bind her hands. She'd be unable to pull a sword—even from thin air—if she couldn't use her hands.

Now it was about payback.

He'd settle the Serb's debt.

It didn't matter if she recognized him. He wasn't vain; there was nothing to be gained in a victim taking your identity to the grave with them. He wasn't about to give her a monologue explaining why she had to die. It was much more effective to let his actions speak. After all, the old saying was right; they were so much more eloquent than any words he had ever uttered.

Tostig held his breath as she called out. The birds scattered, returning to the trees.

He allowed himself a gentle smile as he listened to the crunch of her footsteps on the thin gravel. A few weeds poked through the surface. Around the edge of the path the mud was packed hard from the sun, allowing him to avoid the gravel and move up silently behind her.

He was a ghost in her shadow, listening to every sound she made as she moved inside the church; timing was crucial. He needed to be past the windows before she was completely inside, eliminating the risk of her catching sight of his shadow through the glass.

He admired her body as she moved—feline, feminine, graceful, light on her feet, all lithe and sinuous without making a sound. Tostig liked to think of himself as above the lure of the flesh, though there was something compelling about this one.

It was hard to picture her presenting some dumb television show; she moved with a warrior's poise.

That gave him pause.

It was more than just a few hours in the gym pretending to learn kickboxing when she was working out. She was more deliberate, more aware, than any gym fighter. She'd seen combat. There was a particular manner that veterans had as they moved through the world, eyes moving constantly, attuned to their surroundings. She had that as she approached each pew.

Perhaps this will be more interesting than I'd expected, Tostig thought.

What she didn't have, he was sure, finally, was the sword. That tilted the balance back in his favor. He still had no idea how she'd pulled that stunt on him and the Serb. He remembered the ease with which she had seemingly deflected those bullets.

Annja Creed was truly a remarkable woman.

It was a shame she had to die.

Though for all her awareness, she had no idea he was there, watching her.

She moved toward the vestry door, drawn to it. No doubt the photographer was still whimpering through the gasoline-soaked gag. Tostig didn't begrudge him a few tears; after all, once he lit the fire and turned Saint Peter's on the Lake into a blazing pyre, that rag would burn inside him long before he died. He could beg and plead and cry as much as he liked, soon enough the only thing his throat would be good for was roasting.

Creed quickened her pace as she crossed from the pews to the door.

She hesitated, hand on the iron handle.

It was his signal. The moment she pushed that door open everything had to happen, fast. No time for hesitation. No time for subtlety. Everything changed when she saw the cameraman bound to the chair and knew she'd fallen into a trap. He moved inside, the soft leather soles of his shoes not making so much as a scuff on the cold stone floor. He kept to the shadows, moving down the sides of the pews instead of the aisle.

She didn't looked around.

She stepped through the door.

Tostig moved quickly and silently, skirting the last few pews to stand in the doorway as she knelt to rescue her cameraman, who was desperately trying to warn her that the assassin stood behind her shoulder.

Before she could heed the warning he was trying to communicate with his eyes alone, Tostig hit her. Hard. Too hard.

Creed sprawled out unconscious on top of the terrified cameraman.

"She's not going to save you. I told you not to build your hopes up. Still, you'll find your heaven with a beautiful woman at your side. There are worse ways to go," the assassin mused. "Believe me, I should know."

He wanted her awake before he set to work proper— he wanted to exact some pleasure at least from the murders.

Tostig checked her pulse. It was strong. She was

out cold, though. The cameraman struggled manfully beneath her. Perhaps he misguidedly thought he could save the pair of them even though he was trussed up like a hog.

"You might as well accept it. It'll be easier for you," Tostig assured him, not that there was anything reassuring about being told your best bet was to give in and die quietly.

The next minute would be fundamental to how the killings would play out. He needed to take control.

He slipped the plastic case from the inside pocket of his jacket.

As much as he disliked the use of drugs, they were a vital tool of the trade, and in this case would give him long enough to do what needed to be done.

Tostig was sweating by the time he'd manhandled Creed and the cameraman out of the vestry and carried her back into the main body of the church.

He was getting too old for this, he thought grimly, sweat streaming down his face. Without the Serb things just weren't the same. For the first time in a long while the assassin wondered if this was it, the beginning of the end for him.

The cameraman began to cough and choke around the gag.

He could have let the man die, but that would spoil the fun, so he pulled the gag from the man's mouth and allowed him to suck in huge shuddering gasps of air.

"You're not going to get away with this!" Johan Cheander gasped.

"Oh, please," the assassin said, shaking his head. "Of course I am. I already have. Growing a spine is all well and good, but it won't help you. Now shut up and save your breath."

He regretted engaging the cameraman. It went against everything he held sacred. It opened a dialogue. He didn't want a dialogue. It was a sign that he was letting things slip. It wasn't about the risk of someone hearing; even God wouldn't hear them if they screamed the place down. "Do you want me to stuff the gag back down your throat? One word, that's all it will take."

He looked at the man, then checked Creed again to see if there was any change in her breathing. Ideally he would have moved her car, but there wasn't time. It would just have to remain where it was.

"People know where we are. Our producer for a start."

"Really? That would be the producer in New York? A pity Concord is no longer in service, then. No one is coming to rescue you. You can have that engraved on your headstone if you like. No One Came. You won't be leaving this church until the coroner is struggling to identify your charcoaled remains."

That was too much for the cameraman. He cried out uselessly for help.

Tostig felt the heat of anger begin to rise.

He hit the man hard with the back of his hand. There was no warning. He didn't hold back. The blow snapped the cameraman's head back and to one side. The chair rocked, threatening to tip over again.

Tostig picked up the white gasoline-soaked cloth and stuffed it into Johan's mouth. The cloth quickly stained red from the cut on his lip.

A little blood was the least of his worries.

Thorssen wouldn't be pleased that he was transforming their deaths into a piece of theater, but not everything in life was about pleasing Karl Thorssen. Sometimes it was about pleasing himself. Any satisfaction Thorssen drew from these latest deaths would just be a happy byproduct, not the motive for the killing.

Annja Creed showed no sign of coming around.

Good. That gave him time.

He'd chosen Saint Peter's on the Lake for reasons beyond its location.

Even if this place had been right in the heart of the city it would have been perfect with its great wooden crucifix on the wall behind the pulpit and its ancient seasoned timbers. Even the walls themselves weren't stone, but a mix of natural materials that had calcified over time.

They would burn.

As a boy he'd stared at these walls during the services he'd been forced to attend, imagining what it might be like to nail the people who teased and otherwise tormented him to that giant cross.

There had been times when he'd considered coming back to do that very thing, but had always decided against it. He felt it made things too personal, and therefore, too risky. But this was different. This *was* personal. It was her fault he was alone. The Serb's death lay squarely at her feet.

It was fitting that Johan Cheander was an observer. A watcher. Now he could watch her die without the distance of his lens between them.

Tostig wanted to make it last as long as he could.

He wanted the pair of them to endure long beyond the threshold of pain, and exist in that place where there was nothing—no pain, no relief, no escape. He wanted them to know there was no salvation, and then he wanted them to see his face as he struck the match that would transform the church into hell on earth.

28

In her dream she reached for her sword—Joan's sword, the sword that inextricably joined them across the centuries, Annja and the Martyr—but it was always just beyond her grasp. Tantalizingly close, and yet so desperately far away. She couldn't move her hands. She couldn't will its familiar hilt into her hand.

Annja felt the flames of the fire, heard the crackle and snap of the moisture in the wood, the cross at her back digging into her spine. No salvation, no reprieve, this was it, her wrists and ankles bound to the stake. The air so thick with smoke it seemed impossible to breathe.

Through the confusion she could hear someone calling to her.

She knew the voice.

She recognized the name it spoke over and over.

"Annja! Annja! I'm begging you, Annja! Wake up! Please! Just wake up!"

But it felt so much less real than the dream.

So much farther away.

She struggled against her bonds, trying to pull away from the stake.

She could feel their eyes on her, watching to see her burn out of their lives.

Then she heard a scream.

It wasn't the voice that had called to her. It was another voice. She knew it now, of course. Roux. The old man had lost her once.

Where are you?

Annja fought to open her eyes, willing herself to wake up.

Another scream. Not the old man this time, but she knew the voice every bit as well as his. The scream was her own.

She blinked, trying to grasp what was happening around her and remember where she was. The last thing she had seen was Johan lying on the ground, tied to a chair and unable to free himself. He was still in the chair, still tied to it and unable to free himself, but now he was sitting only a matter of feet from her, with a barrier of smoke forming between them.

"Annja!"

She coughed, trying to speak, and regretted it instantly as pain exploded through her head again.

She managed to crane her neck forward, lifting her chin from her breastbone to see the pews that had been broken and stacked at her feet before being doused in gasoline and set alight. Her arms were pinned to her sides, bound to the crucifix at the front of the church, just as Joan had been bound.

Flames from the pyre stacked around her licked the soles of her feet.

She was suspended well above the fire, but that didn't matter. The wood would burn, the interior of the church itself would burn, the crossbeams that supported the vaulted roof, the broken pews, and eventually her body would all be engulfed in flames.

She *hated* fire.

She really hated fire.

Annja fought against her bonds, trying to wriggle free of them, but they drew tighter, biting into her skin. She gritted her teeth and pulled and twisted at the plastic ties, but that only served to tear the skin around them, leaving it slick with blood.

She didn't need to see the man's face to know what had occurred. Even muggy headed from a concussion, it didn't take a genius to work out she'd been tricked by the man who'd broken into her hotel room—Thorssen's man, the paramedic who had dragged him out of the theater after the rally. Thorssen had signed her death warrant.

Annja willed the blade into her hand, but hands bound tight to her sides, she couldn't summon it from the otherwhere even though it was clear in her mind, there, waiting for her to reach out and take it from the nothingness.

Johan was choking badly. Annja saw he was tied to the chair and, bar dragging it a few inches across the stone floor, hadn't managed to gain any kind of freedom. He rocked the chair a little, the movement threatening to tip over again.

As he did, a burst of air stole into the nave, fanning the flames.

"Is he still here?" Annja shouted over the roar of the fire.

The heat was intense. Sweat stung her eyes. She twisted, trying to get her hair out of her face, only to have her vision swim as she threatened to black out.

A wave of nausea struck. Annja swallowed the rising bile.

"No. He's gone."

"Good."

"Are we going to die here?"

It was a question she had no intention of answering honestly.

"Not if I can help it." She could smell the pervasive reek of gasoline everywhere.

The big man had soaked the interior of Saint Peter's on the Lake in the stuff. Once the fire spread there would be no stopping it. The whole place would go up. Tendrils of flame snaked out toward the walls, reaching up for the timbers bracing the ceiling. She could smell the stuff on her clothes, too. Thorssen's assassin wasn't taking any chances.

A spark leaped from the bonfire and landed on the strip of carpet that ran between the remaining pews. Fire danced along the fabric like a demon, igniting the fibers and lighting up the tiny church toward the door as if in wild celebration.

Annja struggled with renewed energy.

Glass cracked, detonating like a gunshot in the confines of the church as the windows shattered. Fresh oxygen surged into the room, sucked through the window by the hungry flames that roared in delight. Supporting beams creaked and groaned desperately. A shower of dust fell from the rafters.

They were lost and Annja knew it. The fire fanned out to isolate them from the only exit. It wasn't death that concerned her; it wasn't even the fire. It was dying without answers. She'd pinned her hopes on the laptop, which was back at the hotel. It might as well have been a million miles away. Whatever secrets it held, she'd never know them. She could only hope Garin would figure them out and use them to take down Thorssen and avenge her.

Not exactly going to your happy place, Annja, she admonished. But it was true. She should have taken more precautions before coming out here. And as angry as she was with herself, she was angrier with Roux for not answering his stupid phone. She'd told him she wanted him down here, but he was obviously preoccupied with his latest flush or straight or dead man's hand or whatever they called it.

She pulled at the ties binding her, the plastic slicing even deeper into her wrists.

Will the plastic melt before I burn to death or will it just fuse with my skin?

It didn't bear thinking about.

Beneath her, Johan continued to struggle, more desperately now that his path to the door was cut off. The desperation in his face was heartbreaking. She'd gotten him into this, but she was powerless to get him out of it. Somehow he was fighting back the panic as he struggled with his restraints, though no matter how hard he tried, he couldn't wrench his hands free. The fire catching him seemed inevitable now.

The pillar of the crucifix strained as Annja continued to fight against her bonds. Its base began to weaken as the fire gained strength and ferocity. It groaned as she rocked against it, using all of her weight to try and pull it from the anchor points securing it to the wall. If she could just unbalance it enough that she could fall forward, maybe she could carry herself beyond the reach of the bonfire beneath her—not that

that would buy her more than a few seconds from the flames that covered the walls and ceiling now. But it was something. And she had to do *something*. She felt the smoke in her lungs. She felt her head swim alarmingly, but refused to lose focus. If she was going to die here, like this, she was going to die trying to help herself, digging deep, not caving in.

She wasn't Saint Joan, she wasn't strong enough to meet death head-on, fire to skin. Joan was stronger, prepared for her fate. Joan had something inside her, a resolve. Annja could only wish she possessed the same inner strength, and that it might manifest itself as she strained against her bonds, willing the ties to break or the blood pouring down over her wrists to be enough to finally allow her to pull free.

It was a struggle just to breathe now as the smoke thickened and the pain in her head became incessant.

She heard another creak followed by a huge crash as the central joist supporting the timber roof started to buckle. But Annja was bound firmly in place and no amount of fighting it could tear her free. Less than a minute had past since she'd come to her senses, but it felt like forever. If you were going to die, she thought bitterly, that's how you want your last minute to go.

She could hear Johan coughing, but couldn't see him for the thick pall of smoke and the cloud of dust that had risen up as part of the roof came down. More air rushed in, feeding the flames.

It would all be over soon.

She knew one thing, one truth: she wasn't ready to die.

Not yet.

Not like this.

There was another tremendous crack followed by a low rumble she felt deep in the stones that vibrated up through the crucifix. Light speared into the heart of the church, piercing the black smoke with an otherworldly whiteness that seemed to cast the flames aside.

From within the whiteness Annja heard a voice calling her name.

Her time had come.

29

Tostig had the church key in his pocket.

He knew he ought to leave it on the hook beside the door, with it not being there it invited the question Where was it? He could drop it at the scene, but that wouldn't have been much different. As long as it wasn't on the hook there would always be the question of how it got to where they found it. Taking it was a mistake. Worse. As long as he had it with him there was physical evidence connecting him to the church, and that in turn connected him to the fire. But that didn't stop him.

He needed to find the right place to dispose of the key once and for all. And he had an idea where that was.

It was hard to explain why, but this time it was different. He'd told himself it was personal, but it was more than that. It went beyond such a mundane explanation. The assassin needed to stay, needed to see the place burn. He needed to know Creed and her photographer were inside, no matter what the risk. He needed to know she was gone.

So he stood in the doorway, watching the fire start

to take hold of the broken pews and the battered old hymnbooks. He felt an immense wave of satisfaction as he laid the match to the gasoline trail, setting fire to the symbol of those hours of oppression that amounted to his childhood.

Tonight he was drawing a line under so many things; not only was he paying off his debt to the Serb, he was cleansing a hated part of his world.

And it felt *good*.

Almost euphoric. He smiled.

At last he was forced to close the door and turn the key, locking Creed and the cameraman inside. Now the devil could have his fill.

The fire intensified, passing the point of no return. The old church was beyond saving. The fire in the sky must have drawn the attention of people across the lake. They would have called the emergency services to report it. Fire engines would be on their way already. And that meant he had to cut out now, before they were on the narrow road down from the freeway, or he'd run the risk of meeting them.

So he drove, not toward the freeway, but in search of a vantage point. Somewhere he could watch these two deaths play out without being seen. That was a part of his trade he had never indulged in, the voyeuristic aspect of it all. He'd never felt the need to watch what happened in the last few moments of a job, preferring to trust his methodical planning. He was good at this.

But not this time. This time he wanted to see her burn.

By the time the assassin found somewhere suitable, the black smoke was rising in a thick plume and the air was full of the sound of sirens.

He was beginning to appreciate the efficacy of fire. It consumed everything, destroying every last trace of evidence with its voracious appetite for destruction.

He took the cell phone from his pocket and made the call.

"It's done," he said, unable to take his eyes from the conflagration.

"Are you sure?" Thorssen replied.

Tostig had never known his employer to doubt him. Not once in their long arrangement. Yet he was questioning him now. Had his pet politician finally lost faith? Was his trust in him so fragile after everything they had been through together? It wasn't as though he had ever failed the man, even when he lost his apprentice. He had taken care of things before and after.

"It is done," he repeated coldly.

"I hope you are right, old friend. I would hate for failure to come between us."

Old friend. Karl Thorssen had never called him his friend before. That one word was enough to put Tostig on edge. The dynamic between them was shifting. There was something different about Thorssen's voice; he had always been matter-of-fact in their dealings in the past, not one for pleasantries, no lingering on the line. Their relationship had never gone beyond the negotiating table. It was strictly business. A series of transactions to their mutual benefit. The assassin followed his instructions and was rewarded handsomely for his efforts.

The hairs on the back of his neck stood up in warning, prickling against his shirt collar, which was soaked with sweat growing cold.

Now he was certain the dynamic of their relationship was shifting: there was a threat where there had never been one before.

"I have never failed you," Tostig said. "It may be some time before their bodies are discovered, but that is all for the good."

"Bodies? I only asked you to deal with the woman. Who else?"

"Her cameraman. He was there in the hotel room. He was a loose end that needed tying up."

Thorssen was silent for a moment.

Tostig waited for him to respond, all the time watching the fire in the distance. There was no way the fire department would be able to bring it under control. The gasoline had ensured the flames got into the very fabric of the old structure. The church was gone. The fishermen would need to find somewhere else to confess their sins and bury their dead.

"I have another job for you," he said at last.

"Another one?"

"There is a woman making a nuisance of herself. I have agreed to meet her, to listen to her suspicions and offer some platitudes. But I think it is time to call upon your special talents. Dissuade her, Tostig. Convince her there is a wonderful life out there very much worth living and that it would be such a shame if she didn't get to enjoy it to the fullest."

"Of course. Who is she?"

"Una Mortensen, the archaeologist's mother. It seems she has taken her son's laptop from the dig at Skalunda."

Tostig liked control, reason, logic; this situation was rapidly losing all three thanks to his client.

So what if the old woman had some of her son's

possessions; if Mortensen had anything incriminating, surely he would have had it with him, presumably to keep it safe, when they'd stopped him on the road.

"You think there's something on the computer we should be worried about?"

"I'm just being cautious. You ought to be. For some reason she seems to think that I know something about his death. You wouldn't know anything about that, would you, Tostig?"

It was the first time Thorssen had ever used his name when speaking to him on a cell; that was one of the golden rules, no identification. It concerned the assassin that his employer no longer seemed to care.

He was going to have to make his own escape before the chance slipped away.

"No."

"Stay close by," Thorssen said, as though reading his mind.

The call ended silently. Tostig slipped the phone back into his pocket without taking his eyes from the fire. The blaze cast a red glow across the lake.

It was time to leave.

Not just the scene of his latest crime.

It was time to leave Sweden. To leave his life as Tostig. He'd always known the day would come. He had a box—his insurance policy—beneath the floorboards in his downtown apartment. That box contained everything he required to start a new life. It had money, paperwork, plastic. It had an entirely new person with his face just waiting to be born.

To all intents and purposes, as he hung up the

phone, Tostig died. He watched as the last link to his youth went up in smoke.

And like the phoenix from the ashes he would rise again from the flames, reborn.

30

The nurse asked too many questions.

She wanted to know how he'd cut his hand. She wanted him to go to the hospital to get it looked at properly. She pretended concern about tendon damage. Thorssen did not appreciate her clucking over him. And when she reached for the phone to call an ambulance he had no choice but to stop her. He asked her not to. He made her promise discretion, but he could not trust her, that much was obvious.

She became another loose end.

It fell to him to ensure she could not be picked at and unraveled.

The look on her face when she had peeled back the blood-soaked dressing spoke volumes. She had never seen anything like it before. She was out of her depth. Something had changed beneath his skin, the red swelling expanding and causing the wound to open farther, splitting his palm.

"There may be something stuck in there. We won't know what it is without having an X-ray. This is serious, Mr. Thorssen. We can't just stitch it up. It won't help."

"Just clean it up. I'll be fine."

He was used to giving people orders. They did what he wanted, when he wanted. He was used to the power that came with money and politics. He knew what it was like to be feared; people were afraid of him because they relied on him for their livelihood, but this was different. He *snarled* at the woman like a beast. She wanted to cower before him. He could taste her fear. She didn't want to be in the room with him.

"You need to go to the hospital," she insisted, reaching for her phone. She turned her back slightly, and as she punched in the three digits on her keypad to summon the ambulance, he pulled the sword smoothly from the piece of sacking he'd stolen from the sword smith's workshop.

Back turned, she didn't see the lethal arc of silver as it swung for her, and fell before her call could be connected. Not that an ambulance could save her. Nægling dug deep into her neck, severing arteries and slicing into bone. Her weight as she fell forward pulled the blade downward, forcing Thorssen to yank it free from her with far more force than it had taken to embed it.

Without the blade inside to hold the blood at bay it pulsed out to cover his face and chest and the walls and rug around and beneath her.

He didn't regret this, though he hadn't wanted it to happen inside his own home. This was his sanctuary. But she had left him with no choice. No choice at all.

At least it had happened in his den. Any evidence would remain hidden from the eyes of his mother. Neither she nor the cleaner dared venture inside the room without being invited. The nurse's body couldn't remain there indefinitely, of course. Nature would have its pestilent way with her, but he would have time to clean away the mess undisturbed.

His hands were still red with her blood when his cell phone rang.

He should have left it alone, but it was an anchor to reality. The election was two days—three days? Four days? He couldn't remember; even that simple important fact was slipping away from him. It could be important. He needed to act normally, but it had been a long time since he'd felt anything approaching normal.

He gathered his wits and was sure he had control over his voice before he answered, then he listened to the voice on the other end as Tostig relayed the news that he had dealt with the problem posed by Annja Creed and her cameraman. He felt nothing. They were like the nurse whose body lay at his feet, a necessity, a cost of war. He was becoming something more than himself.

Once, he would have trusted the assassin with his life, but no more. Problems caused doubts, which caused more problems. There could be no trust when the man had proven himself a possible liability.

If you want someone killed, do it yourself, Thorssen thought, twisting the old truism.

He had almost asked the man to dispose of the nurse's body, but the assassin had never been out to the house before. Doing so now went beyond the limits of their relationship. It exposed Thorssen to more risks. Risks he was averse to taking. He was quite capable of getting in the nurse's car and driving her body far away from here. It didn't take a genius to dispose of a corpse.

He would be done before his mother returned.

Thorssen had almost forgotten he still had the sword in his right hand.

Nægling was becoming part of him now.

So much so he felt strange when it was not in his grip.

Bereft.

Stranger than that was the craving he felt, the thirst and hunger that pulled at him and demanded to be satisfied.

A single thought dominated his mind: he must move the woman's car. Away from here. As far away from his home as possible.

His hand throbbed with dull agony. He was almost blind to it now. If only the nurse had stitched the wound as he'd asked. But no. She had to meddle. To fuss. Like his mother.

He looked down at his hand. The dressing was almost dry; the cut had clotted but not closed. The red swelling in the center had hardened to form a new layer of skin. He flexed his hand, stretching and closing his fingers, startled to find the skin split a little more, to reveal that the new skin extended beyond the cut.

The metamorphosis wasn't only affecting his mind.

He *was* changing.

Thorssen felt the urge to tug and tease at the edge of split skin and rip it away just as he had with the crusted coating that had shielded Nægling all those years it was underground. Look what had happened to the sword when it had been revealed, the transformation. He could only begin to imagine what he might find growing inside him, the extent of the transformation it was working on him.

But that could wait.

Practicalities had to come first.

He rolled the nurse into the rug she had fallen on and retrieved her car keys from her handbag. It would be easier to dispose of the carpet than to clean it.

The rug was easier to lift than he'd anticipated. He hoisted the carpet onto his shoulder, and felt the back of his shirt stretch and pull. He manhandled the corpse into a comfortable position to carry out of the house.

He opened the trunk of the small car she'd arrived in and bundled her inside, careful to keep the rug wrapped around all of her.

This wasn't his first time disposing of a corpse. He'd buried the sword smith in the patch of ground at the back of the man's house. Even so, the mundaneness of it was distasteful to his new emerging self. He was a warrior. They had fallen. It was not his place to bury the dead.

He looked at himself in the rearview mirror, at eyes he didn't recognize, a question forming in his mind: *If I can deal with death like this, if I can get my hands dirty, why do I need the assassin?*

31

"How's that for an entrance?" Garin Braden looked up at Annja, devilish grin fixed firmly in place as he pulled aside a stack of burning hymnbooks from the pile beneath her feet. He aimed the fire extinguisher at the broken wood, dampening it down long enough for him to climb up to where she hung. "Admit it, it really was a bit impressive. Church on fire, smoke everywhere, me striding to the rescue impervious to the flames. Are you beginning to understand why the ladies love me yet?"

For all his talk, Garin worked quickly and efficiently, cutting through the ropes and catching her as she fell. Annja felt the circulation return to her arms, which, given the state of her wrists and the blood coagulating around them, wasn't the best timing.

"Maybe if you didn't look like a drowned rat," she said.

"Hey, I took a dip in that ice cold lake to save your skin, woman. The least you can do is be grateful."

"I am. Just this once. Don't let it go to your head."

"No, ma'am."

He helped her out of the bindings that still held

one arm tight to the cross. The fire showed no sign of abating. Annja reached out into the otherwhere for the sword, feeling the reassuring solidity of it in her grasp, and then there it was in her hand as though it had always belonged there.

She moved along the aisle toward the door, the flames rippling overhead, the walls bowing under the weight of the roof as she picked a path through the detritus from the collapse. Johan was unconscious in the chair. Annja dropped quickly to her knees, fumbling with the ties binding him, but the smoke stung her eyes and she couldn't see straight. Beside her Garin started coughing. Steam rose from his body where the lake water was evaporating, its protective layer being scorched away.

There was no time. Annja used the sword to slice clean through the ties. Even half blind, her precision with the sword was unerring. Johan's hands came free and he slumped forward, only held in place by the ties binding his ankles to the chair legs. Hot embers stung her skin. She ignored the pain, focusing on freeing the cameraman's legs and getting him out of there. Garin was at her side, helping her.

Together they carried the unconscious cameraman out of the church, half supporting, half carrying each other down the aisle.

"Somehow I always imagined we'd be doing the whole aisle thing in the other direction," Garin said, hacking up his lungs as another bout of coughing hit.

"In your dreams."

"Frequently."

Fresh air—beautiful, wonderful, fresh air—hit them as they staggered out of the church. The doors hung open on broken hinges where Garin had forced them. Annja saw what looked like a portable battering ram lying on the floor beside the doors. She didn't ask. They carried Johan back to a low-slung black sports car not intended for three, and eased him onto the back shelf that pretended to be a seat. The effort brought him around.

"My camera…" Johan murmured.

"Camera?"

"In there," the cameraman managed. "Important…" he whispered, and then broke off coughing.

Garin looked at Annja. "You don't expect me to go back in there, do you?"

"No. I don't expect you to do anything. Wait here." And before he could argue Annja set off at a run across the grass to the blazing shell of the church. The entire structure was ablaze, flames reaching twice its height again into the sky and threatening to spill over into the wooden bell tower in its search for material to consume. The trees were too close, she saw, realizing that if the fire reached even one of those low-hanging branches the danger was that the entire forest would burn, which would be nothing short of an ecological disaster.

She tried to enter, but the heat beat her back.

The camera couldn't survive the heat, surely? The recording would be ruined.

Steeling herself, Annja went back into the fire, covering her face.

Everywhere was aflame, every surface rippled with it. The heat was beyond anything she'd experienced in her life. She felt her hair beginning to shrivel into her scalp and the skin across her face and hands tighten painfully. She couldn't see the camera and had no idea how long she could stand the smoke and flames. The door to the vestry hung open. She'd seen the camera in there, hadn't she?

Annja started to run. Above her, a series of sharp cracks announced another imminent collapse. It felt as if the entire weight of the roof was about to come down on top of her. Annja threw herself through the vestry door. Seconds later the crucifix fell, tearing away from the wall with a scream of tortured metal. She couldn't think about it. All she could do was focus on the camera case. It had to be in here. She'd seen it in here.

But she couldn't see it now.

She wanted to scream.

It had to be in here.

And she had to get out of there.

She was about to give up when she saw it on the floor, partially covered. She grabbed it and turned to run back through the wall of fire and out through the main door as if the devil himself was on her heels. The entire roof fell in behind her seconds after she burst out of the church.

She dropped to her knees.

"You're insane—you do know that, don't you?" Garin said, leading her to his car. "I risked my neck to get you out and what did you do? Run right back in!"

She held up the fire-scorched camera case as if it were the Holy Grail.

"Not worth it. Never worth it. Never, Annja."

"Every time you get out alive it is," she said, earning a grim frown from Garin.

There was no sign of her car.

Picking up on it, Garin said, "I suspect you're going

to have a long and quite awkward conversation with your rental company."

Annja swore under her breath, but the car was the least of her worries.

For a start, she'd hired it in the name of the production company, so Doug Morrell would be getting the bill, not her, assuming they couldn't just use the on-board GPS to locate it. Then again, if the assassin was as thorough as he seemed to be it was probably at the bottom of the lake by now. She'd have to ring Doug and warn him that there might be a particularly substantial bill winging its way to New York. That was a going to be a fun conversation.

She got into Garin's car. Seconds later they were peeling away from the ruined Saint Peter's on the Lake and racing toward the city.

"How did you know where to find us?"

"Elementary, my dear Annja," Garin said. "I'm connected. I have people. Unlike you, they love me. In this particular instance it was the rather lovely young receptionist at your hotel who was only too happy to trade what she knew in return for the promise of a box seat for the folk opera tomorrow evening."

"Charmer."

"And lucky for you, I am, wouldn't you say?" She didn't argue the point. Given the fire in the sky behind them it was difficult to.

"But *why* are you here?"

"Because you said you needed my help. Okay, not in so many words, but it was obvious. I dropped everything and came running. It's what I do. Haven't we established that yet?" The sarcasm in his voice could not have been more obvious if he had tried.

"Right. You traveled all this distance because of the *laptop?*"

"Well, let's just say I wasn't having a lot of luck with the ponies, and the little minxes I'd invited along for a ride were of the pretty, but vacuous, variety."

"Just how you like them."

"Oh, you wound me."

"So, you think you can crack the laptop?"

"Without doubt. I paid handsomely for a little device from someone."

"Someone?"

"One of my contacts."

"That's a bit vague."

"Listen, I can't keep all of their names straight. Do you have any idea how many contacts I have? Aaron? Erin?"

"Sounds like you can't even keep their gender straight."

"Exactly, I'm people blind. Everyone is equal."

"Especially when you want something."

"My contact is confident his box of tricks will do the business with that computer."

"And he knows what he's talking about?"

"Oh, yes, he does this sort of thing for a living."

"What? You hired a thief?"

"What do you take me for, Annja? Again, I'm wounded," Garin said, flashing her a dangerous grin. "Ignorance is bliss, trust me."

As they approached the outskirts of Gothenburg Garin suggested that they lay low, given the fact they'd just stumbled out of a burning building, soot and scorch marks included. It was the kind of detail that stuck in a person's mind and they didn't want to be remembered.

"I'll go in, have a quick chat with the delightful Lovisa. Use my not inconsiderable charms and convince her that I'm sneaking a famous American celebrity into the building and we need to avoid those damned paparazzi." He grinned. "The best lies always have a grain of truth. There'll be another way in. Trust me."

Lovisa? He'd been in the country for three hours and was already on first-name terms with the receptionist, had a date lined up for when her shift ended *and* had thrown himself into a burning building to help them?

Some people were life-size. Some people, like Garin Braden, were larger than life. She watched as he strode through the lobby's entrance as if he owned the place. He probably did; he had his fingers in that many pies. He'd make a joke about not being able to keep his contacts straight, but as he himself had just said, in every good joke there was an element of truth. Garin Braden owned far more of the world than he'd ever admit. He liked it that way, but then five hundred years gave you time to build up a decent portfolio.

"How are you doing?" Annja asked Johan, leaning over into the backseat. He was breathing easier, but he looked terrible. Drained, deathly pale, the only color in his face from the dirt and grime.

"Been better," he said, and then paused. "We should be dead. He saved our lives."

"I know. But don't let Garin hear you say that—it'll only go to his head." It would have been easy to reassure Johan, admit they'd had a lucky escape, but escape meant being free of the threat, and they weren't free at all. The big man—Thorssen's goon—had tried to kill them twice. He was still out there. She didn't even want to think about a third time lucky.

"We should go to the police. We need to. We need to be protected from this madman.... They need to put him away."

"It doesn't work like that," she said, even though she knew he was right. "We don't even know who we're dealing with."

"Of course we do—it's Karl Thorssen. He's behind it all. Everything from sabotaging his own rally—all of those innocent people dead simply because they believed in his hate speech—to Mortensen, the fireworks guy and very nearly us. There's nothing to be gained by trying to kid ourselves here. We've picked up a very powerful enemy—"

"Exactly," Annja agreed, cutting him off. "He's connected. He has friends in law enforcement. He has friends in criminal justice, in customs, immigration, you name it, right across the entire bureaucratic spectrum—and he's connected to so many others through the simplest facilitator of crime ever, money. He owns people, Johan. We can't trust anyone here. We have no idea if they're in Karl Thorssen's pocket. And no, I'm not just being paranoid. I've been thinking about it for a while. We're in trouble here. We need ammunition. We need something we can take out to the world and finish Thorssen once and for all. Let's just offer a silent prayer to whatever devil or deity looks after people like us that what we need is on Lars's laptop."

So much for reassuring him, she thought.

Garin knocked on the window. Annja rolled it down.

"Worked a charm. Drive around to the service entrance. There's an underground parking bay that has a separate stair they use for laundry, food deliveries to the cold storage, et cetera," he explained. "We can get you in that way. The stairs run the entire height of the building, so we just need this—" he paused, waggling a staff security pass "—to get through the lock and we're good to go."

"You're a star," Annja said.

"That I am."

They circled the block, turning onto an incredibly small alleyway, and took the ramp down into the underground parking facility. Garin worked his magic with the lock and they climbed the stairs to Annja's floor.

Johan didn't say one word.

She was worried about him.

This wasn't the kind of thing a hot shower and a change of clothes would fix, either.

Garin saw them to their rooms, made his excuses and left them to it for a while. Annja had half expected him to at least offer to scrub her back, but he hadn't made even the slightest innuendo. *For that, she was truly thankful.*

Annja riffled through her stuff for a clean shirt and jeans.

Then she recalled that Garin had checked himself into the penthouse suite, and it seemed young Lovisa had offered a special turndown service.

Annja was glad to have some time to herself.

It wasn't just about freshening up, though she ran

the shower hot enough to scour the skin from her body. She needed to decompress. She felt like a diver coming up too quickly and suffering from the bends. Her emotions were bottled up inside her, especially how she felt about Roux not being in touch. It was unlike the old man. He'd normally be the first to fuss over her, and no game of poker was that good he'd risk losing her. There had to be a reason Roux hadn't answered her texts. She didn't want to think she was jumping at shadows, but she'd said it herself, Thorssen was connected....

Just call damn you, old man.

She stayed under the spray a long time, head down, the steaming water red at the bottom of the shower from the bloody skin around her wrists. Afterward, she treated and bandaged her wounds, and then dressed quickly. She didn't want to be in her bra and panties when Garin reappeared, and knowing Garin that was exactly what he was aiming for.

The faintest tap on the door caused her to think that Thorssen's man had returned to finish what he'd started, but then she heard Garin say, "Only me."

She opened the door, but before she could say anything, he continued.

"Get your stuff together. You're not staying down here. Not tonight, at least. There's several rooms in the suite—one has your name on it, one's got Johan's. I'm not letting you out of my sight, and don't bother arguing about it. I'll only be forced to call Roux and get him to sort you out." He grinned. "We have one tactical advantage here—right now your would-be killer thinks he succeeded. We need him to keep thinking that for as long as possible. Besides, the suite costs an arm and a leg. No way I'm getting value for money out of it by myself, so raid the minibar, indulge on room service, rack up a small fortune on the pay-per-view.

Johan answered first, appearing behind Garin. "Count me out, folks. This is totally beyond my pay grade. I'm out. I'm heading home."

"I can pay you a lot more," Garin said seriously.

"No, thanks. I'm heading home," he said.

"We need you here," Annja said.

"Sorry. I can't take any more of this. Micke didn't say anything about people trying to burn me alive when he asked me to come and shoot some footage. If I wanted that kind of excitement in my life I'd have signed up for something other than a Swedish election."

"I need your camera," Annja stated, and thought maybe she shouldn't have because it would only serve to make him feel like she'd been using him all along. Still, she wasn't lying. She did need his camera if she was going to get at Thorssen.

"Fine. Bring it back with you if you can avoid getting killed. Otherwise, I'll bill the production company for a replacement."

"Doug's going to love me…bills for cars and cameras."

"You said why you didn't want the police involved, and I listened. You made me realize I can't stay here. I've got responsibilities, Annja. A wife. A two-year-old daughter at home." It was the first time Johan had mentioned his personal life in all the time they'd been together, and she couldn't blame him for backing out. In his place, with the same people waiting for her, she'd have done the same thing. "Every time I close my eyes I see that guy stuffing the rag into my mouth, threatening to kill me…. I can't live like that. I'm walking away."

"Running, you mean," Garin added needlessly, but then he hadn't been the one who'd been tied to a chair while the building was torched around him.

"As fast as I can," Johan agreed, no anger in his voice.

He left them, heading down the corridor without so much as a backward glance.

Annja wanted to go after him, but she knew there was nothing she could say to persuade him to change his mind. This put him out of harm's way. It was a good thing, she told herself. But she didn't believe it. He was going to be out there alone. She couldn't protect him.

"Then there were two. Get your things. Room service will be delivering in fifteen minutes and I'm so hungry I could eat a horse. Unfortunately, they eat horse in this country so I have no idea what I actually ordered."

She threw her clothes and toiletries into her bag.

Garin reached on top of the wardrobe and positioned a small and unobtrusive black box where it could not be seen unless someone was looking for it.

"Camera?" Annja asked.

"Just in case. You never know who might come calling. Especially if they think it's fair game to steal from the dead. I've already arranged with Lovisa for the maids to leave the room alone for a couple of days."

"Uh, what about your hot date? Shouldn't you be wining and dining the lovely Lovisa?"

Garin grinned. "Rain check."

"I bet you're popular."

"Remember, Annja. You can get away with almost anything if you say it with flowers."

32

The suite was larger than she had expected; a small principality could have lived within its four walls.

Annja stared out of the window—a huge single sheet of glass that stretched the length of the living area. The view offered an unrivaled panorama of the city and the countryside for miles beyond.

"He's still out there."

"That he is," Garin agreed. "But not necessarily hunting *you*. That's the important thing here. He thinks he's done his job. He could be out of the country by now. It's what I'd do in his place with everything neat and tidy."

"That makes me feel even worse," Annja said, staring out the window in the direction of the distant lake. "If he's gone, there's no chance we can stop him. He's just out there."

"Point. But you still haven't told me *why* this guy wants to burn you alive." Before she could answer him there was a polite knock on the door and an announcement that room service had arrived.

Garin showed in two members of staff, moving with calm precision to lay out the table and arrange the meal as if it were silver service. They didn't say a word. It was weirdly quiet, until they were gone.

"I wasn't sure what to order," Garin said, waving a casual hand toward the huge meal that had been spread out. "So I rather ordered the lot."

It really was a veritable feast—a proper Swedish smorgasbord with a little of everything from pickled herring to spare ribs, butterfly sandwiches, beetroot dip, avocado sauces, various fish dishes, something Garin described as Jansson's Temptation and a whole host of finger food.

"You could have asked."

"You'd have only said steak, and where's the fun in that?" He laughed and threw himself into a chair, rubbing his hands. "So, you were about to tell me why you've got an assassin on your trail, again."

Annja told him about what had happened in the hotel, about the man that Johan had pushed over the balcony and the fact that someone had ransacked her room the following morning, about the dead archaeologist and everything else in between.

"So your crime is being a nosy do-gooder?"

"Isn't it always? And speaking of… The laptop?"

"Ah, my raison d'être. I'd almost forgotten with all the excitement going on." He pushed back his chair and disappeared into the master bedroom only to emerge a moment later with a small black box, which he plugged into one of the USB ports on the laptop Annja had retrieved.

He booted up the laptop.

"So what does that thing do?" Annja asked around a mouthful of food.

Garin paused and looked at her quizzically. "You

really want me to tell you or is this one of those questions where you're just pretending to be interested to humor me?"

"Humoring you."

"It could take a while," he said. "I'm still hungry, so let's leave it to do its thing and eat."

The device emitted irregular bleeps as it processed various algorithms blind, probing at the password while they ate until at last it fell silent.

Almost exactly at the same time Garin's cell phone chimed with an incoming text alert.

He read it and smiled.

"So, anyone wanna play a game of hot and cold?" His face was split with a grin, the kind of grin that reeked of "I know something you don't know." Annja was tempted to snatch the phone from his hand and read the text herself.

"His mother thought it might have been his first girlfriend's name."

"Well, it's possible. What was her name?"

"Kristina."

"Cold."

"Please don't tell me that it's her name with a number after it."

"Colder."

"Just tell me."

"Has anyone ever told you, you take all the fun out of things, Annja Creed?" he said, laughing as he turned the phone around so she could see the display. One word: *Annja.* "Guess you made quite an impression on our boy."

"Or he was leaving it for me as a message. It's in

there. I know it. Whatever we need to prove Thorssen's in this up to his neck, it's on that hard drive," she said.

He couldn't argue with that.

Garin popped the box from the USB port and stepped aside to let Annja have at it.

She typed her own name in.

The screen displayed a series of icons, some of which she recognized while others were a complete mystery.

Her eyes were drawn to a folder on the desktop labeled Skalunda Barrow.

She moved the curser and double tapped the touch pad to open it, expecting a list of documents, schedules and agreements. Instead, there were a series of photographs.

Rather than jumping impatiently to the last image, she moved through them one by one, zooming in, determined not to miss even the slightest detail. As she balanced the machine on her knees, Garin watched over her shoulder.

There were shots of the site when Lars had first arrived, shots of the caravan, even ones of him staking out the ground. She saw a crowd of people—including the girl, Inge—who were, no doubt, the army of volunteers who would have been working on the site if it hadn't been shut down.

She went through them all, slowly staring at them, hoping to see something, anything, that might shed some light on what was going on.

She found the answer in the last dozen or so frames.

These final photographs looked as though they'd been taken inside his caravan.

The light was crisp and clean, casting strong shadows away from the object in the center of the screen.

"What is it?" Garin asked. "I mean, apart from being a big twisted lump of metal?"

Annja clicked through the final couple of images, putting them side by side while she tried to work out what she was actually looking at. "It's not the same piece—look, it's two," she said. "You can see where he's pushed them together here." She pointed at the screen.

It can't be, she thought.

"Looks like a sword," Garin said.

"Not just any sword." Annja was scarcely able to credit what Lars Mortensen had found buried in Skalunda Barrow. "A broken sword…in the final resting place of Beowulf, a legendary warrior king."

"So it's a king's sword, then."

"It's so much more than that," Annja said, already certain this was what Lars had been desperate to keep away from Karl Thorssen, and absolutely stone-cold certain this was the very reason Thorssen had funded the dig. He'd been looking for a symbol. This was it. "Lars found his holy grail, Garin. Lars found the sword that proves an enduring legend. Lars found Nægling, the greatest sword in the world, the nailer, won by Beowulf after he'd slain the beast Grendel and his mother. The sword he held in death, broken on the scales of the great dragon."

33

The nurse's car was unfeasibly small; how anyone could sit comfortably in it Karl Thorssen didn't know. It was a long time since he'd driven anything so confined. He didn't think of himself as being a large man, but inside the dead woman's hatchback he might as well have been a giant. He wedged his body into the tiny space it afforded. Mercifully, it was a short journey to his destination.

He'd taken as little time as possible to clean up, put on a clean shirt and jeans, throwing the old ones on top of the carpet in the trunk before driving away.

The shirt felt a little tight.

It was new, so he had no way of knowing if his mother had bought one that was a little on the small side, or if he was putting on a few pounds. He felt the ridge of muscles in his stomach: washboard firm. The shirt was tight around the shoulders, too. His mother had obviously picked the wrong one up. Still, it would do.

He drove to a small lockup garage on the outskirts of town. He could have pretended it reminded him of his youth, of getting started back when he was juggling his business from inside it. The truth was he kept it because of something his mother said about it being where the bodies were buried. He'd always assumed his father was in the concrete foundation, but he'd never been inclined to find out.

Despite everything that had happened between them, he loved his mother and if she'd seen fit to do away with the man who shared his biology, then who could have blamed her? He'd seen the evidence with his own eyes, unable to protect her from his anger. Karl Thorssen had always vowed he wouldn't become his father's son, but look at him now, look at the blood on his hands.

He was a monster.

He visited the lockup on rare occasions, not to pay his respects to the old man but to be sure he hadn't somehow clawed his way out of the ground.

He rolled up the metal shutters.

Boxes were pushed up against the back wall. They were full of things he no longer needed but couldn't bring himself to throw away. Little pieces of his childhood, toys, memories. They took up almost a third of the garage but there was still space to fit the hatchback in comfortably. The headlights sent spiders and other night creatures scuttling for darkness, the only witnesses to the car being left there.

This was a better solution than trying to dispose of the car, body and carpet all at once, when the city was already caught in the carnage that Tostig was creating.

Thorssen stood back, glancing up and down the row of garages to be sure no eyes were on him. The place was deserted, and he locked up once again.

He had no idea how many people still used these

garages. Not many, surely? They had an air of abandonment about them. The railway station was only a few minutes away. From there he intended to get a taxi back to the house. He was being overcautious, but the time he spent around the assassin had rubbed off. He was even starting to think like Tostig.

As he walked he tried to slip into his jacket, but found that, just as his shirt felt too tight, the seams of his leather jacket strained across his shoulders, too. So perhaps it wasn't his mother's fault, after all. He resolved to put a few hours in at the gym. In the end, he slung the jacket over his shoulder as though he didn't have a care in the world.

He heard a sudden burst of some too-cheerful ring tone he didn't recognize.

He slipped a hand inside his jacket pocket to retrieve the nurse's phone.

He swore at himself, resisting the temptation to end the call, then to turn it off.

He knew that phones could be traced, that their location could be pinpointed using cell tower triangulation if they were still live—that didn't mean switched on, just that they had juice feeding the SIM card from the battery. He also knew these things had memories, which meant the last recorded location of the phone was less than three hundred yards from where he'd stashed her corpse. He couldn't disable the phone until he'd set up a false trail to lead the police or whoever away from the lockup.

He stared at the screen, which said 1 Missed Call.

What would Tostig do?

He glanced around for inspiration and saw that he was now close to the main road. In the distance, he could hear the sound of a train approaching. He moved briskly, wiping the phone on the lining of his jacket to remove any trace of his fingerprints, banking on the fact that it would be handled several times before the police came to trace it. The plan taking root in his mind was simple: get on the first train in the station and leave the phone on a seat before slipping off again.

It wouldn't take long for the phone to be halfway across the country, and there was no guarantee the person who happened to find it would be some honest soul, either. Maybe they wouldn't turn it into lost and found; maybe they'd look to reset it to factory defaults and have themselves a nice new phone for their troubles.

The kids came out of nowhere.

On skateboards, wearing hoodies and doing everything they could to make themselves look as though they belonged somewhere other than the suburbs. They did a couple of tricks on their skateboards, kicking up the board so it dragged across the ground, then started circling him as he walked, full of threat.

"You don't want to do this," he said under his breath.

He had seen their like before—self-important, entitled brats who wanted to be dangerous, wanted to intimidate, pretending they owned the streets. Good people lived here. He didn't need to see under their hoodies to know they weren't Swedish kids, not born and raised. This was what twisted his gut. This was what drove him. Seeing scum like this terrorize the streets where decent folks had lived all their lives. Too many of these people, frightened to set foot outside their door at night, had sent him letters of support, pledging money to his party.

Thorssen felt the overwhelming urge to lash out and shove them off their skateboards, see how they liked being intimidated.

The rage built inside him, starting low in the pit of his stomach like some furnace being stoked by their mere presence, the coals of hate flaring red hot. He wished more than anything he'd brought Nægling with him; he could have cut them down in an instant. That was what he was born—no, reborn—to do. He was a warrior. It was in his blood.

A smile stole across his face as the larger of the kids approached him on foot, all swagger and ego. He kept his hood up. It was all carefully calculated menace.

Thorssen heard the unmistakable click of a switch-blade being engaged.

His smile spread.

He just watched the boy walk toward him.

"Leave me, boy. If you don't, your friends will be trying to stop your intestines from unraveling around your ankles. Please make it easy for me."

The kid looked at him with a clearly practiced sneer. Oh, yes, he was the leader. The others were his pack of dogs waiting for his signal to attack.

They continued to circle, kicking their boards up every now and then so the wood scraped across the sidewalk. The acrylic wheel created a rhythm on the uneven concrete ground.

Switchblade nodded to the pack; that was all they needed, his order.

The first of them grabbed at Thorssen's jacket, trying to wrench it off his shoulder, but he held on tight.

His wallet was in there along with his house and office keys. Once, he might have surrendered them, let the kids have the cash to save the confrontation, but not now. Now he was a warrior. Now he was on fire. He would burn them.

He felt the hot seething rage threaten to overwhelm him, felt his grip on his thoughts slip. His mind was flooded with memories of brutality and death. He could smell blood. Their frightened heartbeats hammered in his ears. He could taste the rot of their flesh as their bodies decayed, the cloying reek of dead skin, the stale scent of a woman on one of them, all of this and more.

Thorssen threw back his head and roared.

A second hand darted forward, snatching the cell phone from his grasp—the nurse's cell phone—it was all he could do to stop himself from laughing as the kids made their getaway. He let them go. It served his purpose.

He fought to control his bloodlust as he stared into the leader's eyes. His hate threatened to burst through the dam barely holding him back as the kid drew the switchblade across his own throat. A promise of what he'd do if Thorssen made a move toward him.

"Run, little one, run. Run for your life."

34

Annja finished her account of what had happened since the rally, leaving nothing out—telling Garin everything she knew, everything she suspected and everything she feared. Still, it didn't amount to very much.

Her fear was that the two shards of Nægling would have been lost in the remains of Lars Mortensen's car.

But she couldn't believe Thorssen would have given up his prize so easily. Not when his man had taken the time to retrieve the dead man's phone and pretend to be a cop to wheedle her location out of her. No. The sword wasn't gone. His thug had got it before he torched the car and Lars along with it. Karl Thorssen had everything his heart desired.

She needed to think this through, establish a chain of events.

Someone had told Thorssen that Lars was coming to meet her.

Which meant someone had to be playing both sides, someone who was close to Lars and close to Thorssen. It made sense for Thorssen to protect his investment.

The question she kept coming back to was who?

"So, Ugly here," Garin said, pointing at the big man in the paramedic's uniform, "is *definitely* your guy?" He was running through the footage again frame by frame just as she had done so many times already. He paused on the image of the paramedic.

"Definitely."

"Okay, so, we can safely assume that he isn't a caring health professional moonlighting as some kind of a hit man. Why, then, would he masquerade as a paramedic at Thorssen's rally? That seems like a question we should be asking ourselves, don't you think?"

Annja studied the image of the man's face trapped immobile there on the laptop screen, as he helped Thorssen into the waiting ambulance. "Because Thorssen knew he was going to need an ambulance."

He moved the footage to another familiar face.

"And then we have this guy." He jabbed a finger at scar-faced Nils Fenström, the pyrotechnics expert. "Victim of a fire in his fireworks factory. Now call me cynical but why would a special-effects guy be at a political rally?"

"Why indeed…" Annja said, knowing there was only one answer that made sense when all of the parameters were taken into account. He'd rigged the explosion for Thorssen, and Thorssen's hit man, the paramedic, was making sure no one talked.

"It was all for show," Garin said. "None of it was real. Smoke and mirrors. The hit man was there to get Thorssen out. What none of them expected was that the pyro guy would stick around and make a nuisance of himself, hence the little tête-à-tête you saw in the lobby. They couldn't know Johan would catch him on camera, yet there was always going to be a risk with all of those journos around, so they wanted to get him out of there as quickly as possible. Right, Thorssen was never going to need a real ambulance. The explosion was rigged to purposely leave the stage area safe. It's clever. It makes a martyr of Thorssen, without actually killing him, which is always going to be good for votes."

It fit.

He moved the footage on to the dig where Thorssen, wrapped up in the passion of his monologue, seemed not to notice the weight he put on his supposedly damaged arm, backing up the theory.

It fit.

"So what do we do?" Garin asked. "Loath as I am to suggest going to the police, it's rather more mundane than what we usually get involved with. We've tied it up in a nice bow—Thorssen kills the archaeologist for the sword, blows his own rally up for votes and then tries to take out anyone who knows the truth or is likely to try and find it, like your good self. It's all rather disappointingly prosaic and *human*—people never cease to disappointment me. So do we hand it over to the law and let them earn their paycheck? This proves that the henchman was working for Thorssen. Every link of the chain is in place. Even the usual lunkheads controlling the long arm of the law can't screw this one up."

"It doesn't prove he works for Thorssen. All it proves is that he was there, dressed as a paramedic. Thorssen will deny that he knew anything about it. He's a public figure. He'll claim he was a target of the assassin or something. He'll wriggle his way out of it. It's what he does, Garin. He owns people. He owns people in high places. And he wants to join them up there. We're a couple of days away from the election and he's already got an army ready to rise up for him."

"Fine. Then it's option number two. We get the sword," Garin announced. "Like you said, it's a symbol. He's banking on winning this election and riding a wave of unchecked pride to do it, Nægling above his head. That thing was powerful enough to slay a dragon. It's powerful enough to bring down a government."

"Perhaps we should ask Roux what he thinks, if he'd ever pick up his phone."

"I wouldn't trouble the old man." Garin spoke in a way that screamed avoidance. He was keeping something from her.

"What aren't you telling me, Garin?"

"Nothing."

"Don't lie to me. I always know when you're lying. It's why you're a lousy poker player and Roux gets all of your money."

"There's not much to tell."

"Which means there's something, so spill."

"Okay. I've talked to him. He's been here a few days."

"A few days?"

"He's been watching. Making sure you stay safe."

"Well, he's done a rotten job of it, all things considered."

"It could have been worse. Believe me. Anyway, he was primarily interested in the sword, or rather a curse surrounding it."

"A curse?"

"Yeah…"

"Don't make me drag it out of you, Garin. I'm really not in the mood."

"He didn't have the time to go into it. He was tailing Johan, making sure he got home safe, but while he was up in Stockholm he found a book about evil that dates back centuries. Nægling's mentioned in there. Though instead of the biter, or nailer, it's referred to as Grendel's Curse. The blade came from the monster's treasure horde. According to the book it's tainted, and Roux doesn't want us taking any chances."

"So basically he's saying the world will be a better place without Nægling."

"Yes."

"But he doesn't know why?"

"Not that he told me."

"Why do I still get the feeling you're not telling me everything?"

"Because you've been hanging around the old man too long, Annja."

"We'll go after Thorssen. Toe-to-toe."

"Always going to be easier to find a politician than it is a hit man. One craves attention, the other is pretty much invisible. And assuming the killer did his job, Thorssen's already got the sword and has had it for days."

"Biding his time for the big reveal."

"In the public eye, right when people are gearing up to cast their all-important votes," Garin agreed. "So cynical for one so young."

"You don't need to be five hundred years old to know how these things work," Annja said. "There's nothing else on this we need, is there?"

"Short of a note saying, 'Karl Thorssen killed me,' I'd say we've got all we're going to get off it."

"Then I'd like to give the laptop back to his mother. There's stuff on here that might give her some sort of closure."

Annja emailed the photographs to herself in case she should need to use them, then found her phone in the pile of possessions she'd left on her new bed. She was surprised to see that there were five missed calls from the woman.

She played back the messages before making the call. Una sounded calm at first. She asked to meet up for coffee. Then she asked if Annja had any news about the laptop. The third message was apologetic but growing more insistent. By the time Annja reached the final message the woman was emotional, telling her that she couldn't just sit back and let that bastard Thorssen get away with her son's death.

Annja tried phoning her, but the call went straight to voice mail.

She checked the time of the last message; it was almost an hour earlier.

"I think things just stepped up to Defcon 1."

"Not good news, I take it?" Garin asked, slouched on the sofa and watching something on the screen of a tablet PC.

"Lars's mother has gone after Thorssen."

"Obviously she has. Why would life ever be simple? And there was me dreading having words with the lovely Lovisa on our way out."

"To blow off another date?"

"Nope. Not even I am that callous. No, I want to find out why your room was just cleaned. Though 'cleaned' is an interesting definition of the word. As maids go, this one was hardly exacting." He pressed the screen a couple of times, pinching the picture to zoom in, before he handed the tablet to Annja. The maid was certainly taking a good look around, but she wasn't doing a great deal of cleaning.

But then, why would she be?

She wasn't a maid.

"What are you really doing there, Inge?" Annja said, watching Lars Mortensen's student assistant rifle her room.

35

Tostig sat in his apartment, a cold beer on the table in front of him, an old jazz CD playing on the sound system. The television was on, sound turned down. He was waiting for confirmation that the bodies of two people had been recovered from the fire out at Saint Peter's on the Lake.

He rarely drank, but the taste of smoke was proving hard to get rid of.

The pictures on the silent screen showed that the fire had spread into the trees. The scrolling banner said nothing about corpses, only that the fire crews were having trouble dealing with it. The church itself had been completely destroyed an hour earlier.

The cameraman focused on a nearby car that had been damaged in the spread of the fire. It was Creed's rental car. That, to Tostig, was proof enough Annja Creed and her cameraman hadn't escaped.

He'd recovered his insurance policy from beneath the floorboards in the bedroom. There was nothing in the apartment he couldn't live without when he began his new life. Nothing he felt any sentimental attachment to. Tostig wasn't that sort of man.

He had enough money in the envelope to run for a decade without needing to work. He maintained a simple lifestyle. He had no need of luxury. He didn't crave pretty things. He could happily live like a monk.

And yet he was hesitating.

He should have been out of the door as soon as he saw the job was done. But he was here, looking at the television screen, waiting for something to change. He raised the glass of beer to his lips, but didn't taste anything.

Without the Serb to watch his back, he'd been cutting corners, taking the path of least resistance. That meant he was taking too many risks at a time when his employer was asking more and more from him. Thorssen said he wanted the old woman dealt with. Leaned on. That was Thorssen-speak for taken out, no matter how prettily he couched it. He knew the man. He was out of control, seeing enemies at every corner.

Tostig put the empty bottle on the table.

He was done.

Out.

He'd known it since he pried up the floorboards—before that, since he'd torched the church. There was nothing Thorssen could say or do to him. He was washing his hands of the man. Let him find another idiot to do his dirty work.

He picked up the phone and called the one number stored in its memory.

Even as he dialed he knew he should hang up. Just hang up and run. But a voice on the other end of the line growled, "Yes?"

There was still an etiquette to this, Tostig reminded himself. A way of doing things. He needed to sign off on the job. He wanted it done in person, not over the phone. He wanted to see Thorssen's expression when he told him. It was how he could be sure that he was getting his message across, ending their arrangement without him becoming Thorssen's next enemy.

The voice sounded raw, animalistic, unlike Karl Thorssen's and yet still unmistakably the politician's.

"We need to talk," he said.

"Do we? I don't think we've got anything to talk about. Unless this is about money? Are you getting greedy, Tostig?"

"No, it's not about money," Tostig replied. "I trust you to transfer the final payment for the Creed woman."

"Then what is it about?"

"Face-to-face," Tostig said.

"Meet me at the station tonight at nine. I have another job for you. One last one."

"Fine," Tostig said, agreeing to the meeting even though everything was far from fine.

He ended the call and settled back into his chair, as Thorssen's face filled the screen once more. Murders aside, the politician had been the main topic of conversation for the past few days as public support for him reached an all-time high. People were ready for a charismatic leader. They were ready for his message, were naive enough to swallow his rhetoric. It struck a chord with the dissatisfied and his supporters were milking the connection between the attempted assassination and his political enemies who would silence him.

They were sheep being led to the slaughter by media spin.

The picture on the screen changed to show a blackened shop front that had been ravaged by flame.

Tostig didn't need to be able to see the name on the shop front to recognize the small Asian supermarket just a few streets away from where he now sat.

He had heard the fire engine earlier. It always happened. People with their own agendas took advantage of chaos. He'd provided the chaos. There would be riots on the streets tonight, he thought, knowing full well Thorssen had sown the seeds for it. Civic unrest, they called it.

That shop fire had claimed the lives of an entire family. Now there was no family. Three generations wiped out in under an hour. They'd been trapped in the apartment above the store.

This was what Thorssen's rhetoric inspired.

This was nothing short of pure hatred spilling out across the city, fanning the flames every bit as much as the oxygen in the cool, clean night air.

While he wasn't one for long goodbyes, he took a moment to look around his apartment. It had been his haven for so many years, yet the rooms held no real sentimental value for him; he'd never shared this space with anyone, no lovers, no friends. He'd never had a visitor up here.

There were no memories that couldn't be abandoned.

36

Karl Thorssen's mother was waiting for him when he returned home.

She stood in the hallway outside his den, clearly agitated.

"Move, Mother," he barked, the need to be back with the sword burning inside him.

"I thought something had happened to you. I was worried. I wanted to see if you were all right, but the door was locked."

"I'm fine," he said. The words were meant to be reassuring, but he had no control over his voice; the modulation was all wrong, the anger inside him still seething away. He placed a hand on her upper arm. She flinched away from his touch.

"You promised you'd get that seen to," she said, pointing at his damaged and swollen hand. It was his turn to pull away.

"And I will. But not yet. Don't treat me like a child, Mother."

"But you are a child, Kalle." She used the endearment, Kalle, rather than Karl. He hated that, too. It was all meant to remind him where he came from, that he was here because of her, that it was his duty to please her, to make her proud.

"Yes, Mother," he said, moving the hand from her arm to touch her cheek. "But I'm also on the threshold of being elected into the Riksdag, and I'm close to revealing one of the greatest archaeological finds of our time, so I'm a rather busy child." He made a face, willing her to leave him alone.

His cell phone rang.

She gave him a weak smile, and turned to leave.

Ensconced in his den, Thorssen picked up the sword.

He closed his eyes, feeling the static charge ripple through his skin.

In his mind's eye he again killed the man who'd restored the hilt, hacking and slashing until his entire body glistened with a sheen of sweat. His shirt clung to him. His breath came hard and fast, as though recovering from the exertion rather than the memory.

But it wasn't just a memory, was it?

It was in him. Alive.

Unlike the smith.

"What's happened to your back?"

He'd been so eager to get to the sword he'd forgotten to close the door.

His mother stood in the doorway with a cup of coffee clutched in her hands.

He laid the sword down on the floor, and ushered her away from the door. She couldn't come into the room, not with arterial spray of the nurse's blood smeared across the far wall.

"Nothing," he replied, closing the door behind him.

"You've been bleeding? It looks *awful*. Have you been in an accident?"

"I have no idea what you are talking about, Mother." He could feel the swelling beneath his shoulders. The joints burned as he moved. "I'll shower and clean up. It's probably nothing." He kissed her on the cheek and took the coffee from her, giving her no chance to fuss.

In the bathroom he stripped naked and stood before the mirror, looking for the first time at his body's transformation; the fat had gone. Every muscle was clearly cut. He hardly recognized himself. He turned slightly, angling his shoulder toward the mirror, trying to see what had caused the smear of blood that had soaked into his shirt.

There was a wound across his back, running along the line of his shoulder blade.

He ran his fingers along the edge of the wound that he could reach, and just like the cut in his hand he could feel a swelling pushing at the edges, ripping his skin oh-so-slowly apart.

Thorssen picked up the shirt he had abandoned earlier. It bore the same across-the-shoulders bloodstain. He hadn't noticed it when he'd cast it aside, thinking all the blood had belonged to the nurse. The material was still intact, the seams secure.

He remembered that sound, that sensation, when he'd thought his shirt had torn during her slaughter, and realized that it hadn't been the shirt ripping at all. His skin had torn apart.

Something was growing inside him.

Something that was threatening to burst out of him...

Like a snake shedding its skin...

Like a moth emerging from a cocoon.

He was not afraid.

He was afraid.

Was.

Not.

The change was making him a stronger man.

But it was making him less of a man, too.

Less of himself.

He stared hard at his naked body, stunned by the definition his muscles had developed.

It was giving him the strength to become what he *needed* to be.

The sword.

Nægling.

This metamorphosis was connected to the sword.

It could not happen soon enough for him.

Time crawled. There was no point leaving the house. He would make Tostig wait. It would unnerve him. Keep him wondering what this mysterious last job might be.

It was an easy one: to die.

Thorssen ran a steaming hot shower, washing away the sweat that had turned cold on his skin. The pressure from the needles of hot water was enough to sluice away scraps of skin from around the open sore on his back.

He soaped his chest, feeling the flesh bubble as his hands passed over it. The skin was raw, hot, as though drawn tight over a furnace. The soap shriveled and shrank away before it could lather up.

He sensed the change was almost complete.

He was beginning to grasp—or perhaps it was re-member—what was happening.

He would emerge into the light.

People would remember him.

People would know who was the rightful owner of Nægling.

37

Tostig had been waiting for almost twenty minutes when Thorssen's car finally drew into the drop-off zone outside the station.

He did not like being kept waiting, but masked his impatience. He had wanted this. It was public, too. With so many people around, a conversation between two people wouldn't stand out.

The new arrival pulled alongside him and slowly lowered the driver's side window.

"Not here," said Thorssen. "Follow me."

The window closed again before the assassin could respond. The car was driven slowly away, making it easy for him to follow. Thorssen was reinforcing the nature of their relationship—the politician leading, Tostig a follower, as it had always been.

There was no need for it.

Everything he had to say could have been said without either of them getting out of their cars. It would have taken less than a minute to deliver his message. But, oh, no, he was being led to some remote—unknown—destination simply because Karl Thorssen wanted to set the agenda.

He would be glad when this was over.

It only took a couple of minutes before Thorssen turned off the road and drove down a lane to a row of lockup garages that had seen better days.

Despite the hour it was still bright daylight—as bright as it had been at noon.

Thorssen brought his car to a halt halfway along the row.

Tostig felt the hairs on the back of his neck prickle, offering a familiar warning.

He was never comfortable being led anywhere. Being taken to strange ground went beyond uncomfortable. He surveyed the alleyway, the green-painted doors, the buildings overlooking the area, the railway arches, anywhere and everywhere that might be useful or shelter a threat. He swung his car alongside Thorssen's familiar Tesla, and killed the engine. Thorssen did likewise, then clambered out of his car.

The assassin hadn't realized how much his employer had beefed up since he'd been in his service. The man looked like he had been hitting the gym hard.

Tostig had never been afraid of Thorssen. He had no intention of being afraid of him now, either.

Tostig rolled down his window again.

"Why here?" he asked.

"Because you wanted to talk. This gives us some privacy. Out. I need you to see something." Thorssen turned his back on him, fishing keys out of his pocket, and went to unlock one of the garages.

The assassin got out of his car, but left the door open.

"What do you want to show me?"

"In a minute, Tostig. You said you wanted to talk to me? Obviously you have something on your mind?"

Tostig had rehearsed this in his head for the past hour, but now he was unsure. Thorssen had such a powerful presence, he was magnetic. It was impossible to ignore him. But there was *more* to him now, he was more…physical.

"I'm leaving," he said.

Thorssen stopped what he was doing and frowned at the assassin.

"Leaving? As in walking away? The job isn't done yet. I say when you go."

Thorssen faced the garage door and pushed it up to reveal a hatchback on the other side. He stepped forward and popped the lock on the rear door and opened it. He moved so that Tostig could see the roll of carpet inside.

"I've got no intention of making a scene. I've honored our agreement. Everyone who threatened your campaign is gone. We can part now, never hear from each other again. Job done, everyone happy."

Thorssen tugged back the fold of carpet to expose the body of a woman.

"Is this the last job you meant? Disposing of a body?"

"No. It's fine. You're right. We're done. Time to walk away. We have nothing left we need to say to each other."

Tostig turned his back on the car. "Then I'll leave you to it."

"Leave? You won't be leaving, Tostig."

He heard the change of tone in his ex-employer's

voice. What he didn't hear was the sound of Nægling slicing through the air.

He only felt the pain for a heartbeat.

The last thing to go through his mind was, *So this is what it feels like.*

38

Annja called Micke Rehnfeldt.

The filmmaker was glad to hear her voice. The first words out of his mouth were, "Where and when?"

Suddenly she remembered she'd agreed to a date.

"Soon, I promise."

"Why don't I believe you?"

"Because you're a cynical young man?"

"Made that way by life's disappointments," he said, then chuckled. "So if it's not me you're looking for, I assume it's something I can do for you?"

"An address."

"How about mine? Will that do?"

"I was thinking someone else."

"Who are you after?"

"Karl Thorssen."

Micke blew out a long slow whistle. "Big Bad Karl himself, eh?"

"The one and only."

"Well, it's not like its public domain stuff, but he's a politician, his home is on record. All you need to do is call the tax office—they'll even tell you what he earned last year and how much tax he avoided paying.

Albeit that's his official residence—he doesn't actually live there. That's just for the paperwork—a little apartment in Gothenburg, not far from your hotel, actually."

"So where does he live?"

"If I tell you I'll have to kill you."

"And then how'd you get a date?"

"Hmm, good point. I see a flaw in my plan."

"So?"

"Okay, you didn't hear this from me, and the cost is dinner, tomorrow night—you, me, one slinky dress, one proper suit and tie, six courses, wine, music and maybe even a little dancing afterward. That's my price."

"Deal."

"Excellent, then I'll see you at a restaurant called Basement at seven tomorrow. Your mission, should you choose to accept it, is to try and find the place all by yourself. As for Karl Thorssen, the house he actually lives in is on an island off the coast, joined by a land bridge—Marstrand, bit of a rich man's paradise. It's about forty minutes north and west of here, follow the E6 and take the exit for the 168—that'll take you over the bridge. It's fairly remote out there."

"Terrific. I owe you one."

"See you tomorrow."

"Looking forward to it." Annja hung up.

"So you know where he lives." Gavin grimaced. "What's your plan, then? Just go up to his front door and ring the bell? Ask if he has the bits of broken sword, oh, and you wouldn't happen to have seen one grieving mother?" Garin did not bother to hide the sarcasm from his voice.

"Don't be ridiculous," she snapped, although he

wasn't far off; she'd only gotten to "drive to Thorssen's."

She had no idea where Una Mortensen was, and beyond sticking to the politician's side, she could think of no other means to find her, either. But she wasn't about to let her do something stupid.

"How are you with a camera?"

"If it involves using my hands with anything, I'm an expert, Annja. All you have to do is ask."

"Great, you can carry Johan's camera around on your shoulder and pretend you know how to use it."

"Because?"

"Because I'm going to turn up on Thorssen's doorstep, flatter him and get that interview."

"And you think he'll just say, 'Sure, come on in, excuse the dead bodies all around the place, I've been a bit busy'? It'll be the middle of the night before we even roll up."

"You don't know the guy, he's an egomaniac. The entire dig was all about him. He knows I know about Nægling, or at least he suspects. He won't be able to resist one last gloat on camera—"

"Before he tries to kill you. Third time lucky, babe."

"We'll just have to try and stop that from happening, won't we, Garin?" she said sweetly.

"We?" he said, grinning that "why do I always let you drag me into this stuff" smile he'd perfected since meeting Annja.

She knew she was on to something, even if her mouth was moving faster than her brain as to how it would all play out. "He wants the spotlight. The election is three days away. I give him the chance to reveal Nægling for the world, on camera, he won't be able to resist."

"You're certifiable, Annja Creed, you know that, right?"

"That's why you love me."

"Who said anything about love?"

"Tolerate, then."

"Better. Right, you'd better give me a quick lesson how this camera works. I don't want to look like a moron. And you never know, you might want to actually record something. Famous last words and all that."

She took a few minutes to run through what he needed to know, and then they were heading out to the car. Even those spent ten minutes were a concern; what if they were the difference between getting to Thorssen before Una and not?

They sprinted down the back staircase to the underground complex, into Garin's waiting sports car, and accelerated away. Annja urged him to floor it.

"Just let me drive," Garin said, staring grimly ahead as the car drifted across three lanes of traffic as he hammered it around a too-tight corner. The maneuver was greeted by a chorus of horns being pounded by irate drivers. Had it been a couple of hours earlier they'd have been roadkill.

She gave directions as they drove, taking him out onto the E6, the major arterial freeway that runs all the way up to Trelleborg, before hitting Lake Vänern. There, Garin really opened up the engine, hitting speeds more suitable to the autobahn, and then they were off for the 168 as Micke had told her.

It started raining as he hit the road bridge, but a minor shower wasn't going to slow him down. Garin roared into the sleepy island town, following Annja's instructions until they pulled up in front of Thorssen's home.

The huge wooden Viking longhouse-style gates were closed. She could see security cameras set above them.

"Want me to ram them?" Garin asked. She couldn't tell if he was serious.

"That would ruin the whole ego-stroke approach to the interview, don't you think? We play it by the book, Garin. Walk up, hit the intercom, ask for the interview and hope he opens the gates."

"And if he doesn't?"

"Plan B."

"And that is?"

"We improvise."

Would Una Mortensen really have come here?

Would she even have been able to find where the man lived or would she have gone to the apartment in Gothenburg?

The last message she'd left on Annja's voice mail had sounded desperate. Desperate people did desperate things. If not his house…maybe she intended to confront him in public, while campaigning, as he cast his vote even? Surely it wouldn't be too difficult to get a copy of his itinerary for the next couple of days leading up to the election and find out when he was vulnerable to an attack.

There was a screen and a touch pad beside the gate. They got out of the car and went over to it.

Annja hunched forward, trying to shield herself from the worst of the rain as it quickened. In the distance she heard a deep rumble. Thunder. She hadn't seen the flash of lightning yet. Great, she thought as she hit the green button she assumed would call up to the main house. Garin stood beside her.

A face appeared on the screen. It wasn't Thorssen's but rather an elderly lady. His mother.

"Mrs. Thorssen?"

"That's right," the woman on the screen said. "Don't I know you? I recognize you…have I seen you somewhere before, dear?"

"My name is Annja Creed."

"From the television? How wonderful. Kalle will be so sorry he's missed you. But he'll be home soon, I'm sure, if you want to come up to the main house and wait."

Before Annja could answer, the old woman was buzzing them in and the heavy wooden gates were swinging silently open.

They got into Garin's car and he drove up the long road to the main house, fat rain drumming loudly on the roof of the car.

Viveka Thorssen was waiting for them in the doorway of an incredibly modern house that was totally out of keeping with its surroundings.

She ushered them in out of the rain, leading them deep into the home. They went up a wide staircase to the second floor and into an immaculate living space with two large white leather sofas and a huge plate-glass window. The view looked out over a spotlighted Olympic-size rooftop pool and the darkness of the grounds beyond that.

Rain streaked the glass.

"Please," she said, gesturing that they should take a seat. "Could I get you some tea? Coffee?" Her English was flawless, cultured. The woman herself looked as if she was made up of the finest bone china.

"There's really no need, Mrs. Thorssen…."

"Certainly there is, my dear. There's always a need. Civilization was based upon the need for a nice cup of tea." She hurried out of the room, no doubt in the direction of the kitchen.

They could hear her puttering not far away, the tell-tale clink of crockery and the bubbling of a boiling kettle, and then they heard something else: an engine approaching the house. It was followed quickly by the sound of a door being slammed a little too firmly for comfort.

Keys rattled in the lock of the front door.

Then Annja heard Thorssen call, "I'm back."

There was something peculiar about the look on his face when he entered the room. It wasn't purely down to the surprise of seeing her sitting in his living room, either, though his expression soon slipped into that careful public mask she had seen before.

There was no sign of the sling that had been supporting his arm and the cuts and bruises were gone from his face; he'd clearly made a rapid recovery from his superficial injuries. There was, however, blood on his shirt.

"I thought you were dead."

39

"I'm sorry to disappoint you," said Annja. "Hold on there, no, I'm not. What made you think I was dead?"

The politician was obviously struggling to come up with a convincing lie. Annja wondered how long it would be before he abandoned all pretense. Not long.

"I thought I had seen it on the television."

"Not me. Though obviously there've been a lot of deaths on the news over the past few days so I can understand the confusion."

"What are you doing here?"

She couldn't exactly say she'd come to stop Una Mortensen from killing him, or trying to. Or could she? It was an angle. Instead of posing a threat she'd come to him as an ally. It might just work.

Annja saw that Thorssen was trying to shield a bundle he'd been carrying as he walked into the room, doing his best to keep it behind his back. She was familiar enough with the shape of a sword to recognize it no matter how much material he had wrapped around it.

Had he been able to get a replica of the sword made

so quickly, with only the heavily encrusted pieces of metal to go on?

Impressive. But then money can work miracles.

"This is Annja Creed, Kalle. She's from the television," his mother said, reappearing in the doorway with a tray of exquisite teacups.

"Ah, television, then I am afraid I will have to disappoint you. You should have made an appointment through my press officer. I'm sorry I can't help you. I've got to be up in Stockholm in a few hours. Big debate tomorrow, going out live on national television."

That was interesting because she knew he wasn't invited to be part of it—she'd already heard him complain about that—but she didn't say anything to contradict him. They were being dismissed, but Annja was taking no notice of him.

"That's unfortunate. We're leaving in the morning, first thing, and I really wanted to get you on camera talking about Skalunda, the hero buried there and of course the tragic death of your lead archaeologist."

"I'm not sure there's anything to say," Thorssen growled.

There was something different about the man. She didn't feel comfortable in his presence and it was obvious Garin was on edge beside her.

"It's not a problem. I had hoped you'd offer a unique insight into the heritage of your country—this dig is yours, after all. There's no one better to talk about it, but I'll just do a piece to camera, explain that unfortunately your schedule was too full with the forthcoming elections, that kind of thing."

"Perhaps you should do that," Thorssen said.

"Nonsense, dear. You know how much the dig

means to you and to your supporters. Don't cut your nose off to spite your face. Go freshen up. Miss Creed will wait, won't you?" Viveka Thorssen said, oblivious to any subtext playing through the conversation.

"As always, you are right, Mother. Please, Miss Creed, give me a few minutes to get cleaned up and I'll be with you."

Annja gave him as pleasant a smile as she could muster. "Take your time. Before you go, might I ask, have you seen Una Mortensen, the archaeologist's mother, today?"

Thorssen's brow furrowed—the consternation was genuine. "Why would I have? But, to answer your question, no, though my secretary tells me she's been making a nuisance of herself at the office."

The red light on the side of the camera was lit. Garin was recording the exchange.

"A nuisance of herself? That's quite a polite way of saying she was accusing you of being complicit in her son's death."

"Complicit? Are you accusing me of murdering someone? You sit there, in my own home no less, in front of my mother, and throw around wild accusations like that?" He shook his head. "Lars Mortensen was a valued colleague. His death was nothing short of a tragedy. It most certainly had nothing to do with me."

"Are you sure?" Annja pulled out her phone and played back Una's final message on speaker so everyone in the room could hear her voice through the sobs. "Whether she's right or not, she was certainly gunning for you."

Thorssen looked genuinely shocked. He wasn't a good enough actor to fake that level of surprise. He'd had no idea the old woman was possibly coming here. Maybe she'd never gotten beyond picketing his office, or maybe Annja had been right before when she'd thought about a big scene on the hustings, taking him on in front of the cameras. The bereaved mother confronting the fascist for all the world to see?

"I have been out all night. Business in the city. Have we had visitors, Mother?"

The old woman didn't answer immediately. In that pause between the question and the denial Annja knew Viveka Thorssen was lying when she said, "No."

"There you have it, I'm afraid. No one's been here. Now, if you still want me to contribute to your documentary, might I suggest we drop this entire line of questioning? Your viewers aren't interested in this nonsense, and neither, frankly, am I."

Annja could see the anger swell within him. Whether it was a trick of the light, with it finally moving toward true darkness at this late hour, or whether it was something more sinister, it was almost as though he was physically swelling along with his anger.

He threw back his shoulders, pushing out his chest with a deep intake of breath.

In that moment the crimson-streaked shirt he wore seemed incapable of containing him, the buttons close to bursting. Karl Thorssen was oblivious to the bloodstains soaking it.

"Kalle? You're bleeding," his mother said, bringing the seeping red smears to his attention.

Thorssen shrugged. "There was an animal on the track that needed dealing with. It's nothing," he said. There was something of the way he had addressed the crowd at the rally in how he spoke now, but rather than directing them to stand against a common enemy, he was telling the three of them to ignore the evidence before their eyes. He stood there in a bloody shirt, insisting it meant nothing. And if he hadn't seemed so furious she might have believed him. He was that good.

"Turn that camera off," Thorssen snarled, wheeling around on Garin. "You aren't going to make me look like some raving lunatic for your tacky show. Kill it. Now." The red light might be on, but so was the lens cap. She hated Garin at that moment. Thorssen wasn't an idiot; he'd realize her so-called cameraman was a fake. Before she could intercede, Thorssen's rage bubbled over. He advanced on Garin, leaving any semblance of control behind as he let loose a bestial roar, red in tooth and nail.

Annja stared at the politician, not sure what she was seeing: he tore at this shirt, revealing skin covered with splits and suppurating sores, the desiccated flesh sloughed from him like a snake's, dead scales no longer needed. What was it? A sort of virus? A flesh-eating bacteria that had somehow clung to the sword?

She scrambled to her feet as Thorssen yanked the sacking away from the blade he'd tried to smuggle into the house. The metal shone but despite its obvious newness she knew instinctively it was an ancient weapon, not a newly forged copy of the relic. This was the find that had cost Lars Mortensen his life. The blade of a fallen hero, a mythical man, though not so mythical a blade, after all. This was Nægling.

His mother's bellowing cry broke the moment but Thorssen was beyond any compassion or concern. He wasn't in there anymore, or if he was, it was only a shred of the man he had once been. Whatever was happening to him, whatever was happening to his flesh, was changing him. He was something else now. Something monstrous. Something dangerous.

"What's going on with you?" Annja kept her voice steady despite the fear pulsing through her veins. Beneath the ruined skin, there was a glistening layer of new flesh....

"I am becoming what I was always intended to be."

What, not *who.*

"You're in trouble. Karl? Can you hear me, Karl? You must fight this. Focus on me. Look at me," Annja commanded, knowing it was useless even as she said the words.

He lifted the sword, touching it to his lips. "I have been found worthy. Nægling is mine. It always was."

"You think you are Beowulf?" Annja blurted, realizing the man before her had had a psychotic breakdown. Whatever affliction had poisoned his skin had undone his mind to the extent he believed he was some long-dead hero. That didn't make him any less dangerous, only more tragic.

But tragic men can still kill you if you're not careful, Annja thought.

"Beowulf?" Thorssen spat, mocking the name. "The War Wolf? Do I look like a dog? I am *not* Beowulf! He is dead and gone, dust and dreams, long since any use, even as food for the worms. Gone like all mere men."

Annja was already reaching into the otherwhere as he spoke, feeling the imminent threat of violence shimmer in the air between them. This could not end well. She wasn't afraid for her own life; once her hand closed around the hilt of Joan's sword she couldn't be any safer. And she had Garin at her side, a man born to fight, one who had never let her down since he'd first pulled her out of that café in France, guns blazing.

Thorssen screamed again. She couldn't tell if he was fighting whatever was inside his body, or if he was screaming his rage at her, at his mother, Garin and the world.

The animalistic howl tore through the modern architecture, shaking the house to its foundations.

He scratched at the scraps of skin flaking from his face, his arms and torso to display the extent of the damage.

The fragments of his skin seemed to smolder and turn black, falling away like the ash of burned paper and drifting down to the carpet.

Annja stood transfixed by the transformation, her hand still reaching out to draw her own sword into existence.

"Get her out of here," Annja told Garin, not looking away from Thorssen.

"I can't leave you."

"You can. Don't try and be chivalrous, it doesn't suit you. Get his mother out of here. This thing has to be stopped."

No matter what happened next, this wasn't for the old woman's eyes. She didn't need to see her son die.

Garin ushered the elderly lady toward the kitchen.

Annja wrapped her fingers around the hilt of her sword. It was there in her hand, sharing the same moonlit luster as Nægling.

The thing that had been Thorssen gave a twisted smile of confusion as Annja faced him.

"Do you really think you can stand against me? I smell the blood on you. You are a feeble woman. I am hungry. Feed me."

"Feeble woman?" she said. "You've missed a hundred years of suffrage. There's nothing feeble about us these days." Calling him Beowulf seemed to have been the one thing that had finally pushed his buttons. Annja liked pushing buttons. That was just the kind of feeble woman she was. "So, if you aren't Beowulf what are you doing with his sword? Did you steal it from his grave?"

"I am no thief," the thing before her raged, all semblance of humanity lost. There was no coming back now, not for Karl Thorssen. His body had been taken from him by the kind of parasite he railed so vocally against, only the immigrant in his skin was no innocent asylum seeker. "Nægling is mine. Not his. She was never his. Her strength is my strength. Where do you think that thief found her? In my lair. In my cave. He stole into my home and, while I lay dying, took her. But Nægling is mine and I will be avenged."

"Who are you?"

It did not answer her.

Annja rephrased the question. "*What* are you?"

"I am Grendel."

40

Grendel.

Not the hero. Not the shining one who broke his sword in the dragon's belly. Not the man who embodied the spirit of a lost nation. Not the man Karl Thorssen dreamed would change his world, now, slaying the beasts of his generation.

Grendel.

The monster.

That was who he identified with in his disease-riddled mind. He gripped the great blade, Nægling, in a single oversize hand. Any mere mortal would have needed two to wield it.

He swung the sword and roared.

Annja heard the air part as the deadly edge sliced toward her.

She danced out of reach as the gleaming blade hewed close enough for the backdraft to ruffle her hair. She rocked on her heels, then quickly stepped inside his attack, but Thorssen anticipated the move. He lunged in and Annja barely had enough time to bring her sword around to counter his incredible speed.

And again he struck.

And again.

She was on the back foot, being pressed toward the huge sheet of glass that separated them from sanity.

In a curiously detached way she noticed that the storm had worsened, lightning flashing bright and close even as the thunder clapped, booming.

The charge rippled through her sword, the metal as ever in tune with the elements around it.

Thorssen threw back his head and cried out, his voice raw, climbing above the storm to join in the cacophony.

Annja swung again. Her blade drew blood and howls from him. He had misjudged the feeble woman and knew now he faced a warrior whose gender was irrelevant.

"Still hungry?" Annja goaded.

Thorssen rose up onto his toes, stretching his neck and arching his back, presenting his heart to the warrior, taunting her to strike. Annja seized her opportunity, launching herself over the white leather couch at him, only for Thorssen to move quicker than the eye could follow, turning on her and slamming her into the wall.

Annja's face smashed into the plaster, leaving her stunned and dizzy. The world reeled around her as she tried to recover before Thorssen fell upon her again. Though even as she turned, tasting ash in her throat, Thorssen catapulted her across the room.

She came down on the coffee table, sending the bone-china teacups crashing.

Annja rolled away onto her side as Nægling scythed into the wood where her head had been a heartbeat before. She scrambled away on all fours as Thorssen stalked after her.

He launched another blistering attack, preventing Annja from rising.

She slumped to her knees as he hammered a blow into the base of her spine with a booted foot, driving her down onto the hardwood floor amid the shards of broken china.

Annja brought her sword up as Thorssen came for her, cutting deep into Thorssen's his new skin.

He screamed in pain and clutched at his guts to stem the flow of blood.

Annja took no satisfaction in wounding him; he seemed hardly human now, beyond reason. It came down to instinct: fight or flight. It was a miracle there was enough of Thorssen left in there to even feel the cut. He looked hellish, sores weeping, blood running from the two cuts.

"Don't do this," she gasped, pushing herself back to her feet, but there was no communicating with the man.

Thorssen hurled one of the two couches aside, leaving bloody tracks across the hardwood as he closed the gap again, shepherding Annja toward the huge plate-glass window.

She slipped beneath his next swing, dropping her shoulder and lunging, the tip of her blade piercing the muscle of Thorssen's chest. He swatted her attack away as though the bite of Joan's sword was nothing and crashed a fist into the side of Annja's head.

As she spat blood, Annja only grew more determined.

Thorssen threw himself at Annja again, grappling with her toward the window.

Annja was slammed back into the glass relentlessly, until the huge plate cracked, then spiderwebbed, then finally shattered. Together, they went sprawling through the broken window, stumbling and falling as the storm and shards of glass rained down around them.

A fork of lightning streaked down from the sky, spearing the night.

Thorssen rose, blood and rain dripping from his face.

He brandished Nægling.

Annja stood slowly.

"Karl? Can you hear me, Karl? Whatever it is that's wrong, we can help you. We need to get you to the hospital. You're sick."

Another fork of lightning lit his sneering face.

"You think you *know* me? You think you can *help* me? You think I need to be fixed, that I am sick? I'm not sick. I am becoming Grendel. I can feel the fire inside me. I am becoming whole, finally. This is what my life has always been about. This moment." And as though to punctuate it, a huge rumble of thunder rolled out above them. Annja felt it deep inside her chest. "Feed me. I am hungry. So very, very hungry."

He came at her again, Nægling glistening in the rain, the ancient metal slick.

Swords clashed as they skirted the edge of the huge pool. The expensive cultivated foliage that blocked the rooftop pool from casual view wilted under the battering of the storm. The damage to her wrists from where Thorssen's assassin had bound them in the church made every impact from the swords coming together agony.

"Annja!"

The shout came from inside the house.

Annja didn't look toward it, but Thorssen did, allowing his guard to drop long enough for her to deliver a stinging cut to his left cheek, drawing more blood.

He backed up. The deck around the pool was slick with rain.

As they worked their way around the pool, metal sparked on metal as the two blades met. Every muscle in Annja's body cried out from the beating she'd taken, but she couldn't allow weakness to steal in. She launched another blistering attack, gouging a deep slice down Thorssen's right cheek this time. Joan's sword cleaved all the way down into the meat of his shoulder, opening a sickening wound.

She didn't even have enough breath left to waste any calling out to Garin.

Despite his wounds, Thorssen showed no sign of weakening. He was relentless and seemed blind to all pain.

He hit her hard, driving the air out of her lungs.

The deck beneath Annja betrayed her; she lost her footing on the slick surface and started to fall, arms pinwheeling desperately as she tried to catch her balance, but it was hopeless. Thorssen lashed out with the hilt of Nægling, a savage backhanded blow that slammed into her temple and sent Annja into the freezing pool below.

41

Garin saw Annja fall.

He knew he had to get to her. She was out cold, Thorssen on the edge of the pool watching her drown.

He raced flat out around the side of the pool, coming up on Thorssen's blind side. Garin's wild attack caught Thorssen by surprise.

Thorssen tried to turn but couldn't do it quickly enough. Garin slashed at him with a carving knife he'd grabbed from the kitchen. It was more than enough to punch a few holes in the politician. He pulled back his arm and slashed again, opening a wide gash across Thorssen's belly, which had the man staggering back. But that was no more than a temporary reprieve.

Thorssen lumbered around, bleeding, eyes glazed, skin flaking away on his hideously misshapen musculature, and with one clubbing swing batted Garin aside. He tangled with the deck furniture, ending up spread across two sun loungers. For one sickening second, he couldn't feel his legs or anything below the vertebrae midway down his spine, and thought he'd broken his back. It could have been worse.

He was only inches from going over the side of the house.

42

Annja Creed was drowning.

It made a change from burning, was all she could think as she fought toward consciousness even as her lungs filled with pool water.

She coughed, breaking the surface of the water, and reached out for the closest wall, clawing at it and pulling herself up.

The sword was gone.

When it had fallen out of her hand it had returned to the otherwhere.

She was on her knees, soaked, deafening rain drumming down all around. Thorssen swung the ancient artifact once more.

She threw up an arm, knowing Nægling would sheer clean through the bone as her hand closed around Joan's sword in the otherwhere and brought it back just in time to deflect the lethal blow.

Metal struck metal and a shower of sparks stung her face.

The force of the blow shuddered through her arm.

She couldn't hold off her own cry of pain, but something snapped in the attack. Joan's sword had held true. Nægling had failed for a second time, shattered by its wielder.

Lightning, drawn to Annja by the sword in her hand, shimmered down the length of Joan's sword, then spread out in a sheet of electricity across the surface of the pool. Deadly and beautiful at the same time.

Karl Thorssen howled.

It was the most heartbreaking sound she'd ever heard.

He held the hilt of the broken sword uselessly in his hand.

Annja seized the moment. She couldn't afford sentimentality; there was no saving Karl Thorssen. Sometimes that was life. Death. She twisted the blade so it pointed skyward and drove it with both hands deep into Karl Thorssen's stomach.

His baleful cry was enough to make her want to clasp her hands over her ears, but she couldn't relinquish her hold on the sword. Not until he was dead. Annja maintained the upward pressure, ramming the blade home.

His life ran out. Karl Thorssen lacked the will to stand upright, and fell, impaling himself on the sword, collapsing on top of Annja.

There was nothing in his eyes.

No light.

No life.

No sign of Karl Thorssen the man, the politician, or Karl Thorssen the beast, Grendel.

She squirmed out from beneath him, still holding the blood- and gore-smeared blade out in front of her in case Thorssen should somehow rise again, but he was beyond that. All that remained was the slowly growing stain on the poolside decking that was already being washed away by the rain.

Annja doubled over, breathing too fast, her heart beating far too quickly, aware of how close she had come to death.

And then she saw Garin sprawled between two sun loungers, not moving.

"Garin!"

43

He was still breathing.

He didn't move. He had his eyes closed.

"I'll live," he said, slowly cracking a smile. "Don't I always?"

They sat side by side for a moment in the rain. Another arc of lightning illuminated the sea beyond the house, fading so only the moon was left on the water. It was a beautiful sight, doubly so given how close they'd come to not seeing it, or anything else, ever again.

"Where do you think Una is?" Garin said, eyes still closed.

"Back in the city. Harassing his staff, I hope, or plotting a raid on his rally tomorrow morning. Anywhere but here."

"Just because Thorssen didn't see her doesn't mean she wasn't here," Garin said, giving voice to the nagging doubt in Annja's mind that refused to go away.

"But if she was here, surely mommy dearest would have seen her, even if only to send her packing."

"Maybe she did."

"Then why would she lie about something like that? Why would she say she hadn't seen her?"

The scream was earsplitting.

Nightsplitting.

Almost forgotten, Thorssen's mother came lunging out of the darkness on the rooftop.

"You killed my *son*," she shrieked, her voice shrill and piercing. *"You killed my son!"*

Annja looked from her to Thorssen's ruined body and back again.

The mother ran to her boy's side and stroked his head, mumbling over and over as she did. Annja backed away to give them what little privacy she could, given the circumstances.

Viveka Thorssen rewarded her by snatching up the broken blade from where it lay beside her son and pointing it toward Annja.

"Please, think about what you're doing," Annja said, both hands held out as though to pacify the woman. "It doesn't have to end like this."

"You killed my son!"

"I had no choice," Annja said, desperate for her to understand. "There's been enough death today. Please don't do this."

Thorssen's mother held the broken sword out and slashed with it wildly, hacking at the air between them with no skill or control.

Annja intended to wrest the broken sword away from her and stop anyone else getting hurt here to-night.

Even as the thought crossed her mind, a wild swing of Nægling whistled by.

Thorssen's mother swung again and again, but Annja kept out of the sword's reach, allowing Viveka to push her toward the shattered windows into the main house.

The woman was tiring.

The pauses between those huge unwieldy swings of the sword grew longer, the sword weighing on her as much as the death of her son.

Still, Annja bided her time.

The rain continued mercilessly, driving into Annja's eyes. Rather than break her spirit, the breather seemed to reinvigorate Thorssen's mother, who came at Annja with sword raised. Her cry, the same as before. *"This is for my son!"*

Annja had tried to hold the woman off, but it was no longer possible now.

Just as she was about to summon her sword, Thorssen's mother sank to the ground in front of her, crumpling like a rag doll.

It took a moment for Annja to realize that a kitchen knife—the one Garin had lost during his fight with her son—was protruding from the woman's back.

"For *my* son," a female voice said.

Annja could barely focus through the darkness and the rain, but slowly she saw who it was.

It was Una Mortensen, and another son had been avenged.

44

She left Garin to clean up, which in this case meant dragging the bodies inside the house.

Una shivered while they waited in the car. The effects of shock had started to take over from grief. She needed rest. They all did.

"What happened?" Annja asked.

"It was for Lars. And I did it because she *laughed* at me."

"Thorssen's mother? Why would she laugh at you?"

"Because I told her that I was sure her son was responsible for the death of mine. She just laughed, then she hit me. She was a lot stronger than she looked. The next thing I knew I was in the dark with my hands tied. I could hear voices somewhere in the house but I couldn't move. Not at first…" She rubbed at her wrists, the red welts swollen. She didn't say anything else and Annja did not press her.

Garin opened the trunk and dropped something inside before taking the driver's seat. He threw the car into gear and floored the accelerator to take them speeding away down the long driveway from the house.

They weren't even through those huge wooden Viking longhouse doors before an explosion tore through the house, sending debris into the air. As the car zoomed through the open gates, Garin looked back through the rearview mirror. The sky was red, so very red, filled with flame. The fire would be visible for miles around, blazing like a beacon in the night.

45

They dropped Una Mortensen off at the door of her hotel, and then headed to Garin's penthouse suite.

Annja turned on the TV while she began to pack. She wouldn't leave straightaway; she owed Micke Rehnfeldt that date in the Basement later on—but she'd need a full day of beauty sleep before venturing out on the town. As she'd expected, the news led with the fire, another huge one threatening the surrounding countryside, and the fire services already stretched to breaking point.

But before long, the picture changed to show a long line of lockup garages behind the railway station.

She stopped her packing and watched.

The face on the screen was one Annja was convinced she would never forget; this was the man from the hotel, the man who had tried to burn them alive in Saint Peter's on the Lake. She didn't need to understand Swedish to know what was being said about him; it was clearly a crime scene, and equally clear he was the victim. That was all she needed to know.

The image on the screen changed again. Karl Thorssen had perished in a gas explosion at his Marstrand residence. It was too early to rule out foul play, especially given his controversial politics. One thing was sure: without their charismatic figurehead, Thorssen's party was wounded, so much so that it was unlikely to recover.

Its day was done.

Annja slumped onto the bed beside Garin. He barely noticed. His attention was solely on the objects he'd retrieved from the house before tampering with its gas supply. She'd assumed it was Johan's camera, but it wasn't.

"I've been in touch with my people," he said, sounding vague, as usual. "There'll be a story circulating within the hour that links Thorssen and the Serbian mafia. That should provide a believable solution for the recent deaths around him."

"Neat and tidy. So what are you planning on doing with that?" Annja indicated the two halves of the broken sword, Nægling. While she still thought of it as Beowulf's sword, the truth was that it was never really his. It had always been Grendel's.

The sword had a power even if it was broken.

"Let me see," she asked, holding out her hands.

Carefully, Annja unwrapped the sword, unsure if the flesh-eating bacteria that had destroyed Karl Thorssen was still on its gleaming edges.

"Thought I might sell that." Garin cocked an eyebrow.

"Nice try. We'll bury it where no one will ever find it. Put it back where it belongs. In the ground. In the past."

"Fine. But can we eat first? I'm starving."

Annja smiled. "Best idea you've had yet."

* * * * *

JAMES AXLER

DEATH LANDS

Desolation Angels

Bad to the bone...

Violent gangs, a corrupt mayor and a heavily armed police force are hallmarks of the former Detroit. When Ryan and his companions show up, the Desolation Angels are waging a war to rule the streets. After saving the companions from being chilled by gangsters, the mayor hires Ryan and his friends to stop the Angels cold. But each hard blow toward victory proves there's no good side to be fighting for. As Motor City erupts into bloody conflagration, the companions are caught in the cross fire. In the Deathlands, hell is called home.

Available July wherever books and ebooks are sold.

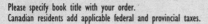

GOLD EAGLE ®

GDL117

The Executioner

Don Pendleton's®

PACIFIC CREED

A terror campaign leaves a trail of bodies in Hawaii

When female tourists are kidnapped in Hawaii, Mack Bolan is sent in to investigate. While all clues suggest a white slavery ring, he learns there is more going on than simply girls being sold for guns.

With his cover thin and his disguise temporary, Bolan knows the only way to find the Samoan leader behind the terror campaign is to prove his worth to the tribe. The Executioner has only one chance to convince the Samoans of his loyalty— and to stop their deadly plan before they destroy Hawaii.

Available June wherever books and ebooks are sold.

GOLD EAGLE®